The Imperium of Steves

The Imperium of Steves

A NOVEL

D.C. PAE

QUARTET

First published in 2009 by
Quartet Books Limited
A member of the Namara Group
27 Goodge Street, London W1T 2LD

A catalogue record for this book
is available from the British Library

ISBN   978 0 7043 7142 2

Typeset by Antony Gray
Printed and bound in Great Britain by
T J International Ltd, Padstow, Cornwall

For my friends, with love

Contents

ONE

Original Madness

Everybody knew it was wrong. Hell, even I knew it was wrong, but Mom never did mind. She always wanted to see the best in me, the goodly woman. She told everyone who would listen that I was going to become an anatomist or a veterinarian. This was the only way I'd learn.

'They cut thousands of people up you know, those doctors, what are they called . . . cadavers,' she'd say and that she thought I was a genius. She was correct as always, a genius am I. But anatomy class subjects are usually dead before the scalpel is applied. Except for undercover operations carried out in secret underground bunkers, but we all know about those. It's safe to assume that life forms are generally, if at all possible, long expired at the point of dissection in modern medicine. Not scurrying around, healthy as can be and without a care in the world, breathing God's fresh Virginia air. Case studies suggest that it is an early indicator of a murderous mind, to attack, maim or kill sweet furry animals without affording them due process and the right to an attorney. Particularly perverse is the art form when the subject in question is the beloved family pet. I had no such pretension toward convention.

Mother pretended the murder was accidental. Little Donnie the hamster had been a victim of circumstance, of hapless blunder. I had been heavy-handed, not foreseeing the strength

I could weald with my bare prepubescent hands. She had acquitted any criminality or motivation on my part. She also omitted the use of the kitchen knife. She simply wiped it clean and placed it back in the drawer beside the sink as though I had cut a slice of ham with it and there was no problem. No problem at all. When she offered a pastrami sandwich to the parson she didn't think twice about using exhibit A to cut the seed loaf. Tiny hamster entrails might somehow add to its ultimate pleasure and taste.

I didn't tell her I enjoyed it. I didn't tell her anything and she never asked. Questioning would only ever be met with lies and a generous helping of bravado. Tiny hamster organs lined up on the cellar step as a coroner might document an autopsy, such precision. The opportunist cat took the rest whilst I had my back turned. I still remember how cute Donnie was making a nest in his straw or taking his water from the dispenser with his microscopic tongue. Or the time he escaped and gnawed a hole in the back of the couch. He lived there for a week until we caught him and committed him once again to solitary confinement in the rodent penitentiary we liked to call his home. Further investigation proved that he was really a she and had been impregnated at the Petmart from which she was purchased. Six tiny pink, perfect, decapitated baby hamsters rowed up on the step, placenta and all. She made a most pleasant squeak as she exited this astral plain. You see, I had started out on the wrong foot. If no punitive action is taken, no crime has been committed. Guilt is unnecessary, one becomes complacent.

Mom scooped up the remains of my experiment and disposed of them in special scented packages she had for her incontinence pads. She never said another word about the matter. It all just got tossed into the garbage along with the memories. She kept a close eye on the cats that came into our yard until neighbourly relations degraded. Thereafter she willed me to perform more surgery in her mind. I never touched those bastard cats alive I swear. I got the blame for everything, not from Mom, but from everyone else. The die was cast. Several field mice and a racoon later, I had been initiated into the serial murderer club and as far as I knew I was the only member, but Mom had a fully paid-up subscription. I saw myself as a scientist. A brave new world of anatomical endeavour and inner knowledge revealed itself. Who needs five years at med school. A Ted Bundy to the animal kingdom was I. I enjoyed my science as much as any ordinary kid would baseball or Oreos. Yes, I enjoyed my craft and all safe in the knowledge that my protection racketeer of a mother wouldn't spill. She was, in her own deluded existence, my inverse nurturer, a facilitator of the perverse.

Like I say, my mom never told anyone, not least my dad, from whom we had become more and more estranged. She knew what was going down, but ignored it, cleaned up afterward; replaced lost animals. I felt she understood me, a silent understanding, a cognisance. A will to preserve the status quo just like with my father who was always in the army, always, even when he was on shore leave knocking up underage prostitutes and high school dropouts. Pop was always at war. Mom told me so. Christ, there had been three major wars since he'd served: Vietnam, Korea and Cuba. The woman had no appreciation for either geography or history, as her bullshit stories suggested. She thought she had me convinced, but I was too shrewd. Mom needed to believe Dad was fighting the good fight. She managed to delude herself so she just kept making up new ones. There had been three in the last year according to her alternative war timetable. We'd finished off Cuba and headed straight to Columbia, through Venezuela wreaking havoc and on to Brazil and Dad had been at the helm yelling 'attack!' He'd been the hero of the hour, the week, the year and he'd be home soon, right after he'd dispensed with Argentina single-handed. This accomplishment was so awesome I often wondered why he hadn't received more honours and why nobody had heard of him. How come our national hero hadn't been more highly decorated, receiving his medals from the president himself. All of this with the use of just one arm. My father must surely be a great man, an icon. He should have had a spot on Larry King by now. Maybe he was shy.

When I got home from school one day Mom was spoon-feeding the cat rat poison. Seemed to me he quite liked it and she certainly looked as if she was enjoying herself. She had fallen out of favour with the neighbours soon after Dad came home and gave her a bad bout of syphilis. The poor soul had only just recovered from the gonorrhoea he'd brought back as a present from his last trip. She blamed it on backsplash from the municipal library toilets. She lied. She had been crying for days and I hadn't helped. The school called up and asked her to collect me for bloodletting in the men's room. I saw it on a TV documentary. An ancient cure for all kinds of ailments, I wanted to release the tension, they swore by it in the nineteenth century. Except I couldn't close the wound and bled all over this girl I liked called Jane. She used to like me in second grade. Now she wished I was dead. Mom had syphilis treatment.

12

The doctor had touched parts of her that Dad wished he hadn't and she was already starting to act strange. I just exacerbated it. She burst the lip of our neighbours' son after he called me a vampire and she spat in the wound to increase his pain. They closed ranks. They didn't seem to like us anymore. I don't blame them. They ran inside whenever we drew up the drive. So I was already starting to feel special. I felt I could function outside the bounds of reason because Mom was always there to protect me.

The next day the cat drew its last breath in the garden. It sat slumped against the picket fence, arched its back, spasmed and stretched its claws out in front, then balled up and relaxed with a sigh. I felt it was only my duty to investigate its demise in a scholarly fashion. I ran to fetch my scalpel, the one I stole from the school lab. After all, a good workman must have his tools. So I set to work to see what was wrong. Cut out its tongue, everything OK there, bit swollen but otherwise fine and continued on to the oesophagus, larynx and trachea. Yes, they were all present, but not quite correct. I'd caught Mom baiting the bastard the day before but that did not matter to me, it just gave me an excuse, an accomplice. Retreating bloodied into the house, I caught sight of the neighbour staring right at me through the window in horror. You know what, I just laughed and flipped her the bird and my most charming smile. So you see, I never killed the damn thing. Mom believed me.

I finally got kicked out of junior high for fiddling with Jane on camp. I nodded off and when I came round Jane was screaming holy hell fire at the top of her voice. I swear on my own life, that priceless commodity, I didn't touch her. I never had a predisposition for sex. I just like to think about it, a lot.

I didn't know what a cunt was when I was ten. I thought it was an affectionate nickname Dad had for Mom. No. I discovered all that in high school. I only got in because of my glorious insights in biology class. Mom persuaded her friend Erma, the academic registrar, to falsify my records. My mom knew lots of middle-aged women. Middle-aged people are everywhere. They make the world turn and she knew them all. Everybody trusts them. They are neither young enough to be swept aside as silly and idealistic or old enough to be bypassed as senile. She persuaded people to do things for me. She commissioned people to let me off the hook. Erma deleted any mention of bloodletting, theft, animal cruelty or alleged sexual abuse of peers from the files. I felt beyond reproach. In spite of all this external help it always amazes me how someone can still fuck up, even with the lifeline of a clean slate. Mom insisted to herself that I would turn over a new leaf.

'My son,' she'd say and stroke my hair with a gut-wrenching sickly smile and a sparkle of madness in her eyes. Still at least Mom was a positive thinker. Dad had all but washed his remaining hand of me.

You might think he had good reason, but then you never met my father. Life was certainly more complex when Dad made his sporadic visits home, as impossible as that may seem. I had barely seen him in the short years of my life. He was as much a stranger to me as he was to my mother, except he didn't give me syphilis. He would swagger in like the lone ranger and people would come out of their houses to greet him and ask him about his top secret missions. The ones that Mother had told them all about in a hushed voice, as though saying it loudly would contravene some secret code of confidentiality. That would never stand up in court. The volume at which her audience was regaled with those tales would not save her from the slammer. He never disclosed his assignments. Maybe there was nothing to divulge. But the deeply penetrating lines on his face and weather-worn look suggested his mind was in receipt of dark knowledge that his lips would never speak and his calm could not quite hide. Maybe they were right. I never found out the truth of the matter to this day. Either that or Dad was an android. He only had to utter the words 'I, Robot' and we would all know he was a knot of electrical circuits connected to the government mainframe. I kept waiting for him to short out. I expected them to refit a prosthetic robo-hand. That way, I would be sure that nothing was ever lost by the amputation anyway. No emotion attached to losing a limb had ever been conveyed to me. It could just be connected back with spare parts, nuts and bolts. They should order a recall. There was clearly a design fault. He was double-hard. He didn't cry. But on one of his visits home it all became clear to me. Dad was flesh and bone with a robotic mind, a super computer all contained in his cranium.

My father had his hand blown off in Nam, although this turn of events is open to interpretation. He was only fifteen. He signed up on the strength of a few strategic lies and the army and the navy were so beaten down by this point they needed all the help they could get. Any little shit would do if only he could take out one of those 'Viet Cong bastards.' Raise the American flag, damn you! He used to show me the stump. It made him feel like a hero. He told me billions of stories about his comrades in arms. One of them had half his left buttock removed after a bullet wound turned septic. Bob was his name. I met him once at some shoulder-punching army reunion. Even at such a tender age I was fully aware that the place was infested with redneck butt-fuckers.

I became obsessed with Bob's ass. I kept right on staring at it, following him round the place. It seemed fine to me, two round buttocks tightly gripped by beige cotton strides. I wondered if Pop had been exaggerating his stories for added impact. Maybe he was the only loser leaving body parts scattered in enemy territory. Bob started talking with a fat guy and turned away from me. That would prove to be a costly mistake. My boyhood inquisitiveness reached a peak and soon got the best of me. I poked him in the ass with a breadstick. No, still couldn't tell what was going on beneath the pants and he didn't even notice. I began a light poking action this time with my finger, seemed hard, so I punched it with my fist. I don't know why I thought he wouldn't notice my investigation, turns out I had hit a raw nerve. Bob spun round red-faced, a rustle occurred in his strides. I'd been rumbled. Pop had seen what I was up to, but was ensconced in conversation with the general and couldn't get away. The solid lump that was Bob's left buttock began wriggling down his leg like a polecat. I had disconnected it and sent it spinning southwest with my right hook, once past the knee it had free descent and sweet release. Bob was calling me every cuss word humanly possible. Pop broke from the general and strode over to us, the robot advancing at pace. I was history. As he bore down upon me, the strange bulge from Bob's pants was revealed to us all; adhesive prosthetic buttock. It lay on the tile by his foot winking at me. There we were; Bob, Pop and me. We all looked from one to the other, to the buttock, in dumb silence. It looked like a giant chicken breast.

The servicemen's wives gathered, everyone stared, seconds of silence ensued, a millennia in length. Then I sniggered. The only noise to break the stalemate was my giggling that turned swiftly into full-blown laughter. Tears streamed down my face. I thought I was going to choke. I just pointed at it and laughed and laughed, nearly pissed my pants. I had broken the silent circle of three.

Bob went for me, Pop went for Bob to stop him beating the living daylights out of me because that was his job. I dove low. Poor Pop, all in front of the vets and their pretty, subservient wives whose reverence for him was slipping away. I would have to be punished publicly as well as privately for this breech of etiquette. The situation, the humiliation, demanded I suffer for my sins; he'd have to claw his respect back. I knew it was me he wanted to kill. He had no interest in restraining Bob, but there were ladies present. Round and round the buttock we went like those ladies dancing round a purse. That was the last time Pop went to a reunion. Bob refused to come around to the house and billed my Dad for the therapy he needed to forget the sorry incident. Still we were all pleased Pop didn't have a swollen chicken fillet for a butt cheek and he could do tricks with his stump.

Pop's stump had no sensation. The nerve endings were decimated in the blast. Raw meat, muscle, cartilage and veins once hung from that stump. They were replaced after many months with a smooth, shiny, discoloured stretch of purple skin protruding slightly more at the top where the bone had broken off at an angle. He couldn't feel a goddamn thing. When he was at home, usually on holidays if he didn't have another war to see to, he'd stick a crochet needle in there, sticking it right in again and again. Everyone watched the spectacle with screwed-up faces, their eyes half closed to feign a lack of gruesome interest, but with the other half eye they watched on, transfixed. It made him feel invincible as he poked his magic stump and felt no pain.

Pop's return often provided the catalyst for another of mother's psychotic episodes, which had started to occur with escalating frequency. I remember one holiday the shit really hit the fan. Mom was tending lovingly to the pot roast. It was the same kind of holiday in which Dad would perform his trick. I guess Mom had seen it one too many times. She was screaming at the neighbour's replacement cat Cojack because it had pissed all over her gardenias for the third time that week and they were withering like grass hung up to dry for rolling. She was calling it a 'fucking, fucking piece of shit,' twitch, 'fuck off and piss on your own gardenias.' She stuck most of her body out of the window and stabbed the air with her fists at the neighbour. 'Fucking take your vermin, you bitch, fuck off with your menagerie or I'll serve it up as meatloaf . . . ' Mom had a mouth like a sewer – the longer time passed, the more the disease progressed. Poor syphilis-addled woman of vast profanity and gross misfortune.

Dad rose from his chair where he had been playing solitaire, a solitary game for a solitary man. He grabbed my mother by the throat and pushed her headfirst with full force to the neck into the kitchen larder, dropping the latch behind. The expression on his face did not change. Still with cold focus as though he'd let the dog outside for a doodle whilst ruminating over military strategy, he turned to the stove and continued with Mom's pot roast in her absence. Mom was pounding on the inside of the larder door, but he didn't seem to notice anymore. He was the kind of guy who got caught up in his own thoughts to block out the outside world. A cold, self-righteous android was he.

He took the vegetables from the hotplate. I watched his every move, frightened to death of making noise so as not to disturb him. On reflection, I believe this was the moment I took a right turn down the slip road to perversity. I had graduated to the torment of human beings. No longer was it confined to the realm of animals, though many would put my father in the same category had they known the truth. Staring out of the window, dreams weaving through his information bank of a brain, filled to the brim with rules and secret codes. He rested his stump on the counter while his only hand stirred the sauce. At least he thought the counter was the receiver of his stump, body weight and all but I had been watching. I saw him lean on the hotplate and I didn't say a word. My nostrils were instantly filled with the sweet, sweet smell of juicy, sizzling meat and I knew it wasn't the pot roast. Must have made his taste buds salivate, that Sunday roast aroma. It was a precious few seconds of relish for my little twisted mind, until the liquidating flesh and fat gave way to raw muscle and a multitude of tiny hidden nerve networks that had not been awakened until now. All hell broke loose. Mom finally broke out of the larder screaming and lunged at Pop with a can of soup. Contact could not have occurred in a more appropriate area of his anatomy. We were pleasured immensely as contact was made swiftly and directly, the can perpendicular to the dripping and oozing flesh of Dad's upturned stump. I pretended to read my comic unawares amidst the screaming and commotion. Pop squealed like a cheerleader as the Campbell's can bludgeoned into his sizzling mushy red flesh and shattered the bone some more. I don't, or choose not to remember much after that, but I remember Mom secretly smiling to herself the next morning as she scraped the congealed fat and burnt skin from the stove and counter, muttering to herself incoherently with a blackened eye.

So you see, Dad could feel pain, he just didn't have the relevant synaptic connections in his brain to convey any emotion. He felt he was immortal but he wasn't. He still didn't cry, not even then, not even after he seared his stump, medium rare. Big boys don't cry, neither do androids, nor do psychotics. So I couldn't cry either if I wanted to retain any vestige of respect from my father. I was a grade A disappointment and a first class embarrassment to him, not a fitting testament to his brilliance. As for my punishment, there were always two steps: the public and the private. The public version always took place in front of his buddies. I was ordered to salute him after a full military style march around the block, butt naked. Later he would take me inside and show me the buckle of his belt all over where no one would see. He'd hit me in the head with a swinging fist so hard I would lose my vision. I'd scramble into the corner and curl up into a ball and tremble and cry as his heavy footsteps retreated down the stairs. His voice carried up the stairwell. I was no son of his. Sometimes I wished he would catch me in the face so everyone would know what a pillar of the community doles out in his spare time. I wished I was dead again. I wished I was dead quite a lot in those days. I wished that Dad had a heart but he didn't. He didn't know what emotion was. He didn't know he was bleeding me dry.

Mom, God help her, was losing it fast. Her friends were falling along the wayside like leaves, but she didn't seem to care. I doubt she even noticed. She had been embarrassing herself all over the place. I wondered if anyone had telephoned Pop to let him know what was going down and if that was why he never came home to his delinquent son and his deranged wife. She'd been acting out all over town. Shouting at people and spitting. If anything happened, just one small thing, she'd head off down the road marked insanity, cussing everyone in her path. She showed her panties in the drugstore just to shut up some old lady who had been complaining she'd taken too long to buy her Bennies, but it was really because she couldn't find her stolen prescription pad. The neighbours were carrying out their very own smear campaign. That was why I stabbed Bobby Schaeffer with a pencil one afternoon and he needed surgery. It served him right for calling me a cross-eyed shit streak with a loon for a mom. The neighbours told everyone all these stories and he repeated them like a little sheep in school. He told everyone she drank her own piss and it was sending her crazy. It was like the Salem witch trial all over again.

It wouldn't be long before I lashed out. There is only so long a person can internalise this kind of maltreatment. It churned round and round my tiny mind. I kept it all in. No sooner had Dad destroyed my confidence and stripped off another piece of Mom's fraying mind than he was gone again on some pretence, leaving shattered sensibilities in his wake. It wouldn't be long before all sense had less than graciously slipped out the back exit, leaving nothing left to tread all over on his return.

It proved to be a negative loop, from home to school and

back and forth and so on. The other kids would laugh and poke fun at me and my good pal Jim. We would retire to corners of the schoolyard to seek solace in fantasy worlds. If it wasn't one thing it was another. My boss eye was a serious source of hilarity until I had laser surgery on Dad's military medical insurance. He wanted me to look him and the general in the eye when he received his medals which would be soon for sure, he could personally guarantee it. He wanted me to see him decorated in awe instead of something slightly to the left of the action. Then there was my mother to contend with. The fact that I was named Theodore was apparently an incongruous namesake because Theodore is no kind of name for a young person to have. The girls said I had no business being named after one of our all time great leaders since I was such a loser. They would sing to me like Marilyn Monroe did for Kennedy and then pelt me with stones. The teachers hated me too and I hated to be called Theodore. In fact, no one ever called me that unless they were ripping me up, except for my Mom and those matrons. Everyone else just called me Steves because that of course is my name.

Jim was a gimp but I liked him. I got the feeling he would always make me feel better about myself. Let's face the facts; the girls were always going to end up liking me more than him. Yes, with Jim stood beside me I would always look cool. Besides, he was the only person who would listen to my constant flow of nonsense. Indeed, he lapped it up. He couldn't wait. He found it all truly, truly inspiring. It didn't matter how trite or ridiculous my words were; he would be in total agreement, in wonderment no less. Sometimes I would test him by thinking of the craziest, most unapologetically stupendous things to say, knowing nobody could think me anything less than certifiable for having such depraved thoughts and Jim loved it. He loved me. I loved myself.

We were little gimps. We had bad co-ordination and our voices hadn't broken yet. I knew it would be better once I sounded like a man. I would boom, I would bellow, it would resound, echo from all walls like James Earl Jones because I had seen *Star Wars* at the movie theatre. I was drawn to the notion of 'Steves: The Dark Destroyer, The Master of Delusion', my hero. I would be Jane's hero too. I'd just take her whenever it pleased me and she'd melt. I'd make her want to do things that she never thought possible because I drove her wild with my burgeoning manliness. She would be the colt to my stallion and Jim would be the Robin to my Batman. Jane would see us juxtaposed and I would make the finest comparable companion. After all, everything is relative to something else, like the lesser of two evils. I fancied myself the champion of the independent cause as I always felt different somehow. It comes from being abused so very often. Anyone with half a mind knows the value of the intellectual, independent choice over the marketed mainstream strategy. This would eventually be my strength as inversely as it had always been my weakness. I would turn it all to my advantage. I knew I would never make a Jock, never toe the line.

I told all of this to Jim and he inevitably agreed. Jim ruled my world because I ruled his. My every action condoned with blind faith and the unconditional bonding of youth. His subservience was to be commended but only if his allegiance remained in the right place. Testing times were ahead of us for sure. I wasn't certain that I had as much loyalty to Jim as he did to me. I just didn't know if I could give what I received. You see, I knew it was Jim who fiddled with Jane at camp. She blamed me because secretly she wished it were true. Jim was certainly a sneak and much more cunning than I had given him credit for. In some part it was my fault, I suppose. Jane was much more developed than the other girls. She started sprouting in single digits and I told him I'd seen inside her shirt; that her breasts were firm to the touch and smooth and her nipples were like silver bullets. I read it in one of Mom's special books, the ones she kept under her bed for night-time reading. She came alive in the night. They weren't the only ones I had felt, I'd boasted for the purpose of gathering kudos. Yep, I had been slipping my hands down shirts left, right and centre and all willingly received. I guess Jim thought this was acceptable behaviour because I had legitimised it in some way.

The unauthorised communal tent was the perfect ruse for phantom prying hands. Who would know whence they came. I certainly had the proximal advantage. When Jane awoke undressed to the waist, it was I who just so happened to be having a wet dream and flailed murmuring. I rolled over at the wrong moment, my nose tickled by a lonesome, stray breast hair, inhaling nipple. That's when I was rudely awakened from my steamy chance encounter with Princess Lea by the most piercing, murderous scream that I had ever had the misfortune to hear. Even worse than Mom and that was truly a feat in itself. Jim felt bad, worse than hell, but he was impotent to do anything. He couldn't look me in the eye as they marched me back to school. I was called to account in the principal's office. Jim just hung around outside for what seemed like years. Mom was there. I was there. The principal was there. So was Jane. So were Jane's nipples and they were piercing through her shirt, pointing at me accusingly.

It seemed futile to protest or to say anything at all. The teachers had been waiting for such an opportunity to eject me from the institution for as long as I could remember. If I told the truth they would say I was lying. Jim wouldn't speak. If I came clean they would've hauled him in there within the blink of an eye and he'd have pissed himself on the principal's plush rug. I didn't really care if they let me go. They were doing me a favour. I'd have more time to get up to mischief, less time to get yelled at. Actually, I was a little proud of Jim. In many ways this ritual had been a kind of coming-of-age for him. We could join forces once again and sweep on ahead in our two-man misfit band. After all, I knew he would do all he could to make it up to me, grovel for a while and repay my kind gesture with favours. Whatever I asked he would do. Maybe one day he could take the wrap for me. It would only be fair. So I just sat there with my arms folded, eyeing up Jane's tits insolently. A junior high reject. All in a day's work.

A semester passed. Mom called Erma.

Erma turned out to be a tricky one, bent, but she looked so straight down the line. All the better, for she wrote me references that would have put Mother Teresa to shame. I owed her a great deal, though I never showed it. It was by her hand that I managed to get into private high school. Dad's money proffered as his last ditch attempt to correct me by allying me to the well heeled set. A doomed plan for certain but subsequently, I finally managed to get closer to Jane. She still refused to let me touch her. Spoil sport.

Jane, my Jane; by the time I got into high school I had matured somewhat. I felt like a stud already, a pseudo stud at any rate. A semester passed, my voice dropped and my shoulders rivalled the Jocks' for breadth. Yeah, sure, Jane wanted to know me now, for appearance's sake. She would never separate the new improved Steves from the kid she had grown up with, familiarity breeds contempt. OK, the other girls had caught up with her in the womanly stakes, but she still cut the finest figure. I still yearned to squeeze her and do bad things. But I just didn't really know her. I superimposed my own dreams of what she might be onto an empty shell of a girl, a girl who was so lacking in substance it was infuriating and I became embarrassed by association. All the time life was passing right by her and she didn't even notice. It was fortunate that she liked to do guys' stuff like play basketball and smoke and watch science fiction and war movies, but there really was no substance to her when I actually thought about it. Things weren't ever going to change. She was the girl who settled down and had kids as though that was the pinnacle of achievement; without ambition or drive, a conformist. That was when she started to bore me. I was going off her already and if that wasn't enough to seal the deal, she ratted on me. She turned out to be more experienced than I thought. This expertise was the work of our science teacher. She was not to be trusted. A she-devil disguised as the girl next door. Jane ratted on me for trying to save her virtue. I wasn't to know she didn't have any to lose but I found out. Talk about trying to do someone a favour. I resolved never to bother again.

It was a Friday evening after class finished for the weekend and we were all feeling celebratory. We had been hanging around behind the Plaza galleria, sniffing glue and assortments of household and industrial detergents. High as kites were we and ready to fly to the moon. All this mingled with testosterone made for a potential chemical imbalance. It was just Jane, Jim and I and a couple of other guys and girls. We were doing no harm. Jim and I sloped off to get some beers with our fake IDs. Whilst we were sourcing supplies, some old guy, must've been around forty, was busy accosting my favourite girl back in the alley. He invited her back to his new apartment, the one he kept for flings with underage girls behind his wife's back. She said yes, the tease. He was sliming all over her and licking her face in a styleless fashion no decent woman would have contemplated in a million years. We made our way back in defeat, my mood dampened. Not only did we return empty-handed, but I came around the corner to see this guy draped all over my Jane. In my stomach was a seething ball of fire. We stormed over, puffing ourselves up against this large, suited business-man. Jim followed my lead. I suppose he thought we were no match for that business tycoon. But this was to be a David and Goliath rematch, director's cut. He did something much worse than trying to steal my girl; that fool. He actually laughed in my face.

'Go home Kiddo,' he chided. Then he began to walk off with his arm around Jane. Kiddo saw red.

Bludgeoned. Yes, that is the term necessary here. In order to facilitate utmost pain and because it seemed to be the only rudimentary weaponry around, I grabbed some old bicycle chain from the garbage skip we had been leaning on. The thought process was fairly hazy and poorly planned but brilliantly executed. Some award winning moves were on display.

I squared up to him, blocking his path as he pulled Jane away from us, his arm still round her shoulder.

'Where do you think you're going?' I inquired.

'Back to my pad with your girlfriend, by the looks of it. That's right, isn't it beautiful?' he letched. Jane nodded in the affirmative. He grabbed her breast as though that proved something other than the fact she wasn't worth my affection. As though it proved he owned her. He was welcome, I didn't want soiled goods. But the sleaze still needed to be taught that undermining Steves will never do. She didn't even protest. I closed my eyes for a second and imagined restraint did not exist. Then I unleashed the fury.

'I'm going to whip the fuck until he squeals.' I rasped the chain against the concrete. Everyone dispersed. Jane retreated. Neither of them was looking so smug now.

Once, twice . . . six, seven, eight times, I couldn't stop. Girls screamed, I laughed, Jim cried. The guy's friends were following shortly behind him but beat a hasty retreat as they turned the corner to see my display of youthful might. They didn't stick around long enough to see my face. There was nothing they could have done. I was venting all my frustration in full flow. I warrant I would have survived the stab of their fountain pens had they attempted to intervene, office boys. Rip, tear, thud, splat, blood spattered across Jane's face in a ribbon of red flecks, thrust at a pace so that they elongated and bled into each other. The chain, swinging back and forth as if by its own volition only inches from Jane's pretty, corrupted face. I stopped just in time, just as he was at the edge of consciousness. We had to flee the scene. We stood there frozen for precious seconds until sense returned to us. Then we sprinted away at ninety nine times the speed of light. No one would be able to prove anything because the only witnesses were my friends and they would never turn me over. There were rumours spreading like wildfire though and Jane finally spewed it all out to the science teacher she had been seeing without my consent. The school notified my mom of the impending expulsion, but she did not understand the nature of their proposition.

'Thank you.' She responded and scratched her crotch.

I was no longer welcome in the bastion of the articulate and educated. Yawn. Although they dearly would have liked to go for prosecution, it turned out the guy was a school governor; happily married with two lovely daughters matriculated into the very same institution. He had a reputation to safeguard that attempting to sleep with a minor would not withstand. Thus freedom was mine. I didn't even have to get Jim to make the false confession I still felt he owed me. That could be saved for another day. Jim was my get out of jail free card although he didn't realise it yet. If he did, he did not dare to question my judgement, not after that.

I had achieved a certain degree of celebrity, no, infamy from all of this. Everybody was talking. They had seen the guy around, his face all mashed up. I think some of them were secretly pleased that the pious trumpeter of big business solutions was now the walking wounded. He deserved it anyway for pensioning off half the local workforce; sending their pay packets to Bombay at half the cost, without a second thought for their livelihoods. Perhaps this would keep his ruthlessness and his arrogance at bay. A few of the kids from school started following me around. I would just be walking to the store. As I turned they would be ten paces behind, looking around for inspiration and scratching their heads so as not to look like the sycophants they were and because they were scared of me which pleasured me immensely. Some of them just did it because they lived nearby and thought they might do a little detour so that they could check out what Mom was up to today. It wouldn't be long before they got what they wanted and she'd flash someone. I just knew it was on the cards. She had become rather partial to letting it all hang out in public.

I also gained the attention of the little guys' moms, well at least one anyway. Mr CEO had fired her husband, so she condoned my actions in secret vindication. I was considering her now that I had gone off the idea of Jane. I wondered if she would consider adopting me and get her husband in on it. I could try and make them feel sorry for me. I was the victim of an underprivileged upbringing. I couldn't help it. Then I could lay this little guy's mom whilst his dad went out and bought me a Corvette since I was old enough to drive now. I could endear myself to them and play them like fiddles. She certainly had a special new glint in her eye when I walked past the house. Maybe she liked a little bit of rough. But reality crept in. Perhaps I could go along with it for a while, but I knew I would have to be prepared to use my imagination. She wouldn't be as lithe and taut as she used to be and dad might still have a fair left hook. He'd probably been doing some weights in the back yard since he reached the mid-life crisis. His new bulging arms would be backed up by a sledgehammer of cholesterol in that thickened, solid body. Take him on and he might just have a coronary and then I would be doing time. Still, it was a perverse fantasy and I liked those a lot. Still do as a matter of fact.

What Mom failed to tell me was that as a concession to the school for not fingering me, I must attend therapy with the local psychiatrist. Mom had been seeing Doctor Burke for a few months now. Dad thought he was helping her, although he didn't seem to realise she only needed treatment to undo all of the damage he had done. I knew better, she had only got worse. The Brain Butcher, I liked to call him. He took his two hundred bucks an hour and ran all the way to the bank in disbelief, clicking his heels along the way. I knew it would only be a matter of time before he scrambled my brains too. I would have to keep his efforts in check.

During her semi-insanity, Mom turned from religion to the cult of therapy to soothe her pain and banish her demons. She was into fads. Anything that promised much more than it could ever deliver. Ever faithful in the quick fix approach was she; a perfect target for pyramid selling schemes, psychics, hypnotists and such like. She was taken in by everything that promised her security, leaving me to look on cynically, sadly shaking my head at her every half-assed attempt at redemption. I went along with it. Sneering and playing up to the maudlin game of voyeuristic confessionals that I knew would ensue. My plan was to throw the Doc off the true scent by inventing things and lying. He would sit with two fingers propping up his withering head and nod and ask for more. He wouldn't respond to my statements but continue to stare at me until I added more and more, like a particularly bad interviewer on TV who can't think of any intelligent questions or deviate from the script. He would wait until I got to a point that was fitting for his next question. Questions he had memorised because he seemed unable to improvise. I saw this as a failure on his part. I already knew he was a failure anyway as he had done nothing to benefit my dear mother in her quest for sanity.

'More, elaborate, tell me about your childhood, your father, your mother.'

Of course he already knew. It was all in his casebook, the file marked 'Steves' was bursting to the brim. Mom was the guinea pig for all his new methods that needed to be tested to prove safe for human exposure.

'Do you expect us to hypnotise mice in the lab, or ask rats about their family history and their feelings? This is the art of the mind,' he said patronisingly when I took the opportunity to question him, 'a human process, rats have inferior conscience and lack the ability to speak.' Clearly he had never met anyone like myself before. I fear the rat to be the king of communal living and the purveyor of fine morality by comparison. Foolhardy old goat.

He had all kinds of tried and tested methods up his sleeve. Each one designed to extricate the utmost personal information. To torture the individual in question by confronting them with anything unsavoury that had gone before, that once resurfaced, could possibly drive them nuts. Yes, all of this designed to bring the most brutal and hurtful feelings that remained hidden for years to safeguard the owner, bubbling back to the surface and send them plummeting in a downward spiral. I imagined his expertise used as a new torture device by wayward regimes. Suppress and avoid, that is my advice to you. We have the ability to forget for a reason. All of this pain generated for the exclusive purpose of adding a few more

morsels to his salacious new book, to be marketed as a testament to his gift of understanding, a shrine to celebrate his
superior professional prowess; his gift from God to prove his
worth as a true healer of the mind. Instead, he just waded in
there and got bogged down in it all. He charged forth like the
proverbial bull in a china shop and smashed and mashed and
fried people's brains and disconnected their minds from their
lives. Then let them go like helium balloons to float around
almost endlessly before reaching the stratosphere and bursting
on impact.

I had to write everything down like homework and I should
try very hard not to miss anything out because I might neglect
the key to my madness. The Doc told me I should get a pen
and paper and make a list of all the good points about myself
and all the bad ones. This process was adapted person to person. Then a list of all the shitty things that happened to me and
why was compiled. We could talk about how I had channelled
my negative energy in order to unwittingly bring about catastrophe upon my own shoulders. Break it all down and analyse
the death out of it. He liked that. He said it was good for me,
only I didn't know it yet.

'What about a hit list?' said I.

'Theodore, what is the purpose of such a document? Write
me a passage about why that is of interest to you, with
examples.' He knew he'd be high up the list, top three easily. I
leant in closer to him and announced I had a proposition for
him to consider.

'I could dissect you and list all your body parts if you like.
We don't get the chance to do it at school. We just look at the
pictures in books. I'd like to see it close up. I might do com-

munity service down at the morgue.' I was joking, but I said it dry. Doctor Burke looked like he might cry. I relaxed back into my chair and smiled at him. He called Mom to ask for more money for sessions because I sure as hell needed them. Every time I came by his office after that he had a bodyguard frisk me for knives or anything that could be construed as a destructive projectile launched at his balls. However, he could not confiscate my fist. I was beginning to see the irony of the world and his flagrant lack of systematic planning. That precisely that lack of planning can lead to destruction and failure. Of course, the best-laid plans can and will go awry if you neglect to govern them in the strictest of manners. Tight controls, checks and balances are what are needed. We all know the benefits of self-regulation. Doctor Burke had not ensured a failsafe plan to govern his own well-being.

So I wrote everything down in order that he could pinpoint the moment, the emergence of madness, its embryology documented. The seed could be small, seem insignificant, but become cataclysmic when analysed twenty times over, after fifteen other things had been read into it. Thus something that seemed so unimportant had suddenly become enormous and pivotal and had morphed into something entirely different to that which was real. This was par for the course as the Doc seemed impervious to the truth.

I was not privy to the fact that Mom had filled him in with useful anecdotes already. Perhaps he had tired of her and now he had moved on to another victim. Mom's sessions became supplementary to mine, fact-finding missions, like preparatory research. He poked, prodded and cajoled her for more juicy morsels and half-truths; any superfluous detail that might lend a new light to his enquiries into my wanton mind. I got the feeling that my leading him astray with wild stories was clouding his hypothesis, for I never had any intention of even grazing the truth. The therapy was merely a mild irritation and somewhat fun whilst he wasn't on to me. I had no intention of letting him in, for that would prove too unsettling an encroachment. The fool was intent on burglarising my mind.

On her last visit, Mom furnished the Doc with my scrapbook. The one I had filled with press cuttings of things that I found interesting. The one no one else ever saw because it was so dear to my heart. I felt violated. I was as angry as hell when he pulled it out of his top drawer and wanted to know more.

'Now let's see,' he said putting on his glasses and clasping his hands. He read out loud into his Dictaphone, slowly for added impact, raising his eyes over his glasses intermittently in an enquiring manner.

'Scrapbook entitled "The Empire of Steves".' He licked his finger and turned the page. 'Potential members.' Pause for effect. 'Joe Derek Spangler, convicted February 14. Convicted by unanimous jury after five minutes of deliberation. Dissected his victims into cubes.'

'Leroy Gilman. Shot his mother in the head, decomposed body found buried under his porch. Sentenced to death by lethal injection November 19 1983, sentence commuted to life imprisonment, pending leniency after child abuse allegations surfaced and were corroborated by family members. Escaped during transportation to maximum security prison. Deemed to be harmful to others. Really.'

'Fugitive on the run. Nathaniel Bartlett Junior. Suspected of four drive-by and two sniper-style shootings, total fatalities sixteen. Last seen in the Houston, Texas area. Considered to be armed and dangerous.'

'Kathryn Monroe, 16 years of age, committed to state mental facility, Tucson. Convicted of arson; burning her entire family of six to death in their own beds, June 16 1980.'

'Is there anything you would like to share with me, Theodore?'

This was not looking good. Not good at all. I refused to elaborate on my plans. So we sat in silence for the rest of the session. I had an unhealthy interest in the macabre. I wished I'd brought my darts with me because he had my back to the wall and I imagined spearing him right through both of his pupils to stop him from staring. I dreamt of paying him back one day. The ceiling looked nice; I stared at it until it was time to go home.

With that I felt the Doc was on to me and he was closer to the truth than I felt comfortable with. The wild goose chase had proved to be a poor ruse, a botched fakery. I reasoned that I would have to kill the Doc if I saw him again or burn the files. With no infiltrator in residence at his office there would be no chance of an inside job. So I would just have to go along with it, with the corrective conditioning and so fool him into believing my behaviour had been adjusted. He preferred to call it 'behaviour modification'. I informed him that he could dispose of my collage of perversity, it was just research for a class essay anyway. I paid Erma a visit. She felt sorry for Mom, knowing that she was getting worse every day and not wishing to overload her with undue stress. She sent the Doc a letter on school headed paper, forged the principal's signature. It turned out that the scrapbook had been important research for a paper and that I had been a prize student torn down by an isolated incident of juvenile revelry, a one off. I had been such a good boy that I had continued with the paper even after I had been ejected from school. I deserved a gold star and a pat on the back. I was a committed class genius. I should have made Prom Queen. The Doc felt suitably embarrassed by his imaginations that he gave the scrapbook back to me. With my precious personal research restored there would be no need to spend valuable time in the library studying microfiche to re-establish my findings. I could steam on with hatching my plan, as yet in its embryonic stages. The Doctor didn't know what he had done.

So the sessions went on, covering the same ground over and over. He wanted to know about all the things that Dad did to me, how I felt about Mom, what I thought about myself. I omitted the truths. It whirled round and round, stirring up anger and bitterness. He would take me to the edge and I'd want to stab my father through the heart. I was a mass of pent-up hatred, frustration. I felt heavy and weary of it all and uncommonly bilious, my stomach churned. The Doc didn't care; it was all ripe for the files. I felt sick. It had all come back. I couldn't help feeling that I had been cosmically shit on at every juncture, every stage. With every one of Mom's schizoid episodes and every outpour from Dad's raging pseudo-heart. I was a cosmic shit magnet and I was about to repel. He was playing with fire. I'll give him his dues; he certainly did some damage in there. How I would love to drive by his surgery now with bloody hands and smear them all over his face, all over that grey moustachioed face and laugh. Just to let him know his little experiment didn't quite work in the long run. Just so he'd know that, before I drove a stake through his pre-eminence. I'd watch as they rescinded his honorary degree and professorship. So people could see that you can't turn a hospital porter into a psychiatrist on the strength of a silver tongue, a fake CV and one stinking case study. As I left his office for the last time, I turned to him at the door and raised a fist to his chin. 'If I ever see you again,' said I, 'I'll kill you.' And one day I just might.

That night I got home to find Mom's home help waiting for me in the kitchen. Mrs Johnson had arrived to deliver exciting news as Mom sat in the corner dribbling. I suppose she thought the impending arrival of my father might be a comfort to me. She wasn't to know she was announcing the ascent of the devil from the bowels of hell. Mrs Johnson, Mom's general dogsbody and victim of persistent abuse, told me to remove all sharp implements from the house. I should stay inside. Mom was effectively under house arrest until Pop came home, like some Burmese dissident of the junta, held captive. He would be back tomorrow. I'd only have to hold out for twenty-four hours. Mrs Johnson was taking a short sabbatical. Just twenty-four hours to go, surely even I could manage that. She was due to leave the next day. Yes, Dad was on his way and I felt compromised. I began to hate him for it. The Doc had brought all the pain back. All at once I wanted desperately for Pop to return so that Mom could get more help and at the same time, when the word came, I felt dead. I knew he was coming back to sever ties and finalise things with Mom and me. I'd be alone with her, with no chance of escape. I couldn't face a lifetime of that. You see, my mother was as incapacitated by her state of mind as I was to be mothered by her. I could do nothing to break her mould and she could do nothing to release me of her grip. She had me unwittingly imprisoned by her own lack of rehabilitation. She had come to require the curative, not preventative method. She never took her pills. She had herself to blame. She was beyond saving. Any perceived connection with the real world was by now severed. She could no longer fend for herself and interpersonal relations were mere memories. The only human interaction she allowed or was offered was with Mrs Johnson whom my father paid off handsomely so that he would not have to do the job himself, or even to see Mom at all. I could not be trusted. I was sure to neglect my mother. The call would come to him that she had been found wandering the streets in her night gown, barefoot. Everyone would know she had gone crazy. They knew anyway, but Dad felt he could pass it off, perhaps as a short term hormone imbalance, a fleeting lapse never to be revisited. By now my resolve to escape my heritage had the will of the Bengal tiger and the strength of the fearsome bear. Dad was coming home for the first time in nine months. I would tell him then. I was ready. June 16 1987 and I'd be gone.

On June 17 1987 I was still begrudgingly in residence. Pop hadn't come home yet, nor had he regarded me highly enough to call and tell me he was going to be held up. Worse still, Mrs Johnson had headed off on her two week break to Hawaii. I had been reliably informed by the hospice that due to staff shortage, a replacement dogsbody would not be available until Pop returned. Therefore it would be down to me, a sixteen-year-old waster, to tend to every need and whim.

Two weeks passed and Dad was a no-show. It was the worst two weeks of my life so far and that was no mean feat. I loved my mom but she was a bitch. I dodged a constant stream of foul language, foodstuffs and anything that wasn't nailed down. She wouldn't eat so I stopped making her meals. I knew I'd be wearing it no sooner than I'd handed it to her. She pissed herself and looked pleased about it. She locked herself in the bathroom, ordered pizza for half the street and defecated on the front lawn. She fiddled with herself over and under her skirt. She didn't have crabs; she hadn't seen a man except for the Doc for months. She did not need to for she had me. She dribbled. Every once in a while I thought I saw a flicker of hope, as though she recognised me. Her face would soften and you had to really look to see it, but the twinkle would definitely come back to her eyes. Then it was gone as soon as it came. It was as though a wave of hope rolled over her for just a second and then headed out to the horizon and beyond to who knows where. Mom was like a little bottle lost at sea, bobbing around, looking for solid ground and never finding it, getting dragged back into the swell by the current. I wanted her to be happy again. Maybe it would stop her. She used to be happy in her own way. That slightly crazy happiness, when she knew she was crazy and that's OK. It is when you stop knowing that you've really lost the thread. But happiness now, for her, seemed far away, eclipsed by something malevolent and all-consuming. I never thought it would come to this. I never thought I would have to wipe my own mother's ass as she cried and didn't know why.

I must keep an eye on her at all times because she had called Pop and told him she was going to kill herself. He didn't want her blood on his hand; surely he could be tried for neglect. Perhaps if she had issued him with a joint suicide pact, my own demise included in the threat, he would have considered it as a lucrative trade-off. After all, if I wasn't a bum, I was a waster, no-hoper, loser, scab. Dad hated me. He hated that I had half of his genes. He hated that Mom's had managed to override his in the genetic power struggle. The quality of the nucleus had been poor, his material compromised. I looked like her, failed like her. I even ate like her with my little finger in the air. I had no balls and neither did she. I was to all intents and purposes, my father's nemesis. I was a mongrel and he was a pedigree; inconsistent and intangible, prone to mood swings, uncertainty, paranoia, and delusions of grandeur. It seemed so clear that I belonged to the travelling salesman who stopped by one day and gave Mom something she'd never forget. To his mind, I made her mad. I ruined her, not him. I was obtuse, impulsive, repulsive, reckless, a liar, a swindler. I would amount to nothing. I already amounted to less than nothing so I would have to make further improvements in order to reach mere nothingness. I was the true embodiment of insignificance, an amoeba. One day I would die and before such time I should be neutered in case I attempted to reproduce myself; to further corrupt Dad's dud chromosomes, creating another perfect example of derangement and delinquency. There was no point. There was quite simply Theodore Steves, and that meant zip.

He would have to face his conscience in the final judgement; that he had made me this way and not by small contribution. A rounded individual does not result from being ruled with an iron fist. He would learn that childhood traumas create wounds that never truly heal. Nevertheless, he spent years wondering where he went wrong, only to gloss over every good reason that he knew to be true, in order to point the finger of blame at someone else's door. I felt like the centre of the universe and one of its outermost satellite moons, an ice-cold wasteland, all at once. I didn't know whether I was coming or going. I felt omnipotent and like nothing at all, in unison. If I really meant so little, why did Pop hate me so much?

The burden of his return was bearing down on me, but I couldn't leave Mom to his mercy as much as I wanted to hot-foot it out the door. I imagined him on the train, busy calling round sanatoriums for the cheapest rate. I wished to God I'd been dealt a better hand in life. Pop was on his way home and it would be like the holocaust, Armageddon. Dad would rip Mom's heart out. I knew that he'd finally had his fill and given up on her as it seemed he had years ago. Something had to be done. This disastrous chapter in my life could not be resolved by proxy killing. No. I couldn't solve this problem vicariously through animal carnage. I realised I'd have to take matters into my own hands; action must be effected, like taking an enema, I must cleanse. I must finally do something positive for Mom instead of careering through her life disrupting everything and causing her pain and heartache. I would set her free and in doing so set myself free. I would save her from herself. She could then be my angel and look after me from on high as she had always done before.

I loved Mom so much and it broke me in two. She was nuts. She never did anything unkind to anyone before she got sick. It ate away at her mind. It changed her but she didn't know what she was doing or saying. People laughed at her and pointed. They had no respect. They never saw Dad hit her. They never saw him hit me. Both of us cowering together, wondering what his blackened heart would conjure up next for our punishment. Punishment for something we didn't deserve. It was always the war with him. Everything. The war was in his head, playing on repeat. They were both killing me slowly in their own special ways, a slow and secret death. Something inside me had died. I had to set things straight.

There was no strategy. It all happened in a flash. Jim was due to arrive at any moment. I'd arranged to meet with him so I could say goodbye and clear off well before Dad got near the house. It was now or never. I arrived back home, my arms full of the groceries I intended to leave for Mom so she wouldn't starve. I still wasn't sure exactly when Dad would be back but it would keep her going for a few days, assuming she didn't smear it all up the walls. Mom was on the kitchen floor, her face illuminated by the half light, the slits of the roman blinds throwing shafts of moonlight onto a tortured expression. Tears glinted, streaming down her face, drawn out by years of self-loathing, self-harm and self-neglect. I stumbled on some newspapers she'd scattered all about the floor. I almost stood on her hands as she crouched before me. I set down the heavy paper bags and began to cry.

'God?' she said in a soft whisper. 'Have you come for me?'

'No Mom it's me. I got some stuff from the store. I'm back now, it's OK.'

'Who are you? I don't know you. Theodore!' She hollered over her shoulder as though I were in another room. 'There's a man in the house.'

She looked so scared. She started to hit me with little clenched fists. She had no strength, her hands just fell at the ground

43

and she started to wail. Silence, suddenly punctured by shrill wailing and then the silence returned again. I couldn't allow her to suffer anymore. Everything came and went from my mind in a blur, a void, gone so fast it felt like the laws of physics rearranged and time ceased to matter and splintered. Moments like this sucked into the vortex. It was black and still as though time had stopped. Looking back, I see images in double, triple, time speeding through the cosmos, screaming through my mind at one hundred miles per hour. A flash and it all comes back. Mom, I'm going to make you proud.

I charged upstairs to Mom's bedroom to find the gun Dad kept in the dresser drawer. I had stumbled upon it once before as I rummaged through her belongings looking for her rude books way back before I knew the facts of life. I never thought to investigate it further until the last time I was in there. Turning the place over for any spare cash I could find to buy her food and to pay for her pills. The pills she needed but never took. The ones she kept under her tongue and pretended to swallow before spitting them out behind my back. The Smith & Wesson was loaded. That was assured. Dad always said there isn't time to load a weapon when the enemy is about to strike. Should an intruder reveal himself, he must be disabled immediately with a swift and fatal blow. It was just like the war. A man had the right to defend himself just as I had the right to defend the dignity of my mother. A dignity that the callousness of life had seen fit to strip away. I would save her from herself and from the cruelty of everyone else. I could no longer help her and no one seemed to care at all. Lost in the system and in her head was she.

I grappled with the thing. It was heavier than I'd expected

and I had to hold it with both hands to get a good enough grip to euthanise with expedience and accuracy. The barrel slid forward in my shaking hands. I caught myself in the mirror and looked a little. I didn't posture or pose. My dark twin stared back at me, my stooge. I would close my eyes whilst he took care of this for I couldn't bear to think for myself anymore.

I jumped down the stairs two at a time, hot and sweating and shaking. An out-of-body experience was upon me, light headed and heavy footed. My heart ached inside. I focused on nothing to overcome the schoolboy anguish I was feeling at my core. I blanked reality out for the greater good, for if this was to be the rest of our lives, we might just as well both be dead.

Mom was still on the kitchen floor. I left the light off. I didn't want to see her like that anymore, but to remember her laughing and baking brownies and cleaning my knees when I fell, like normal moms do. Kissing it all better and remembering I was her son. Because she didn't recognise me anymore. She thought I was God and that I had come for her salvation and I would. Because when I asked the angels or anyone to help, they ignored my pleas. If only I could muster the courage to stop crying for long enough to see clearly through the tears that had me blinded; the inertia that had my hands incapable of mobility. I could do this. Fate had come calling and it refused to take no for an answer. She looked up at me with those big eyes. She could see right through me. She always knew, she said the eyes are the window to the soul and they are. Hers were telling me to stop the pain.

As I wavered, I put a hand on the trigger assembly and tripped the trigger early. I wasn't ready. I wasn't aiming right.

The bullet tore through Mom's shoulder, ripping her dress and obliterating the collar bone at point-blank range, she shuddered violently, thin and slumped, her shoulder hung. I smelled burned flesh, jolted backward, thrust by the blast. She coughed and spittle and blood trickled from her mouth. I could hardly see her, but I could hear the gurgling sound and her calling my name softly. I couldn't even shoot her right.

'Mom, I'm sorry. I'm sorry. Sorry. Sorry. I'm sorry.' I kept saying it over and over again. Tears were all in my mouth. My head was about to explode. Then the click of the door came. No. I swung round expecting to see Jim stood there in the doorway. I reset the trigger for Mom. But it wasn't Jim at all. It was Dad. He lunged at me.

'No, son, no!' His voice tailed off as he dropped to the floor. I shot him with the round meant for Mom, but I don't remember doing it.

Mom was pulling herself toward me with her good arm, legs trailing. There she was, hanging on to life, just to will me to take it away from her. I couldn't move. The gun still smoked in my hand. I had prolonged her pain by forcing her to bring herself to me. Until the end I'd caused her more suffering than could ever be justified or necessary. As she reached me she outstretched her arm, thin fingers clawing, scarlet with holding her wound. I dropped to my knees. I know that's what happened because she put her hand to my face, the moistness transferred to my cheek to join the tears. She stared into my eyes with that sparkle and whispered in my ear. That's when I pulled the trigger. I had the gun to her head. She slipped down my body to the lino floor. Her eyes rolled back and her mouth was still open. A dark pool began to form around her head almost immediately. In the

46

darkness it looked black and grew larger and larger. It crept toward the dark pool that had seeped from Dad's head and thickened. I continued to stare until the two masses reached each other. Mom and Dad together again, except he was going to a different place.

I don't know how long Jim had been standing there when I finally noticed his presence. The room filled with something, some aura or whatever you'd like to call it, but it was there all the same. Jim sensed it I'm sure, but he couldn't tell me because he couldn't move his lips. He was frozen in the moment he stepped into the room when he heard the shots go off. It may have been dark, just silhouettes and outlines but I could clearly make out the whites of his eyes and the place where he was standing in the pool of Dad's blood, seeping up his sneakers and his too-long jeans.

I shook violently. I was going to be sick. I shook my head and cried uncontrollably. Then I wiped the gun on my jeans and took off into the yard and over the fence. I ran and ran into the night, leaving Jim to his fate.

TWO

Eugene

I headed straight to New York as all waifs and strays do. For the young and free, the city is a dazzling abundance of undiscovered treasures. Mesmerising and tantalising with its fluorescent signs and its whispers of fortune. Watching the girls stalking the streets, looking for nothing more than the thrills that summoned me to this place long ago; fresh blood, easy pickings. Life is uncomplicated because nobody cares what you do. Lost in the big smoke, coasting all day long with the boys; lounging in cafes, smoking in the springtime and drinking dry the bars at night. The noise and pollution sucked up your nose seems like the best thing you ever inhaled, ever. Every bagel the best you ever tasted. Take the dew in the mornings, glistening in the park or walking over Brooklyn Bridge on a crisp winter day, the sun streaming into your eyes and making your heart warm and satisfied, even though your hands are like ice. The wonder of it all allowing you to forget the past, every little discovery a new surprise, a new opportunity. All of it waiting for you like a dream you had when you were a kid. No one can ruin it because it's yours. It's just so inspirational, so perfect, brazen in its glory. The city sprawls out showing you everything it's got to offer, just waiting for you to help yourself to a piece of the action. Those were the best years of my life. Yes, life was good. Before I got bitter,

New York was the place to be. Like no place on earth.

Inevitably this would be subverted. It was only a matter of time. Some day, some place, the little threads would begin to unravel and fray. It nagged and goaded me from the back of my mind, subconsciously waiting for the inexorable moment for the bubble to burst or for the cops to come calling. Always waiting for Jim to squeal his heart out; rotting in the bowels of some godforsaken prison cell for my crime. I thought I'd just about run rings round it. My wallet was swollen from the fruits of the newest enterprise. I could do pretty much whatever I wanted, whenever I wanted. I had friends, we'd kick around laughing. We'd spend our time fooling around, ripping off old guys who couldn't run any faster and ripping off young guys who didn't know any better. Virginia seemed a million miles away. The channels of enterprise appeared to be endless and bountiful, within the confines of my youthful outlook. One in which there never was too much ambition, no resignation, just contentment. There was never any reason to think we didn't have enough or that we really wanted more. We epitomised the carefree existence of the young before they've bogged themselves down in the mire that they call their lives, creating their legacy and losing their identity in the process. It's the power of suggestion that really screws people up. For a guy like me, it screwed me even more than bowing to the weight of expectation screws the others. For me it was the suggestion that somehow, I wasn't quite good enough, that I lacked moral fibre, being an urchin and all. Mommy and Daddy didn't hire a nanny or take me on foreign holidays. They didn't destroy me with the high expectation that kills the rich kids' resolve to live with even a smidgen of self-determination or self-respect. It was the insinuation, compounded time after time with the sly looks and superior glances, that I was an outsider that pushed me further and further to the hinterland. It's the guys in the suits with the big houses shoving you around in the drugstore, jumping the line because they think themselves more important. It's the smug self-righteousness of the bourgeoisie that really made me see red. When I resolved to change the world, when I decided to control it, I didn't do it because I didn't have enough to eat or I saw kids in Africa who couldn't get medicine. I didn't do it because I wanted to make the world a better place, stop global warming and save the seals. I did it because some fat, fucking, arrogant, Rolex-wearing, Martha's Vineyard ass bastard pushed me in the Five and Dime and didn't say sorry. Actually, it was outside the Ritz-Carlton, Central Park South but that's beside the point. I never liked tyranny wrapped up in middle-class values. I never liked the keg parties we'd sometimes raid on balmy summer's evenings just for fun. I never liked being told I was anything less than some bastard just because he had a buck in his pocket and I didn't. I knew I was destined for a purpose higher than the nine to five and God knows, I knew I was better than he would ever be. All I had to do was prove it.

By the time I moved into apartment 1B of the Creswell building some years had passed. I was thirty-five years old and all out of love. My girlfriend had just bust me for forging dud cheques and selling the diamond tiara her daddy bought her for her wedding to some guy he deemed far better suited to her than I. Could have been almost anyone, but it sure as hell wasn't me. She threw me out of her apartment but only after I staged a sit-in for several days. I hated the world and everything in it and who knew, I might even have started to hate myself, but just for a minute, then I saw the folly in that. In the years preceding I'd been on the streets selling all kinds of hash and coke, skunk, meth-amphetamine, acid; whatever I could lay my hands on. I thought I was acting pretty competently in my new role. I made a passable pretend boyfriend of sorts and I was all cleaned up as far as my dealing pursuits were concerned. I managed to save my own money by spending hers and that's the way it should be at all times. So when the kitty ran dry, I figured I could afford a nice place, or something with at least the pretension towards being halfway decent. I studied the classifieds for weeks, but whilst I'd been kicking back in the lap of luxury, I'd been priced out of the rental market. Maybe I just got used to the grandeur of Central Park West. One thing for sure, Central Park West never got used to me, but that's a different story. Brooklyn's where it's at now. Three cheers for Crown Heights! Yeah. If I kept telling myself that shit, one day I'd come to believe it. But don't bet on that.

Of course this was before the boom days, before the renaissance, regeneration. Back when the place was no more than run down warehouses and cafes and proliferated by the less than genteel. Back when Brooklyn had character, you might say. It had plenty of people willing to rip off your wallet or whatever else it was you had, no matter how worthless. Sometimes just for the sake of the high. It was essentially a dysfunctional sort of place where poor families existed and converged. It had a heart of gold and an exterior of pure arsenic and a whole bunch of students plotting existential, intellectual rebellion.

I realised I could only afford the Creswell apartment after a budgetary meeting with myself. It was decided by both parties, only prudent to avoid spending all my hard-earned cash on a joint I'd only see the inside of every once in a while if I could help it. I'd need a place to hoard my effects. The place was run-down and smelt like a burned-out car wreck. Drug-addled reprobates collected in the stairwell. Two of them, track-marked twins who only let safe passage from the ground floor if a person contributed to the heroin fund. So, I generally made my way outside after they'd had a hit so I didn't have to pay the toll. Those crazies were capable of anything. The cops never came near our block unless someone reported a homicide. They were too scared of all the other deviance they'd find inside. That would give them way too much work to do. There were a caseload of felonies going down every day behind those closed doors and the NYPD don't like that kind of thing at all. They're too busy posing by patrol cars for tourists' photographs. So it was a strategic move, partially borne out of necessity, but not an insurmountable hurdle to overcome for my resourceful mind. I was not as fussy as vanity had led me to believe. Indeed, it served my purposes very well not to be. I would be left to my own devices, an option that I found to be both beneficial and positively superior to any other outcome. If any one of those bastards, whoever they were, so much as looked at me wrong, I felt I might flip out and destroy the lot of them. I had no intention of spending the rest of my days rotting at someone else's behest in the belly of the county jail. I wouldn't have left Jim to serve my stretch otherwise. No.

Without a doubt, I have no intention whatsoever of doing anything at anyone else's pleasure ever again in my goddamn life. Amen.

The day I moved in was a small victory for me, like the liberation of western Europe but in microcosm. I divested myself of the tyrannical woman and all the limitations that come hand in hand with acting 'the way one ought to'. God knows those people make their own ideological prisons, Park Avenue fools. I was ready for some grit. I didn't see any sign of Eugene for the first few days for he was ensconced as always in his hidey hole apartment, hermetically sealed from humanity. What reason he would choose to relate with I, of all beings, could not be fathomed by even the most genius of minds. He could have tried to make friends with any normal person, instead he chose me. For a precious few days I had the safe-guard of anonymity and ignorance on my side, good defender. For a few days I could pretend that no one else existed. Until he heard some fool had moved in next door, then came the knocking on the wall, supplemented with quiet moans.

At first I ignored them as any practised selfish person would. I had not learned the art of empathy. I had not cared much for it when it was never reciprocated and had abandoned it as a life skill not worthy of my concern years ago. My apartment was all peeling wallpaper and exposed piping, dreary and small and dim. The toilet had no seat. The refrigerator didn't work. There were cracks in the walls, moving toward precipice pro-portions. The lights had no shades. I would have no need to apologise for the dilapidated state of the place since I had no intention of inviting anyone inside. It was the ultimate bachelor pad for the man who no longer had any women or any friends to entertain. But you wouldn't see me cry for that is the way I liked it.

It could have remained that way for weeks or even months or years, stalemate. He continued knocking, waiting for a response. I, on the other side, waited for him to stop waiting and throw in the towel. I could have endured it if I hadn't been kept awake night after cursed night by what sounded suspiciously like the death throes of some deranged animal. I was away from the manor most of the day, co-ordinating my mules or buying shit in the projects from some crazy gang members who were clearly trying to both rip me off and kill me. None of which they managed to pull off, I might add. Eugene zoned in on the only downtime I ever God damn got. He seized it and sent it hurtling to kingdom come. On the fifth sleepless night it seemed only reasonable for the farce to stop and I would make it so. If whatever was in there, at this point undecided, didn't cease and desist immediately, I would have to turn loco and do away with him once and for all.

It transpired the fifth night was a legitimate attempt to garner the attention of his neighbours in order to summon forth the emergency services to extricate him from the sorry state he'd got himself into. So was the screaming of the first, second, third and fourth nights, I later learned. Eugene had indeed and, in fact, got himself well and truly stuck on the can. He had been surviving on the hope of being rescued by some good Samaritan. Even the forcibly-inflicted four-day diet hadn't afforded him the weight loss necessary to create space to inch himself out of his predicament. I'd have to bust down the door with my bare hands . . . Yes. I stomped round there.

'Take it, you fiend!' I punched at his door with my fist and recoiled in utmost throbbing pain. Damn it. I began beating it with frustration, both fists and not much coordination. They bounced off without making any impression on its surface, but my hands were sore as hell. I sprang back to take stock of the situation. I was getting nowhere like this. So I ran at it full pelt from the living room, smashing into it full. Bastard! I bounced off again like a rubber ball and ricocheted around the corridor for several seconds. It always works in the movies, those lying script writers. Bastard, why couldn't it be forged of plywood, those old buildings are made of solid iron. I was angry with it now and no mistake. I'd teach it a lesson it would never forget. So I went off back to my apartment to fetch a sledgehammer and hacked that disobedient bastard to bits, splinters flying. Take it, bitch! That done, I intended to assail my aural assailant and make him the sorriest he'd ever been in his whole life. I was braced and ready for confrontation. Gene looked horrified as I entered. I resisted the temptation to growl 'Heeere's Johnny' as I poked my head through the hole I had made. My eyes were met with what looked remarkably akin to a giant baby. The largest nude person I had ever seen; pink, round and wedged firmly between the narrow walls of the toilet cubicle, hovering over a broken basin. It had held its resolve for three days before realising the futility of such an ordeal. It relinquished its porcelain mould and with it, its will to go on, cracking into shards now wedged into inches of blubber. Blood had trickled down this curious beast's butt, down his porky legs and dried to a deep scarlet just above his elephantine ankles. His lips quivered as he mouthed the word 'Mommy.' Oh dear Lord above in all his finest glory. What is a man to do when confronted with such a pathetic sight? I spun round on my heels and slammed the bathroom door behind me as I made my way out of his apartment and into the street.

Of course one will ask oneself: how could a man be so cruel? Easily. But as surely and keenly as I tried to avoid the thought drinking my final whisky of the evening, even I couldn't do it. In a move closely related to lunacy, I appeared to have had a change of heart. Although where this strange new emotion came from I cannot even begin to contemplate. So reluctantly the next morning I strode back in there to save the pitiful brute from himself and his porcelain captor. I gave him a few hours to see the error of his ways, naturally. By the time I arrived he was a strange purple colour. He hadn't moved for hours and his circulation was faltering. Watermarks stained his face. He gurgled. Pity that man. I hoisted him free. My arms shook under extreme duress, him squealing and whimpering as his fat sides scraped against the walls, leaving long horizontal grazes on his flanks. He clung as tightly as a limpet to a rock or a baby to a mother's bosom; the humiliation. I ordered him to dress before I allowed him to speak to me, for I felt a little sickened by the sight of his cascading rolls of blubbery fat. I wafted him into the bedroom in disgust, not looking at him as he trudged with heavy footsteps and a wheezing wind pipe. For the execution of such a selfless act one expects a fanfare and a ticker tape parade. Eugene offered me a cup of tea and a wide-mouthed grin once the pain had ebbed away. I had compromised my pride and lost essential kudos for an infinitely smaller reward than was just or expected. Never again would I commit an act unmotivated by my own gain, for it was just plain impolite not at least to proffer some monetary incentive for my heroic efforts. I wished to prize him back into the spot where I found him and level his head with the sink.

Sitting pondering such glorious retribution, I had a moment during the interim tea making period to eyeball the strange world I had stumbled into. I had never seen such adornments since the day I ran out of my parents' house with blood on my hands and gladness in my heart. I had come to a parallel dimension that would make Martha Stewart beam with pride and happiness in the knowledge that someone, somewhere was following her doctrine with gay abandon. I was a man of the world and had been to botanical gardens before, albeit for a coke drop. Now I felt I had once again been beamed into the flower garden at the end of the world. I was in some strange Eden and a distant nagging feeling that nothing this perfectly honed could fail to be inwardly subversive enveloped me. It must be a cover, perhaps he was a spy. No one could be so conservative, not in New York. The man was surely crazy. Everywhere I looked I could see nothing but paradise print and chintz, glorious chintz. Help me! There were cushions with frills and place mats with small animal scenes. I edged backward, in fear of such domestic overindulgence and lolled back unwittingly into a rose bud patterned couch. Before I could move an inch I had been topped with a cushioned tray bearing tea and tiny cakes; trapped in Stepford was I. I shuddered from head to toe in revulsion.

Having lumbered into his wheelchair, Eugene wheeled round and parked opposite me, directly in front of the television, his usual outpost. The treads of his wheels could be seen grooved into the carpet beneath him. The brake was applied. I had to sit for two hours listening to his outpourings of self-pity, tedious they were at the best of times. He regaled me with them whenever he felt my sympathy levels were failing. I felt I may expire from sheer boredom alone. I felt I might attack him but these feelings all melted away as he described his second home and his family fortune. I could see I was in for the long haul here. Eugene's mother was teetering on the edge of this astral plain apparently. She being his only living relative left him the last seed of the Steadman family tree. As the only living beneficiary of prodigious fortune, he was fully entitled to an uninhabited ranch in Tucson with four thousand acres of land thrown in for good measure. I had truly been blessed, rewarded from the heavens for my good deeds and kind gestures. Mother had been putting in a good word for me as always with the gods and the angels. Eugene was eternally grateful for my help, I can assure you. I would be his new best friend, with my fingers crossed behind my back and an evil, yet undetectable glint in my eye. Friends should share their wealth I'd suggest and if he found this to be an unpalatable plan, I would prize it from his dead fingers, the bloated, gullible fool.

So, I had made good and there was all to play for. I had to get him out of New York City and down to that ranch. I had to have it. I took to visiting Eugene every day with food parcels and helpful and interesting, although made up, anecdotes about my life outside the apartment. He could not make the stairs. He could hardly wipe his own behind; however, I was not desperate enough to do it for him. I could tell him anything, for he had no idea about the outside world, not since 1999. The world for him was perpetually wedged in the twentieth century. The last time he went for a stroll, he looked

58

up in awe at the Twin Towers whilst comparing their relative size to the two tacos he was eating. There wasn't much in it. He pretended those buildings were still there to preserve the status quo. He turned off the TV news whenever he heard the theme tune, just in case something horrible had happened that he would subsequently have to erase from his memory. A master of blocking out unpleasant truths was he. He still ate two super size tacos at once, for a snack. That was plain to see. You see, Eugene was too fat to walk more than a few paces without losing his breath. He could waddle to the window with his stick and glance outside for a minute or two until his legs began to wobble and cave under the sheer weight of his girth. He had resigned himself to such a fate. It rendered him dependent on others for almost everything. He had a nurse and now I guess he had me too, for a price. But it was better than peddling low grade drugs on street corners. For this investment would reap an exponentially higher reward for far less hard graft.

This was all incredibly frustrating. I hated to be nice to anyone. Now I must apply myself to the cause of goodness. I must feign compassion and perform servile tasks. All of these alien concepts. What a dreadful waste it is that the most undeserving fools get the prizes, those that neither have the balls or the imagination to mobilise themselves to constructive endeavour. People like Eugene, the inherently stupid. It's shameful; I became bitter and debilitated with envy. Furthermore, I feel another pang of it coming on as I recant. After all, Eugene would only spend the money on pizza delivery and Pillsbury dough I fancied. To spend his entire inheritance on edibles would only accelerate his morbid obesity, if he hadn't reached critical mass already. I feared his days might end with a heart attack before he could write me into his will. All my good work would come to nothing so I would have to be swift. He had the stomach of a Santa sack, that man. He would heartily munch his way through a week's worth of meals in one sitting and smacks his lips wetly after each mouthful. It was more than enough to put a discerning man off eating forever more and in the afterlife too. I began to view food as dirty and as an indulgence rather than sustenance. I resolved to eat all of my meals alone and instructed Eugene to do the same. As a result he would either spend the rest of his days alone scoffing or emerge a sylphlike silhouette which he'd secretly envied for as long as he could remember. He was alone in his mind, he was an island. He was larger than some small charted islands one can easily find on any map of the world published today. And he was petulant. Not since my days as a small child had I met someone more so. He did not make any demands. He merely made strange unrhythmic breathing noises when he didn't get his way. He hyperventilated by his own volition. He would learn that this was no means to an end by my hand. I rather enjoyed the spectacle of ignoring him until he turned red in the face and looked fit to burst.

'Look, we could be like this,' said I, pointing at the two little china men on Eugene's wallpaper.

'This is us tending the land down at the ranch. I tell you. The writing's on the wall.'

Scenic decor is never a fashionable choice. His had little people raking on the range. The tiny scene repeated over and over in sepia hues.

'This is me and this is you.' I pointed. 'It's us on the ranch. Look, this one's even wearing plaid just like your favourite pants. That's settled. You can't escape fate Gene, don't even try.'

Eugene rolled his eyes toward the heavens. I'd got him there. This was surely prophetic. I'd clutch at any straw in order to swerve the stubborn mind of my curmudgeonly, half-witted accomplice by coercion if necessary.

'Steves, I cannot live my life according to the predications of interior design. Where would I be if I had, say, a Superman motif as I had when I was a child? Where would I be then? Under the wheels of a speeding locomotive that's where. You can't move me. You just can't. I won't have it. Go if you want to. I won't cry for you.'

Eugene turned his back towards me in his seat. Perhaps feeling that he didn't have the correct angle to signify his disdain, he swivelled his chair around so that he faced the window. He sulked. I couldn't see his face but I could tell. His bottom lip thrust forward, he held his ear. I could tell he was angry and felt exposed because he always held his ear when he felt confidence slipping away. I was on to a winner. I'd just have to try harder and once gaining foothold, I mustn't stop. Beat the will out of him, metaphorically speaking. Get on a roll and steam ahead, not giving up until his spirit is broken.

'Do you know that for every birth in New York City, there are two deaths?'

'The product of changing demographics; there is a growing elderly population eclipsing the youth of today. More are older, they die more often. Next!'

'And that one of those deaths is always a murder.'

Eugene turned his head half round so that I could see the side of his face, but not so far that I could see his eye.

61

'Liar.'

'One is always a murder and sometimes the birth rate is at a ratio deficit of three to one. On these occasions, the causal nature of such deaths is always disease. So that three people in New York City, every day this is, die by such channels. One shooting or could be a stab victim. One riddled with disease because of the stench and filth outside these very windows. One just dies because nobody bothered to check whether he was still alive and died of heartache. That's true; I read it in *Time* magazine.'

'You read no such thing in *Time* Steves and you know it. I once read that the world would be overrun with nanobots. It hasn't happened yet, never will. Now stop lying.'

'No, I told you that.' Sigh. 'You have no power of foresight, man. New York is old hat. They have nanobots in Tucson now. Now that's true.'

'Did you read it in *Time*?'

'No, the *National Enquirer*.'

He knew I was right. His demeanour suggested it and his passion to refute my claims suggested he believed them to be true. If not the whole truth, it was all in the name of progress. A lie is not a lie if it is told for a good reason, I always say. The pursuit of happiness and self-preservation demands it. Thoughts of murder left and right pervaded Eugene's mind for the rest of the day. Soon I would make him hate New York. Job done. Smirk. In order for these perversions not to drift from his memory overnight, I needed to cement it into his psyche the next day.

I was thinking an aggravated burglary may just do the trick. Standing on my head, thoughts meandering, a rape would be good to effect his detachment I perceived, or a shootout. How could this be achieved? My head pulsed. Standing on one's head enhances the thought process; a rush of blood to the brain, flooding capillaries, creates a tension from which rapid and crazy thoughts are derived. It is precisely this pressure which achieves results. I was thinking hard about which crime to commit first when something thudding at the wall from the other side clouded my brainstorm. I got down. The hooker at it again no doubt, plying her odious craft. I lost count of the times I had lain in bed listening to nocturnal pursuits of the witch next door. There was actual structural damage, plaster falling onto my head in tiny pieces in the night. One day I feared I may never wake because she had unwittingly murdered me from a distance by causing plaster subsidence and release. The wall caved in on one Mr Theodore Steves. I could see the obituary. I was not having it. I resolved to go round there and tell her to sew it up for all our sakes. Chastity is virtue after all but this time there was a hell of a thwacking going on in there. Goddamn. She was a busy girl. The thought of it made me sick. Once an ambulance had to come and take her away because one of her clients got heavy. I listened. Silence. I listened some more. Thud, smack. Yep, the beatings continued and I had a theory.

My apartment separated Eugene from the brothel that operated next door. It was a buffer zone, an intermediary between him and the unsavoury. I would not become his security blanket. I had grown tired of that game and refused to collude in his denial any longer. I concluded this would be the perfect time for the good old boy to shake the shameful hand of society. Take it by its clammy hand and see for himself the horror, the tragedy. One day I shall burst down the door and roll him in there, thought I. This would be as good a time as any, if not the very best. Let us see if my theory was true; some fat, panting loser that can no longer face up to his wife, so he comes downtown to take out all his frustrations on a whore he neither knows nor cares for. He's the guy who drives the kids to school. He's the school bus driver, wait, no, worse than that, he's the disabled kids' bus driver. He takes the Down's syndrome kids to the park sporting his fluorescent coat that screams 'You can trust me little ones. I'm a good guy' and his jaunty cap. He's all smiles. He's up for the Care in the Community Award and everybody loves him. His wife couldn't conceive, I fancied, so he had no kids of his own to dote on and instead he bestows all of his burgeoning, mis-placed love and pride on to a bunch of underprivileged kids whom he thinks of as his own, or what he has had to settle for. Really he's thinking 'Dumb bitch, call yourself a woman, you can't even give me a child. How useless can one be?' So she spends her whole life trying lamely to appease him and sometimes it works, but it's all just faux sympathy until he finds it's him that's shooting duds. His inconsequential, in-adequate body is just a shell that lacks the virility necessary to justify his status as a man. So there's nothing left to mask his weakness than to beat the hooker to a pulp of an evening. It prepares him for next morning's revelry with the kids at camp. At least that's what I imagined anyway. I had great stories in my head, great imaginations. I'd like Eugene to see that, I mused. To open his eyes, a little education into the seedier side of life. The madness, the vitriol, the blame displacement turned into rage and deflected on to some poor hooker who can't look after her own child or pay the gas unless she gets her ass busted every night. Her son was one of my mules. A prize student, he shifted ten times more hash than the other kids. So I sent him out on a made up job. I couldn't let him hear that, the screams of his own mother. He would be half dead. He was a good kid all told and she was a bad mother and Eugene was a poor quality liar if he expected me to believe he did not see what was right before his eyes. I heard the Strauss go up in his apartment, so I knew he was listening but he simply refused to hear.

With this in mind I set on my trajectory to Eugene's place. Knocking the door almost down before he mobilised his ass. I knew he was peeking at me through the peephole. So I duly pressed my eye up to the door. No, I couldn't see him through the one way device but I knew he had magnification behind there, maybe a corneal scanner just to make sure I was no impostor. After two, he let me in and the Strauss almost deafened my perforated ear drums and sent them to kingdom come. I felt compelled to turn the volume down. Eugene scowled in a boyish manner and yet resigned himself not to even protest at the rudeness of my gesture. This maddened me, so I switched it off. Pah! Silence. I expected at any moment to hear the hooker's brain being splattered up the interior of the adjacent wall. I wanted him to hear it but just to reiterate my lifelong predisposition to bad luck and cursed poor timing, there was nothing. Nothing! No whimper, no banging, not even the smallest of screams. Surely she could manage that at least. It all went quiet. Not the deep throated growl I had been expecting, denoting the release of force by its owner. What? Not even a scuffle? Poor show indeed.

'Listen.' I pressed my ear to the wall. 'I heard it again. Just like the fourth of July when the ambulance came. Just like Independence Day when her teeth gained their independence from her filthy mouth.'

'She had a health issue is all. I know because I talked with one of her gentleman friends. Some nice men came over to comfort her. One of them told me it was a burst appendix. It could happen to you'.

'You'll get gallstones,' said I. There came a muffled sound.

'See. I told you everything was fine, it's just the TV and, there, she's going out, I just heard her door.'

'No. Something's not right.' I scratched my head. 'All hell let lose in there not five minutes ago.' Maybe I'd missed something somewhere between my apartment door and Eugene's. 'I'm going to investigate and you're coming with me, for protection.'

It was a poor cover story. I reckoned Eugene would make the worst body guard in the world. Although on reflection, if the assailant shot wrong and missed his target he could take a bullet. It wouldn't be like Kennedy and the governor. No, it wouldn't be like Dallas, Texas, 1963. Not even a scud missile could burrow its way through all that fat and gristle and come out on the other side. He could be my bullet-proof vest. Perfect. We had to go in there. I was quite sure something horrible had happened to convey my message so much better than words ever could. Quite sure of it. Very sure of it. We would need imagery and that was just what we were going to get. What great sport indeed! But I would have to move with speed and stealth.

Eugene always did this thing when he didn't want to be

moved. He'd try to slide from his chair onto the floor so that I couldn't wheel him around. He hated people, of any persuasion, driving him round the place 'willy-nilly.' Even when I offered to recreate the Gumball Rally over Brooklyn Bridge he declined. There were hours of fun to be had, seeing his face screw up and his little eyes disappear into his fat cheeks like piss holes in the snow. With speed on my side I could negotiate the brake off and lunge from behind in order to create the force necessary to set the thing in motion. I caught him out. He'd barely managed to lift an ass cheek in downward movement before I had him out of the door and almost crashing into the corridor wall. With such a heavy object, one needs a clear area to turn. Ninety degree angles are out of the equation, so one must revert to the wheel spin method for manoeuvrability. A short straight along the corridor and the wheel spin method was employed once again. Eugene shrieked with terror and anticipation, not knowing whether to laugh or cry. I like to think he enjoyed it. Having rallied in such an abstract fashion to the hooker's door, I noticed perplexingly, that it appeared ajar. Yet in my merriment, I had failed to internalise this somewhat irregular factor and pushed the wheelie chair right in there. I should have realised this was not the normal course of things. The damned whore had twenty padlocks behind there. A regular came by and he'd be freezing his balls off outside for several minutes before she opened up. He'd mostly look embarrassed and would nod courteously as though we didn't know his business there. He would suddenly find his shoes interesting, tying and untying his laces, trying to avoid eye contact with passing residents. I pushed Eugene in full force and stood for a moment smiling and watching him career into the room from my rear vantage point. I was like a proud father watching his son cycle for the first time without stabilisers, not knowing I had let go. Whoosh! He was riding free. Doing it all by himself with propulsion and gravity providing safe carriage. Unfortunately Gene had full comprehension that he was a lone rider as I slapped my hands together with glee after finishing the job. It was barely two seconds of sheer pleasure and pride before I heard him wail from inside the hooker's lair.

'Oh, dear God Almighty!' Scream. 'Oh! God help me. Save us all. Save me! God!!!'

At last he knew my name.

We'd rolled into a goddamn, twenty-four carat slaughter house. Eugene sat motionless in the centre of the room. His body facing the window but staring to his left, his eyes wider than the lids should allow. This looked like the scene of some kind of ritual sacrifice, as though a chicken had been gutted and slung around until drained of all its bodily fluids. The worst part was that there was no discernable body there, globular anatomical secretion but no secretor, no source. No context in which to place such a sight. It was blood alright. It had that translucent quality that so evades movie set make-up artists until the correct mix of corn syrup, detergent and pigmentation is met. I knew she hadn't been screwing a special effects man. She was far too cheap and unimaginative for that. So I headed intrepidly into the kitchen to find the evidence like an explorer in deepest Peru. The paraphernalia that littered the place would be completely unnecessary in the average family home; suspicious contraptions of all kinds. The sleaze was veritably dripping from the walls. I'd have to steer clear of the hypodermics, rubber straps, a guillotine! Gods, nothing would have surprised me in this, the condo of the denizen of depravity. Eugene wanted to leave.

'Call the cops!' he hollered but I failed to see his point. I had to be privy to the culmination of such a feverish and ill-conceived attack. I wasn't about to leave until I'd scoped the macabre scene to the fullest of my ability.

'Close the door!' I yelled. 'Rock up to the door and close it. I'll just be a couple of minutes. The witch has to be in here somewhere.'

'She's in here, in there. For the love of the mighty power Himself Steves, she's everywhere!'

Nevertheless I left him to carry out my instruction as I knew he would. Even he wasn't stupid enough to continue shouting the odds whilst surrounded left and right by body parts. I pressed on.

It was like a warren in there, not so much the architecture but the soft furnishings. I couldn't find the walls for scarves and hangings. Curtains and cushions were scattered around like a harem with hidden depths. It wasn't dirty, just untidy and all lit with red light so that I couldn't determine the trail of blood. I could have been standing in it for all I knew. It must have seeped into the carpet because I wasn't slipping around and the pile squelched underfoot. My snakeskin shoes, my poor snakeskins, ruined! Travesty! I felt compulsion driving me onward. I couldn't leave now. It would be torturous watching the cops wheel her out in a bodybag. It would drive me mad with frustration, nuts. All the time thinking about its contents, all night long, night after night of spurious speculation. Was it mutilation? Was it strangulation? Did her eyes pop out of their very sockets? Like a child watching a movie and staying up all night, I had to see it with my own eyes, I simply had to. I'd seen it all before. Eugene could not comprehend it all as he sat wedged against the apartment door and I could not achieve clarity. There was no scent to discern in the hallway and I had not heard sounds that could afford a greater understanding of the events leading up to this puzzling crime scene. So I must fulfil my sensory inquisition, gratification almost, with exposition. I would refrain from allowing Eugene to see any enjoyment derived at the moment of discovery but I knew that I was going to, in a sinister, inhumane fashion.

You know, you just cannot imagine death so lucidly as to see it in life. The carcass bears no resemblance to its portrayal on celluloid. There is no removal when you are the witness, no space and no distance. Believe me if you will, death is much, much worse than your imagination will allow you to comprehend. All of the waxwork creations could not recreate the scene. Mannequins do not spasm, do not let out gas and they do not stare at you fully in the eyes as though they would blink in a second and move again, get up duly and pour a cup of coffee. Have you ever seen the victim of a fatal bullet wound? Perfectly preserved, save for the small entry hole cauterised at the edges with a slim rim of charred skin. Precious seconds pass by before the realisation dawns that movement is never going to happen, but looking closer, one is tempted to think it just might. Just like Mom, watering the gardenias in heaven.

I found no remnants in the bathroom. It looked as though it hadn't been touched. Just as I suspected the filthy woman had no hygiene-related scruples. Neither did I discover any signs in the inner sanctum; the boudoir itself. The most likely candidate I felt. I stood in the doorway. The place smelt of sexual conquest. I overturned the mattress and scrambled to see under the bed. Nothing but sex aids and lubricant. Well, there could only be one place left to scour. Oh tell me it isn't true . . . I approached the door of the kid's room; an abominable aberration, pure, unadulterated sickness beyond even the bounds of my own, tormented imaginations lay in store. Swinging open, the door seemed heavy and the air was heavy too, musky. The scene cloaked in black. I felt around for the light, the switch was one of those cord affairs with a bead on the end. It tried to outfox me for a couple of seconds by swinging pendulous out of reach. Once I had mastered its dimensions, I pulled down with a swift jerk. My heart almost jerked out of my chest, for stretched out all over the single bed lay a hulk of a man, once anyway. A hulk of a corpse was looking me right in the eye. Soft rolling wheels advanced behind me. The corpse looked me and Eugene right between the eyes, spread-eagled over the smiling face of the Tickle Me Elmo-motif sheets.

For once I was stunned into silence. This I had not been expecting for a second. I just stood there wondering how in the name of God the woman had inflicted such devastation upon the man. What were the logistics involved in such an operation? I had to size it up, turning my head sideways like an inquisitive mongrel, to scope all angles. The answer proved not to be forthcoming. This guy had to be two hundred and fifty pounds. He was torn, ripped to shreds as though he'd lost a tough fight with a wild beast. He had fought to the death. His greying shirt unbuttoned and splayed out on the bed. His bulging belly lacerated with vertical strokes up to the jugular, not one inch apart. Blood had seeped down his rounded belly into his shirt and then onto the sheets, a great gaping chasm for a stomach. His pants were still fastened and his ankles were tied to the bed posts with duct tape. The same held his mouth closed and was now peeling away due to the saturation of blood mass that had oozed from the mouth. I got in closer. Eugene held my shirt tails, pulling me back. I peered straight into those glassy eyes, the yellow teeth, swollen tongue. I suspected that had he been breathing, halitosis would have sent me reeling backward in disgust. His tongue was black, lips blue, eyes bleeding ever so slightly at the tear ducts. That's when the motherfucker twitched. I was but six inches from that putrid face. The spasm sent it up in a judder toward mine; his legs briefly left the bed but were harnessed back down by relaxing muscles and duct tape moorings. He had soiled himself before death and the movement let out a fresh plume of faecal miasma into the air to seek out my nostrils and contaminate within. Although the movement was geographically small, my mind imagined the bloated beast hurtling toward me with unparalleled speed. I lurched backward, recoiling onto Gene. All the hairs lifted on our personages. I was frozen in semi-recline over Eugene's sitting frame.

'Let's just get the fuck out of here,' I stammered.

Eugene suddenly found strength to wheel himself in reverse, out of the poor kid's room quicker than I've ever seen him move. My enduring vision was one of a retreating bloodied corpse, zooming away from me but still head on like a camera trick. I saw everything retreat after that, getting smaller as we went. Eugene wheeled backward all the way to his apartment two doors away. He whimpered and bellowed for the duration of the trip. He'd summoned ten times human strength to save us both from the death zone and sent us hurtling into the wall of his living room, sweating, trembling and I, strangely aroused.

There wasn't a moment to spare. We hadn't been out of there for a minute before sirens sounded outside, followed by the heavy footsteps pounding on the stairs. They stopped briefly to push past the hypodermic twins. We were frozen in anticipation. We knew they would call by to see if we had heard anything untoward. Eugene, to me to Eugene, sideways glances. We must appear to be unawares and continuing some domestic task. They must never know the truth. Eugene flicked on the tube and I began pouring cold coffee into tiny tea cups. How civilised. They were all I could find in my haste. After five minutes of routine questioning we realised we had been 'watching' re-runs of *Days of Our Lives*. Ass! Damn it! How incongruous. The cop smirked at us patronisingly, assuming us to be gay lovers. The whole time my snakeskin shoes were dripping with plasma, winking at me from under the cop's chair.

God, I broke a sweat. I rubbed my clammy paws up and down on my strides slowly and covertly to transfer the moisture. For surely the guy would shake my hand on departure. Then he would become suspicious. So when he was done with us, he suddenly wouldn't be done with us because he'd know I'd got something to hide. He would jump straight to the wrong conclusion. Mother always did tell me that I looked guilty, even when I hadn't done anything to look guilty for. Although usually to be fair, it was my fault. I just lied and said it wasn't. If they took me in for questioning they might start asking questions about my folks and then I'd be in trouble.

They might realise they had imprisoned the wrong guy and Jim would be released and I'd be finished. Paranoid delusions were gaining a foothold. I must retain my customary cool. Eugene was uncommonly calm as though denial had blocked it all out and we'd never been where we had just been. That we'd never seen what we'd just seen. My glands were going haywire, seeping into my palms to hide the tense reality of our secret intrepid journey into the whore's crimson lair. He wouldn't know we'd only had a little peek inside. He wouldn't know that the lie we were covering was a smaller lie than the one he would suspect we were covering and then we'd be prime suspects. *Stroke, stroke.*

Eugene was letting him in on our weekly Saturday afternoon high tea and matinee to cover the ridiculous scenario in which we now found ourselves. He was telling the inspector how it's not like the good old days when one could enjoy the simpler things in life. How, for sure, we'd heard a couple of bangs but put that down to home improvement. In any case, the woman wasn't a social animal and we hadn't seen her around too much. Good old boy. He even managed a soft-voiced diatribe into the tendency of modern society to eschew community spirit and the sliding of social values. How Brooklyn was going to the dogs. Genius. *Stroke.* He did it all with the voice of an angel and his cute face. The one that made you think he'd never heard of violence or theft or prostitution or even of masturbation, or any of the onerous things in life, never mind the concept of murder. Throughout, the cop was eyeing me, befuddled. I was busy looking around the room stroking my sweaty palms down my pant leg. And, oh no, too close to the groin region and he was hastily out of his seat.

'Well,' he cleared his throat and coughed, 'I really must continue with my investigations. I, I must be getting along now . . . '

I rose in order to escort him out, to make sure he was really gone, but he waved his hand at me in a halting, defensive gesture.

'No need to see me to the door, I think I can find my own way just fine, don't trouble yourself.'

He avoided eye contact as though I didn't exist although I was the focus of his attention. Oh dear. Sweat transference mistaken for lewd conduct and immoral advance. He near ran out of the place, couldn't get out quickly enough for his own liking. I could hardly help but wink at him as he left. I licked my lips too. That would see him off quickly. He never turned his back to me. He daren't leave himself vulnerable from behind. I guessed he wouldn't be back in a hurry. There would be no attempt to nail my ass even if he suspected duplicity, out of the fear that I might try to nail his first. Even so, I hosed down those snakeskins just to be sure, my favourite pair, my shoe of choice. I resolved that they could indeed be saved, hardy reptiles and good Italian craftsmanship. Think I did more damage with the hose.

The boys in blue were swarming around for days, ensuring Eugene stayed tense, very tense. He spent the whole time impersonating an owl on surveillance, watching and listening and worrying that he would be implicated by association. He had started to feel uneasy in his homestead. He wouldn't admit it yet, not now. After a couple more homicides on the block he would have no choice but to give the place up. To flee the scene as he bore witness to the demise of the last bastion of the good, now handed over to the satanic hordes and entered into the clutches of evil. Yep. He would have to up sticks and I knew just where we would go. Of course I had just the place in mind. The rot was setting in. I sat there dreaming of the ranch. Thinking for the fiftieth time or so, just one or two deaths would be what we needed here. What are a couple more homicides in Brooklyn. It would tip the balance. They didn't have to be on the block, could be in the vicinity or thereabouts. The nurse who came to deliver her thrice monthly day care visitation to Gene would make a fine candidate. I could accost her next time she came to deliver 'essential personal services.' If all of these things were to happen, wouldn't that just be damned fortuitous. I shall personally guarantee it, thought I.

First I had his mother, the old hag to deal with. How rude of her to keep me hanging on like this. Would it be too much to ask for her to just roll over and die like a good girl should. The widow Steadman had become a thorn in my side and one that would need to be extracted immediately. Eugene decided the only course of action was to retreat to bed for a few days to sleep off the horror. Go to bed and forget. He had stocks of food piled by his bed for easy access and a bucket for his ablutions. He wouldn't move for two days at least, which would give me ample time to visit the widow, just to make sure she was alright, you understand. If I had a soul I would have been worried for Eugene's sanity, rolling round in bed. He hardly dipped into his food mountain so I knew that something was deeply wrong. I left him for a while until he surmounted the point at which histrionics ceased. Yes, our fortunes would turn as a result of his apathy, for a change is a good as a rest. He was resting up nicely, recuperating before the second assault. I checked him briefly to make sure he was truly ensconced for the duration. I was met with groans and two fat white feet poking out from under lilac scented sheets. His self-absorbance was complete. He was retarded by events, entirely disabled. He took full advantage of his misfortune in order to affect utmost guilt and outpouring from I, his cohort. I fostered this none-theless in light of its obvious benefits. He would try to suck me in with his wallowing ineffectual guilt-mongering before he'd lift a finger to help himself. I pondered as to whether I should change his locks so he couldn't escape should he have a sudden burst of energy. I reasoned that with his dedication to the cause of self-pity, he would remain inert to secure full effect. I would have more than enough time for the round trip to Jersey, even to take in some sights. Nobody would ever know I had gone. I would repay him with matricide by proxy. Poor bloated being of self-loathing; there never was a more fitting martyr than he.

It only took a few hours before I slipped my nimble feet out of those complimentary flight socks and into my snakeskins, pounding the streets of Camden County, NJ. Eugene had given me enough points of reference in his ramblings as to his mother's whereabouts. With a little detective work I'd be swooping in on her like a vulture in no time at all. There was also the letter I had procured from his safe, on headed paper, detailing the address, room number and name of the insti-tution in which she resided. But there never was more fun to be had than to make a caper out of an investigation, to play James Bond for a while to brighten up one's day. Alas, I deferred to the easy option after a couple of hours treading the streets until such time as I had become bored with my game. I disembarked the cab at 15.07pm precisely and took great care not to let anyone recognise my face, just in case. The cabby left believing he had dropped off a nurse Bobby Westway of Cleveland. He would think nothing more of his fare.

The widow Steadman looked awful pale. Eugene claimed he'd her packed off to New Jersey so he could be closer to her if she took a turn for the worse. I never once saw him burning down the turnpike due to a state of matriarchal meltdown. I never saw him spurred out of his own habitat by purpose of compassion. I think it was all for show. I had to act quickly and decisively. Straight for the kill and there might be something of our inheritance left standing to collect. I must be shrew and cautious for this exercise. I tippy-toed to find my charge.

I found the widow languishing on the fourth floor of the geriatric wing in the New Jersey Salvation Army hospice. It was a converted mental asylum with barred windows and shadowy corners in which to hide. I thought places like these existed only in the movies and was pleased to find this a falsehood. Having perfected my finest skulk whilst dealing hash on campus at NYU and Columbia, it was all too easy to slip past the scant security operation unawares. This, far less down to my ingenuity than their engrossment in poker playing, but no matter, I felt the accomplishment was mine. Take credit for everything even where credit is not due. The wearing of my blonde wig would aid me in the event of minor skirmishes or close shaves with hospital staff. As I trekked ever onward and located the widow's room, my heart began to pound in my chest with the adrenaline surge that always accompanies a kill. An old man stood at the end of the corridor. He was oblivious to the world around him. He stared into the wall drugged up to the eyeballs, inspecting the peeling plaster. Some ex-corporate hedge funder I thought, getting his dues. It didn't seem like any of the cronies in this place had much to live for. They were squatting on the last step on the stairway to heaven, all comatose and dribbling. Left there by people they called their friends. More like the waiting room at the gates of hell. The widow Steadman was no different. She looked like she had expired and been buried for several days only to be exhumed and placed back into her bed, sallow, hollow and wretched was she. Now I knew the reason why Eugene never came to visit. His mother was nothing more than a *corpus horribilis*.

The hideous sight violated my whole personage and unsettled my aura. I shirked back with my hands up to blot out the sight. Oh my eyes! I had to defend their virtue. Nevertheless, I would have to face physical contact with this withered, wretched beast hag, if I ever hoped to get my most ambitious plan to date off the ground. I could have detonated the west wing with high explosive if I'd wanted to. It would have been a more palatable plan. Since I was there I may as well strangle her. Silent and still, I imagined her peeking through her stumpy lashes ready to pounce. One assumed this woman had not been touched by masculine hand for many a year, if not since the conception of Eugene. The horror of the woman and the resulting chimera of a son was the likeliest reason for that. As strongly as I felt the urge to follow suit, I would have to buck the trend. The ace card would be a closing hand around her stalk of a neck. A nuzzled pillow stuffed into Grandma's dribble-stained face and pressed down with my full body weight. Force it down, then force it down further until it breaks her teeth, burying the shards up into her gummy jaws. Her swelling throat a lake of blood, her mouth its waterfall, tearing the veins too close to the surface, varicose and twisted through the paper-thin skin. Yes. For this exercise I should have worn a top hat and tails, thought I, but now I was the blonde Samson, drawing all of my strength from the hair.

I approached her from the left as if on the verge of liberating the contents of a vial of concentrated Ebola. I was cautious, calm and sure. Quiet as a church mouse at Sunday Mass was I. The only sound was a faraway screaming, some other old bastard that needed putting out of his misery. The coast was clear as intended. The corridors were subliminally resounding with the quiet creeping of death, but one could only sense it if one was finely attuned. The widow would soon be all ears.

Hospitals make it so easy to kill their charges. Why else provide a killer with so many pillows. The stack on the chair beside me was brimming with extra weapons in baby blue; feather-stuffed implements of murder. I took my pick and lurched forward. I would give her just long enough to look into the eyes of her killer before finishing her off, but not long enough to gurgle or scream or whatever noise a really old person makes before they shuffle off this mortal coil. Not a peep. I buried that goddamn pillow into her face, kneading it for a couple of seconds like dough. The fists weren't clenching. Adrenal surge. I assumed a pulsing action. Maybe that would wake her up. If I took it away and the bitch was laughing, goading me, I'd rip out her spinal cord with my bare hands. I poked her full in the hollow of her hollowed cheek. Nothing. I stopped short of drawing blood, corkscrewing my finger in there. Take that, you hag! And that! I slapped her.

Well, if that's not the rudest thing I ever came across. She could have had the decency to wait for me to kill her before she went and died. Unfathomable, barefaced insolence. I felt piqued. The staff here must be a touch lackadaisical about the concept of death, not to have sent her on her final cruise to the morgue in a timely fashion. She'd been dead for hours. To add insult to injury, she wouldn't even get a post mortem for her troubles. This behaviour was indefensible. As surely as I wanted to punish her rotten old corpse, I realised that even now the commode nurse was wheeling her pee-stained charge down the corridor for the relief of the widow's bladder. I must flee and flee I did, snagging my left knee on the abseil down the parameter wall.

Upon my return to New York I felt mightily disheartened. Shredded plans swirled around my head. I wondered how long I would have to keep the secret until the appropriate authority divested itself of the news of the widow's fate for Eugene's pleasure. Nothing would have satisfied me more than to be the bearer of this bad news. Even so, it would be several degrees less than prudent to let the news slip and ruin the whole thing. I brought my heavy limbs back to the apartment, schlepping down the street. My mind clouded by the unfairness of life. My greatest hope, that I would find the hypodermic twins over-dosed on the stairs to appease my thoughts of failure and that nothing deserved ever comes of life. I was in a blue period, brought on by my inability to slay. I climbed the stairs. The twins weren't even there. Probably won the lottery and were off sunning their track-marked limbs on golden beaches, such is the indecency of the world. Pout. I expected to find Gene in a state of disarray upon my return. My internal doom mongering for the entire journey allowed me to see this as the most fitting end to my travels. I would revel in his malaise to lift my spirits. I expected nothing more than a grunt of a riposte to my enquiries as to whether he was bearing up well under the circumstances. Truth is, he'd had time to contemplate the issues at hand and was gladdened in his heart to be able to close the door and seal himself into this utopia of his design.

'I won't leave this place, Steves. It keeps me safe and out of harm's way. Nobody bothers me here. I have been cleaning whilst you were away. My beloved Nancy helped me. I didn't allow her to clean the toilet though. Everything's back to normal, cleansed of evil, just like the good old days.' He swirled around in the centre of the room, much like a prima ballerina but fatter.

'Aaaahhhhh!!!!!' I clasped my head in disbelief.

God save me from Eugene's own brand of hedonistic armchair nostalgia. Spare me one more moment of self-indulgence. Take me now and sweep me away like the wind from his lavish pining for the good old days. Since when in this godforsaken hellhole did the guy ever have a good day in his life. Was I missing something? He just looked off somewhere into the distance in a dreamy trance. I wondered if somebody hadn't pumped hallucinogens into the apartment through the air vents each time I went out. Or hypnotised him whilst I had my back turned. He had illusions of cloistered youth and peachy days gone by in the floral apartment his grandmother decorated for a joke – only didn't tell him. He'd brainwashed himself to augment his uneventful, mediocre existence and to imbue himself with Walton-esque serenity. I could have spewed right there. Clawed my own throat out attempting to expulse the offending vomit stuck fast in the back of my oesophagus. The events of the last couple of days had not taught him anything about the futility of such positive thought. That was the final straw. Nursey would have to go!

Nurse Fanny, I liked to call her because historically, all nurses are called Fanny. In fact, her name was Nancy, which Eugene could never utter without prefixing the words 'my beloved'. It upset him that I could be quite as impersonal and facetious as to call her Fanny as he thought it a basic and coarse name. Nancy had never been either of those things, with her tiny hands and her ear to ear smile. I preferred to think of her as a state-sponsored whore although he never did fully explain to me precisely what 'essential personal services' entailed. For the housebound, I could have a very good stab at a guess. She could have made more money going freelance, without the justification and assumed professional stature of introducing the clinical element into the mix.

Whilst she may have been prim, she was quite pretty in an unassuming fashion so I can't imagine she enjoyed her employment for a minute, knowing that she had options. For on the couple of occasions I intercepted her in the lobby, she had a smile so fixed it looked almost painted on, as though she had donned a smile mask in the car before disembarking. All of this made her look unnatural and remarkably sinister. So it didn't bother me any to think of her death as a conduit to securing Eugene's departure from Brooklyn. I could only think of her amusing corpse, her perma-smile drawn on by the mortician shining out at us jovially from her casket, happier than ever not to have to relieve Eugene for the cause of medicine one more lousy time.

Nurse Fanny visited on a Monday, but not on the last Monday in the month. She was procured by triage on those days to administer dressings to accident victims when the other nurse Fannies took vacation leave. I singled out the next Monday to intercept her visitation as I believed time to be of the essence. My patience, at an all time low ebb, was beginning to wear extraordinarily thin. Nurse Fanny being another ton of ballast to be thrown overboard thus allowing my plans to take off. I thought the strategy through one evening in the usual fashion of standing on my head, plotting her schedule and her route. There was very little to detail or make contingency for as she always arrived at 3:00p.m. and left at 4:00. She pulled up outside in her car, paid the meter and entered through the lobby, making straight for Gene's apartment. She did not diversify in any way from one appointment to the next, creature of habit that she was.

Annoyingly, the next Monday happened to be the last in the month. I had to put my plans on ice for a full fortnight, which frustrated me more than words can say. When *the* Monday arrived I awoke with a sense of great wellbeing, considering that I would be doing something constructive during the day ahead. Breakfast tasted more gratifying than was customary and the sun shone gloriously through the blinds. It was very apt thought I, that Nursey would at least see the sun glistening over Manhattan before she took her dive into the river. 'Meet my friend Hudson,' I'd say with a smile before pushing her in with my little finger. It would all work out and by God, there was nothing I had missed.

As the clock struck 2:58p.m., I moseyed on down to the Chevrolet and sat for precisely thirty-six seconds awaiting her arrival. Looking like I was rummaging around in the glove compartment for something or other so as not to draw unwanted attention. By 3:06p.m. I was really beginning to lose my patience and enthusiasm for the plan. The only thing there was to do was to smoke a cigarette so I turned on the engine to heat up the lighter. I waited some more. Oh hell, thought I, once I'd smoked it. Maybe I'd better take a drive around the block. Of all the days to be caught in traffic or on some extraneous errand, why must she choose today? Of course and as always, being miffed is not the best aid to the responsible driver. I realised whilst pulling onto the east side of the building that I might miss her on the south side. The entrance was situated on the north-facing street so I would have to hurry around the back a little. I careened that car round the corners, narrowly missing some bum drinking whiskey from a paper bag. As I mounted the curb, who would have though it possible in the universe? Nursey parked up on the west side. Some fool had pulled into my space out front. As misfortune would maintain its almighty governance of all things and ruin them, misfortune put paid to my 'swimming with the fishes' idea. At first I thought I had run over a small bump in the road in my haste, perhaps a manhole cover or some small rodent. No. It was none other than Nurse Fanny crumpled under the wheels of my sturdy old automobile. I crunched into reverse and crunched Nursey in unison. Back and forth I went gaily. I retreated and jettisoned myself just out at the next block. By the time I'd brushed myself down and sidled round to the scene, quite a crowd had gathered. They had engulfed the place. It was really a spectacle. I had a miniscule look, nothing too indulgent. I winced. The axle had ripped her throat clean out but nobody had seen it happen they said, there wasn't a bang. She had only made a soft thudding sound, such a giver in death as in life. Well, we were out back after all. If the old bum was still hanging around and had seen what had ensued, he'd only reason that he was hallucinating in the same way that he thought he was Father Christmas or the Easter Bunny or the President. The chattering grew and the sirens grew. I'd been in close proximity to too many of those of late so I took a walk in the park to clear my head. The car was stripped by the time I returned. Three more cheers for Crown Heights! No matter. I wasn't registered for it or insured on it anyway. Damn that woman though. I hadn't even seen her face at the end, it had been so unexpected. I preferred my actions to be determined by my own volition, not guided by chance or fate except for the fate that I chose for myself. I sulked for a while, my power taken away. Nevertheless, the final result had been tantamount to that I had planned so I would resign myself not to be disheartened after all was said and done.

When Eugene got the call I was lying in the bath tub reading a dog-eared, outdated copy of *New Scientist* magazine that I procured from a park bench. It must have been lifted from a doctor's surgery as the thing was two years old. Since I needed something to take my mind off the day's trials I read it anyway. By rights the science I was perusing was old hat, embarrassingly behind the times and not worth the paper it was written on. My head full of retro science, things passed and gone and the world moved on, I wondered whether there were clones lined up in Perspex cases in secret labs as it alluded to. Like in the movies or just walking down the street twitching and squinting in the first manifestations of genetic meltdown. Then came the shrieks from next door in true Gene style. I was being hailed. I responded to those shrieks as any good actor would. Only after towelling myself off and applying cologne did I patiently dress. I gave myself the old once-over in the mirror before departing nonchalantly towards his apartment. The wailing ceased. I heard the shrill become more transmuted until it waned after a spell into a low gurgle. Only then did I set foot out of my pad. By the time I swung open his door, unlatched for my speedily anticipated entrance, he was sprawled out over the carpet, dislodged from his chair and barely able to breathe. His face streaming with a mixture of sweat and tears, he lolled onto his side face down and embarked upon a muffled grizzle. He held his ear.

'Oh Good Lord,' I threw up my hands, 'What misery has become you? Gene, speak to me!'

'Ste–e–e–ves!' his big arm lolled toward me, 'They said her throat had been slit from ear to ear!' He enacted it with his chubby limb.

'Who, man? Speak up.'

'Nancy, my beloved Nancy, my caustic-smelling beauty. Her apron . . . and . . . ' sob. 'Her apron clean over her head! What kind of indignity.' Grizzle. 'What kind of world are we living in? Insanity! Where is my solace now? Where is my paradise?! Lost!'

I pondered. What embellishments people are inclined to make. Her apron over her head? I never touched her skirts. I certainly did not disrobe her in any order. This was not my work. Those lousy rubber-neckers copping a feel. How distasteful. One must never exonerate taste from their workmanship.

'I am aggrieved!' He went on and on. 'I feel as though I have been raped of my sanctuary and my sanity! And Mother's dead too!' Wail.

My God, the man was beginning to dramatise in almost as accomplished a fashion as I. What a malleable soul and a speedy learner, even if he had plagiarised my style, he had learnt from the best. Kneeling over, a sudden unfettered, if not fleeting spasm of guilt, no, of opportunity enveloped me. The good feeling rose up inside. This terrible event had worked for me far better than anything I could have imagined in my wildest dreams. This brought about a warmth that descended for at least a second as an outpouring of feeling for Eugene.

'That is the final straw!' I stroked his head, hamming it up for all it was worth. 'For your sanity, for your piece of mind and to save your bleeding heart from haemorrhaging as that of your precious Nancy, we must flee, Eugene. There are no more matriarchs to fall whilst we look on without the power to save them. We must salvage ourselves whilst we still can. First your mother and now this! We must disembark this debauched, rotten city. We must go to Tucson!' I raised my fist to my heart in pride and with a wet eye. Then, cupping that swollen, hairless head in my hands, I gazed into his watery eyes. He needed no more convincing.

Fortune had indeed struck me that day, my fine friend. For these developments would signify the point of no return. My position was secured at the head of the top table. I had mounted the launch pad to thrust us on to the trajectory I had worked toward for so long. It was the day Eugene severed ties with his precious empty life, with his four walls and had quit the city in his subconscious. After all, the mind is the hardest to conquer, to button but I had it nailed. He turned himself over to me as his guardian. All of his worldly possessions would now be mine. Oh sweet surrender. I loved this guy. I loved his fragile mind and his bleeding heart.

Eugene finally wanted out. In a three-week stretch he'd seen his neighbour slash a client and sling his innards all over the walls. His mother had an unforeseen and sudden exit. The nurse had been squished under the wheels of a speeding Chevy, limbs and spleen asunder. He'd seen more body parts than he'd ever been subjected to in a whole season of *ER*. He'd developed palpitations, a furrowed brow and premature hair loss had accelerated to obliterate his lonely last hair. His bubble had well and truly burst. Rural idyll seemed a comforting prospect by comparison. He revelled in the idea of me lying horizontal on the ranch porch with a cigar in my mouth, watching him tend to the herb garden or some green fingered, wholesome task. All the time he remained as intended, blissfully unaware of who was pushing his buttons. Even better, he felt he had come to the groundbreaking decision by virtue of his own determination. There was no need for him to feel compromised or resistant. He imbued himself, thus, with a sense of pride to have happened upon a life-altering resolution without the prerequisite of a lifetime of deliberation. Give that man an award.

He put off the reading of the will for a few weeks after the widow Steadman passed over. He said it was too painful but then he already knew the determinations of his benefactor in any case. Now as we walked in to the lawyer's office to hear the news, I held his hand rock steady and told him it would be alright. I was there for him always and forever. His mother would've wanted him to prosper on the nuggets of her life's bounty. If he didn't graciously accept, well, that would be as though he'd kicked her corpse in the teeth. I told him that to appease his aching heart and guilty soul, he must put his inheritance to good use to help those less fortunate than himself. A commune, yes, what a fantastic idea I'd had that very minute, naturally. We could set up a commune on the ranch, gather new comrades. We'd send out our new friends to do good deeds for those who had lost their way in the world. They would all join us with glee in our worthwhile enterprise and feel nourished and good and kind. We sat.

'Felicia Mary Steadman bequeaths unto her son, Eugene Edmond Steadman (I laughed inaudibly) named as sole beneficiary in this last will and testament, her Tucson, Arizona Estate, Steadman Range (we'd have to change that for a start). All of its four thousand acre grounds (wow). In addition to this, the sum of five hundred thousand dollars (yahoo!) and her treasured Charles Bronson collection, including the life size waxwork currently on loan to Grauman's Chinese Theatre in Los Angeles, California. The latter, to be transported to the benefactor, after full duration of terms, stated in the signed contractual agreement, due to expire July 28 of this year.'

I almost pissed my pants.

'Five hundred thousand dollars!'

So did Eugene.

'She left me Charles Bronson!'

I could see he had missed the point entirely.

THREE

Dissidents of Virtue

No sooner had the will been read we were off on the road to find our fortune. Indeed, the very next I saw of Eugene, a mere hour after returning from the widow's valedictory speech from the grave, there he was perched aloft his chair. Barely visible behind a huge leather trunk he had placed on his shallow lap. I could hardly see him save for his feet and the shiny dome of his enormous head. The case was patched with stickers from fat camp in Wichita. His hands were quivering and veined from the strain of holding that huge case over his huge body. For most, the lap would provide a ninety degree angled ledge onto which a case could rest, but Eugene had a large distended belly instead and therefore had to withstand its whole weight in his hands to prevent it slipping down his ski slope of a figure. When sitting he appeared to half stand owing to his bodily protrusion. His face as pained from exertion as confusion, as he considered his aged mother's passing. I let him hang.

'Can we please go now?' he groaned, painfully.

Whilst I would have preferred to make a road trip out of the journey, a cross country adventure no less, Eugene proclaimed he couldn't countenance such a thing. He said it would be like the Paris–Dakar challenge with me at the wheel. He had no basis on which to form such a poor forecast of my driving skills, having never actually set foot inside an automobile with my greatness before. Yet I felt to a certain extent he may have made the correct assumption. His evidence perhaps derived from my wanton and somewhat maniacal wheelchair manoeuvring skills. He didn't even know about my incident with Nursey so I felt slightly cheated. Instead we must fly internal and take our chances with airport security and an automated pilot as our safety mechanism. Eugene was both overcautious and fastidious in his packing. He packed wet wipes and almost everything else he owned into his case and nearly had a coronary when I revealed I'd packed a Swiss army knife and a stun gun in the secret compartment. He scared easily. Luckily I wasn't packing his shadow so he would have no need to be afraid of that. He insisted he wouldn't be my travelling companion any longer unless I removed my pointy objects. Perhaps a wise move in these times of elevated security, so somewhat begrudgingly I left behind many of my essential personal effects at Eugene's behest. Thus my luggage became somewhat underwhelming. It appeared most of my cargo could be interpreted as threatening at best or completely illegal. So it was down to the smalls and shoes, a photo of Mom, one of Charlie Manson, my personal documents, a wad of cash and of course, my able mind.

The cab pulled up but thirty minutes later and the driver wished he'd gone elsewhere for his five dollar tip. It took the two of us and two random strangers to heave-ho his bulging case into the trunk. They agreed to help out only after lengthy coaxing and a couple of tokes on my reefer. Our taxing endeavours lasted fourteen minutes precisely. There was only groaning and supervisory comment from Eugene's quarter, beside he had not the muscle tone for manual handling and so was impotent to aid our Sisyphean task. Luckily we had bulging biceps, for it took proportionately the same degree of man-power to load the giant into the back seat. And we were off!

As our fellow passengers found to their cost, there is something to be said for air travel with a morbidly obese sidekick. For a start you get to board the plane first. We strutted by the other passengers waiting patiently in line at the departure gate, us grinning all the way and saluting. They already hated us before we had even taken off. There we were sitting comfortably in the best seats in the house with maximum leg room for mobility. Conveniently situated next to the emergency exit, should there be any complications during the flight, which may or may not be caused by us. Fat Boy was snoozing like baby by the time they took receipt of their complimentary papers. A grand start to an even grander journey said I and Gene agreed when awoken by my elbow. We must have a celebratory drink to toast our genius.

This most harmless of celebration got me into quite a bit of trouble, all told. The flight took a turn for the worst after promising beginnings. I swear to God, I had no intention of assaulting the air stewardess. I had no ambition to draw blood. Usually well considered plans of carnage end in total failure and genuine good intention conversely ends in a bloodbath. Once again, attesting to that theory, I found myself maiming without intent. Murphy had been employing his law with pre-cision and he had his eye on me as always and forever, uneasy bedfellow that he is.

The reality of the situation was this; I had merely been edu-cating the lady as to how an authentic measure of whiskey should be served. What kind of damage can you do with a couple of Jack D's? Then the whore of Hades proclaimed that I tried to glass her. The bottle was plastic for Christ's sake. The pressure in the cabin must have addled her mind. Nothing could have penetrated that make-up with any level of success, for her face was as plastic as the airline food.

We settled down into our seats, one for me, two for Gene, he was paying after all. Smiling and posturing at the other passengers were we, their feet to their chins in their tiny little seats. They were all packed in there like little sardines in a can, poor souls. I got the seat next to a hypochondriac from Detroit, squeezed in between my wide-buttocked steed and she, with her seething neurosis. I started to get a little nervous after take off. Restrictive conditions are not conducive to soothing an unstable mind. It reminded me of when Mom used to lock me in the cellar when I was a kid. OK, so I did mail dog shit through the pastor's letterbox but that was a mistake. I thought it was the principal's house. I took my mind off the flashbacks by watching the in-flight film; *Panic Room*, not ideal viewing under the circumstances. I passed on the luncheon which Eugene took off my hands with glee. The hypochondriac from Detroit described her hysterectomy, in detail which made me feel decidedly sick and glad for the millionth time to be a man and not a woman in this unfair world of ours. I drank another miniature drink. You know, miniatures do not satisfy the needs of a seasoned drinker such as my good self. One must empty several into one's glass at any one time to be truly sated. Everybody but the puritans and the prohibitionists knows this but try telling that to the damn stewardess from the fiery furnace. You'd think she was dispensing a prescription drug.

'Only one at a time sir, airline policy and only on three occasions during this flight.'

Now, I don't like to be difficult. As Michael Jackson once said 'I'm a lover not a fighter, Paul', but I don't much care for the corporate spiel. I don't need to hear company policy quoted chapter and verse, thank you. I do my part for the industry. I keep several workers at bourbon production facilities salaried for the year. All I wished to do was educate. No less than three miniatures to a full serving of your finest American whiskey said I, nursing my prescription single. I had merely been trying to apprehend a couple more measures from her trolley to decant into my plastic beaker covertly, sneaky beast that I am. It was she who applied the force, not I. I admit there was a struggle. She started wrestling me for the pilfered whiskeys. That is what happened right there. I could feel the screw top coming loose. If I could mentally calculate the exact angle of the beaker to impending stream of whisky with expeditious verve, I could have at least a double downed before she had time to react. But she seized the bottle and I fought her for it.

You know when events happen in slow motion right there before your eyes; but you are powerless to stop them mid-flow? I saw it coming. I relinquished my grasp, she was still tugging on the damn thing and the top found freedom. Whiskey exploded all over the hypochondriac from Detroit who reacted as though she had been sprayed with sulphuric acid.

'Aaaahhh!!! My eyes! Aaaahhh! My stitches have ruptured. Nurse. Aaaahhh!'

The bottle flew as though ejected from a cannon, flying over Eugene's portly frame and clipped the stewardess' mouth like a newly sharpened Stanley knife. Blood, whiskey, stumbling backward movement; I just turned away and faced the window, sulking. I felt like a kid again, didn't mean it. The next I knew, I felt myself being hoisted from my seat by a waiting marshall, still in the foetal position as he carried me to the back of the plane. I spent the remainder of the flight harnessed in the flight attendant's chair unable to move, glancing about as the other passengers' eyes bore into me as though I had just yelled 'highjack' and lit an ACME bomb. Eugene held his ear and pretended he didn't know me, turncoat.

We finally landed safely on soil, gleeful to be alive after our in-flight assault. We were greeted on arrival by two large officials of the law, badges flexed. How wonderful it felt to have a welcoming party and a police escort. They must have known we were VIPs. Still, rough treatment to dole out to such cele-brities of conscience, thought I. My shirt sleeve was almost ripped from its cotton bindings and hung forlornly at my side during the debacle that ensued. No better treatment for my good steed Eugene either. I will call them Officer Dick and Officer Asshole for purposes of identification. Officer Dick was solely responsible for buckling the front wheel of Gene's chair, mid-scuffle, creating more of a problem for himself than for Eugene since he was now responsible for guiding the thing into the awaiting vehicle. All it wanted to do was career to the left in a fashion most resistant to his intended direction. Eugene balled up in the seat like an armadillo in defence mode; he had learned my tricks well.

It is inspiring and heartening to know that we could again prove to be such a thorn in the side of law enforcement with-out actually having intended any harm. Officer Asshole rived me around like an overzealous Salsa partner and spun me with hurtling velocity into the car. No apology for ruining my houndstooth suit jacket then or my wide collar shirt. Just as I thought, the man had no taste or style when it came to the fashion stakes. A leisure suit and fanny pack wearer if ever I saw one, even in his uniform you could see right through to his redneck roots. They would soon learn how insignificant this whole scenario proved to be by comparison to the malice we were conjuring up for future confrontations. They would never have let us go with a mere caution had they any imagination. But we do not pay hefty wages and swollen pensions to the law for their power of foresight. They are expected to be bumbling fools who cannot contain criminals and so we accept them as they are. Besides, if they did a more comprehensive job of incarcerating villains, they would have nobody to police and this would wipe their very need to be from existence. You know they set minors free so they may guarantee their future employment. Anyway, what transpired from this innocent misunderstanding was a night in the cells for us both. This was a fine thing indeed since it saved us $200 in hotel bills and $35 for breakfast. That was money that could be better spent on munitions.

With no charges to answer we were relinquished begrudgingly by our porcine jailors and ejected from the building unceremoniously, our belongings nowhere in sight. The first glimpse of Phoenix was from a heap on the floor, from the standpoint of a small child. Even from this view things looked decidedly smaller than New York. I warranted minds would follow the same convention. Still, one cannot observe the reality of life from ivory towers. I collected myself from the sidewalk and rescued the destroyed wheelchair from the lobby entrance. I wheeled it round to Eugene who was lying face down on the concrete like a walrus. It took me seventeen minutes to load him into the chair. I had no strength left for conversation or any further physical endeavour. What we really needed now was a bus heading south toward Tucson and that was not going to be easy. Eugene looked fraught. Two hours of searching for the bus terminal without the aid of map, wandering and wheeling a defunct chair round in circles in the baking Arizona heat will drain anyone's enthusiasm. We started with less than the average terminal depressive. I made an executive decision. It was high time for us to buy some wheels of the automotive variety. With our belongings evading us it proved good sense on my part, as always, for packing the essential paperwork and monies in my underpants. They never searched my groin, the homophobes. Yes, my briefs were a good tight fit, safe as houses. The car salesman wasn't overly impressed at handling the notes I produced from my undergarments but he soon got over that when we plumped for the vintage Mustang Boss 351 over the less impressive but far more affordable Ford Taurus. It's all in the name of style. Whatever, I figured we were worth it and I still had a ten-thousand-dollar incontinence pad.

Eugene fit most snugly into the passenger seat once I had managed to stuff him into it. So snugly in fact, that I would not allow him to drink or pee at all during the first leg of our journey for fear of further logistical complications. I would have to cut him out of the chassis if removing him from the vehicle bore even a passing resemblance to getting him into it. Then there would be his repatriation to contend with. He was nominated map reader, I was nominated evangelist.

'Thank God we have disembarked the onerous city. Won't you just look at this place, my friend,' said I as we rolled down the highway, desert landscape on all sides. Sigh. 'It's just like coming home, Dorothy.' Imaginary tumbleweed rolled by, Eugene tutted.

'Oh spoilsport, you'll see. Our neighbours will welcome us with open arms and be brought to the brink of tears by our timely arrival. This place needs the spirit putting back in. Here we are to give them just what they need. It's all about the giving.' I whistled. I was really enjoying the freedom of the open road with the wind billowing through my hair. I ran my fingers through it to make Gene jealous.

'Steves, has it not occurred to you that our neighbours will be prairie dogs and coyotes? The last time I saw the neighbours they lived three miles away. I only met them because the Sheriff brought them round to identify my mother. She tied their son to a tree for two days for stealing apples. He was reported missing. I hardly think it likely that they will cry for joy. They'll probably run for cover.'

'So they should, so they should. People are always afraid when they witness greatness, they feel intimidated by it. No matter, they will crawl from their holes eventually and we will ensnare them . . . I mean, welcome them in, yes, with open hearts and a clenched fist. It is the way of the world. Mighty fine thing it is too, you have perversion in the family, Gene. I shall have more respect for you now.'

'Oh what on earth are you talking about Steves?' He ignored my last retort. 'I thought this was to be our retirement, our twilight.'

'Thirty-five is too early to give up on life, my friend. Don't throw in the towel now. Let us be steely in our resolve. No more sitting round on your fat ass, rotting in your little room, wishing the world would come to you and fall into your lap. It's all here for the taking. That is precisely what we shall do and I'll tell you how. Don't you trust me, Gene? I've saved you from a prison of your own design. I have.' I patronised. He scowled, looking ahead thoughtfully.

'Well yes, I suppose so. You know Steves, you are just about the best . . . actually you are the only friend I've ever had. But what exactly do you mean? I'm confused? Who will be joining us? Will there be ladies?'

'Ah, to the crux of the matter! There will be a fine choice for you. Fine ladies of all shapes, sizes and persuasions. There shall be festivity and joy, a collective, a coterie, comrades to pick you up when you are down, to tend to you when you tire. We shall work together as a family. You've always wanted one of those, haven't you friend? And it shall be so, I personally guarantee it. You stick with me. I shall make us heroes!'

Eugene nodded furiously, his eyes wide with anticipation. A small amount of spittle collected in the corner of his mouth, salivating in anticipation of the friends he'd never had.

'First we must set up the ranch. Set everything up so comfortably that they cannot possibly resist, with creature comforts; a workshop, subsistence farming, an armoury. We may keep animals if we please, emus perhaps. We shall not rely on others, only ourselves that we may never have to beg or ask for anything ever again. We shall be our own world. We'll forget those people who have hurt us. Or if we see fit, which we shall, we can exact out most fervent revenge on those who have spurned us. Divine retribution, now isn't that a fine thing. We shall make them pay.'

Eugene's eyes glinted. The power of suggestion, the suggestion of power; power bestowed. Nobody is immune to its allure. Not even the nicest man in the world, sat right there next to me. He pondered just how glorious it would feel to drive a stake through the foot of his beloved Nancy's killer or the boy at school who tried to flush his fat head down the toilet.

'I have a name by the way. I've been creating my, I mean, *our* legacy for as long as I can remember. We shall be a strong outfit, a fighting force to be reckoned with and we shall be called . . . wait for it . . . It's good.' I gesticulated wildly, briefly forgetting about the job of steering. We veered slightly but I saved it. 'We shall be called "The Empire". Now isn't that prestigious? No one will remonstrate with our unyielding solidarity, a united front.'

Pride overtook me and I saluted my steed and he reciprocated. That, I told him, would be our sign of respect, of greeting, great salutation for such dissidents of virtue.

Eugene would still need to be worked on some more. As yet he had not reached his comfort zone with the whole military strategy I had planned. I would ensure he felt the weight of the great debt he owed me for saving his sorry ass from bedsores and solitary confinement. If he didn't bend to my whim I would rescind my friendship and its associated benefits. It would kill him, for I was his only friend in the whole universe, ever and he knew it just as well as I did. I would use it as a stick to beat him with if he ever stepped out of line. He capitulated as I knew he would, for the moment at least. Although his bladder's resolve was beginning to cave and spoil his attitude toward the plan, which would never do.

'Yep, evermore shall we be gone from that place Eugene, for we are dissidents of virtue. We are Empire. It's hard to be humble when you are holding imperium in the palm of your hand, yet be humble we must. It's a shame that secret gods must fill their own tanks with gas and pay up to the minion at the cash desk and such menial tasks. It's only under the cover of this anonymity that we may propagate our greatness and so it must be done. What are we?'

' . . . tut . . . Empire, we are Empire.' Eugene wiped sweat from his brow and rolled those cynical eyes.

'And . . . ?'

'Oh, don't make me.'

'We are Empire, quite right. Yes. And then what do we do?'

'Salute.' His hands rested on his hips. Except he had not actually felt his hip bones for years, if ever, but I assumed they were there somewhere.

'Well, come on then man, get to it!' Eugene managed the most half-hearted of one fingered salutation. 'That's better, if lacking in enthusiasm. We must work on that.'

'Why don't you salute?'

'Because I *am* the Empire, Eugene. I hold superior imperium above all earthly and celestial power. Without me you'd be nothing. Nowhere! I am the Master of Ceremonies. Goodness me. I do hope this isn't dissent I'm witnessing, at such an early juncture too.'

'God help us and save us.'

'I heard that. Now, do twenty "Hail Steves" as penance for courting discord. We must be in unison with the doctrine. Come, come, only twenty miles more to go, let us be jubilant and start as we mean to go on here, with love in our hearts.'

We drove all day which certainly took it out of Gene. He was complaining of the onset of deep vein thrombosis before we reached the city limits. He felt sure he had ruptured his tormented bladder; his contorted visage spoke volumes about its incompetence. It is the penance to pay for consuming the world food reserve thought I, so the whining to sympathy garnered was not tipped in his favour, exceeding even my usual level of failure. Life is for giving, for giving to oneself, I say. Today's personal present would be to see Gene wet himself but a few steps from the can, seeping into his pants with the possibility of it dribbling into his shoes. No better reward for my hard day's work than to see such a gratifyingly humiliating sight. How pleasant that thing they call Schadenfreude, it is one of my favourite indulgences. If that wouldn't quell his sniping, nothing would. He did impress me in several aspects all the same. His map reading skills really proved to be of a high standard. He had found his calling. The organisation should be left to him, with my imagination its nemesis.

He managed to hold onto his urine and let out a sigh as we bore down on the ranch, which thankfully appeared to be exactly where he'd left it. We tore up that drive like we were striking victory in a NASCAR final. We did it in the Mustang with panache. Gravel flew hither and thither, flashing past the screen at speed, flickering like diamonds through the beam of the headlamps. It was as black a night as I had seen for many a year and the stars shone down on us hazily. As they only can without the city glare to obliterate their existence from our tiny, tiny world. I was filled with anticipation, for long drives like this only ever lead to great sprawling mansions. I could see precious little except for Eugene's eyes eagerly staring forward for what seemed like hours, but was in fact only a couple of minutes of wheel spinning ascent. A fortress atop the hill was what we needed. That would be the ticket indeed. I had grand ideas and I wasn't disappointed. Good Lord! I never knew Eugene was the product of landed gentry. I should call him squire. Dreams will come true my dears, if you concentrate hard enough for long enough, never ever let go and strangle the shit out of life trying. We were upon it.

A husk of a giant mansion on the hill rose before us, but a husk with potential nonetheless. Who in the world needed a place so large except me, I mused. Did they know when they were laying down these very foundations that godliness would dwell here in years to come, I mused again. And design it so that he could have a room for every one of his twenty comrades or more. Who knew how many we would number by the time I had put the finishing touches to my daring plan. The whole state could bunk up here and there would still be room to spare. I'd have to fill up the empty space with guns; guns to shoot critters and trespassers. Grenades and bombs for any assaults we might undertake and there would be many, possibly millions, if not trillions. I will stop short of calling them crusades, more like excursions out into the field, because of course, home turf should never be the theatre of war. I dared not comprehend the true possibilities of just how magnificent this place could become, just in case I jinxed the whole endeavour. Eugene, with typically defeatist tendencies equipped himself with mumbling disclaimers following along the lines of 'This place just isn't what it used to be,' 'I don't think a feline would attempt to climb those stairs,' 'Where's the door, roof, floor?' and all other manner of petty complaints, but then he never had vision. There was no space in his mind for innovation, just process, mainly featuring the process of sloth.

I hate to say that I was excited, because that would compromise my cool, but the grandeur of the place certainly beat the crap out of anything I have ever grasped with my own hands. I mustn't let it slip away. Work must be done. There were plans to be forged and forged they would be, right after a good night's sleep on the porch. I prayed to the god of all fine things that it didn't rain on the snakeskins since the place was sprouting leaks like a colander. I felt Eugene would grasp the facts come the morning, dawn light rising above the place to light it up as though a temple on the hill, blackness lifted to reveal the truth.

I bedded myself down on the decking with some dust covers we found over what ancient furniture was left behind in the widow's haste. Alas, the Chippendales had been purloined along with the Ming dynasty vases, I imagined. There was nothing of note but old junk. I banished Gene to the great hall where his snoring filled the huge empty space and disappeared out up the chimney, drifting toward the city. If the locals didn't know we had arrived already, they soon would when they heard the giant's snore. It was his roar. I drifted off to sleep upwind, fully clothed and shivering in the desert night. I dreamt of my rightful place in the universe as Lord of the Manor, King of the Hill, the finest despot there ever was.

Poke. Poke. I jolted up. Something dug into my shoulder like a swift butt from a giant salami. Just like when I worked in an Italian restaurant washing the dishes in Little Italy. The retarded owner Sal would jab me awake at night with large meat products, screaming and ranting about the unwashed dishes and the sudden absence of gin in his personal stash under the sink. But I try not to make much mention of my menial past. A sausage-like finger bore down on me once again.

'Steves, the roof is gone and I'm quite certain there used to be a west wing.'

Who was this cretin. Didn't he know Rome wasn't built in a day? My eyes were welded shut by sleep, but still I staggered round not really seeing but imagining the construction. Surely this was no time for a sane man to be awake. This guy was getting more and more like my grandfather by the minute, 5am! Where is my breakfast chef? It must be served on a silver platter. I was god-awful hungry and now I had meat products on my mind. I checked my snakeskins, still there; all was right with the world. So I decided to put a positive spin on the proceedings, even though I wished to punch him on the nose. He handed me a sheet of paper onto which he had documented the items present and items that were missing. The absent list was greater by a ratio of 10:1.

'Hmm, I see. Should we not dwell upon what we do have, Gene?' Defeatist fool.

I inspected the absent items as per the itinerary once my eyelids had released themselves from their glutinous anchors. I did it very slowly and without much zeal.

'We have walls, we have floors and ceilings on the first floor. We have rudimentary plumbing of sorts, mould and dry rot. We also have rats, good work.'

'Rats aren't a good omen, Steves. They are in my negatives column, see? Vermin detract from the overall effect we were hoping to achieve. They're dirty. We must get rid of them.'

106

'Ah, but they are not stupid, sir. They know when they are on to a good thing. They wouldn't invest their time here for nothing. I intend to discover their motives.' He batted a hole in the wall with the broom he was carrying in an attempt to flush the creatures out. As any credible entity would, they ignored his protests. I'll bet they were laughing their little asses off in their comfy cavity-wall home. They probably had the Ming vases in there.

I wanted to know which bastard came in the night and removed half our inheritance anyway. Maybe Dorothy flew away with the west wing and left it in Oz. Nothing to show it was ever there. Should it have fallen victim to some hurricane, there would have been fragments and foundations. Some bastard spirited the whole construction away in the dead of night, hitched it upon some super trailer, a palace on wheels. A hick's paradise, complete with spiral staircase and his and hers double sink bathroom suite and towelling set. We were left with a robe. Fine lounge robe though, claret silk embroidered with the initials TS. Good news for me and really a message from above. Eugene's long-dead father Tobias Steadman had abandoned it when he ran away with the maid. TS, is that Theodore Steves . . . ? It is now. A message of divinity, meant to be. I appropriated that. I had my completed outfit, my snakeskins, lounge robe, cigar. We should take some snaps for posterity.

Gene wheeled off a few feet, hoisted himself up with the aid of his broom and stood in the clearing. Something similar to ground zero lay before him. Apparently, this had been the site of his childhood playroom, now gone forever. He was feeling tearful. So many memories; when his au pair used to creep into his bedroom at night. That made me smile as twisted thoughts of under-age perversity entered my mind, but he confessed he would read her poetry. The man had never been entirely, or even partially male. I cannot conceive of it.

And do you know, suddenly the man could stand, oh, it couldn't have been easy. Where is the fucking wheelchair now, thought I. Not two days earlier I was pushing that fat sot around twenty-four seven. The man could barely put on his own damned shoes, never mind survey his land, itinerary and god damn it, I swear I saw him gamble around those grounds like a new born lamb when my back was turned, devious wretch. He froze whenever he thought I was paying attention.

A psychologist would tell a different story. He would say that as his freedom insinuated itself upon him so the veil of depression lifted. His resolve to conduct himself in a fashion of independence was restored. He was merely regaining his confidence and appreciation for life. When the mind bursts back into action, so the psyche doth follow. Personally, I felt embittered by the wheelchair absenteeism. I would break both his legs and stuff him back into it if I didn't need him for hard graft. The man was clearly a mongrel, but a most obedient one in the main and he was too fat to run away from me. So I would let him off for now.

It wasn't long before we had a makeshift canopy erected of tarpaulin and wishful thinking. We would need a handyman around the place, a carpenter, plumber, and electrician all rolled into one, a handsmith and in the not too distant future. Preferably before our own handiwork had the place rocked to its very foundations. We managed to cover both the bathrooms and a couple of the bedrooms. The most important area would be my study, the hub of operations. I set about creating my own unique atmosphere in there, at the rear of the property, in front of the back porch. It would be the place where I could sit for hours or even days casting an eye out of the window, surveying my grounds, my country. Producing plans so complex and wickedly insane that no one would dare question me for fear of a harpoon attack or some such crazy retribution. How exquisite. It had to be done correctly. I would sit and stare at the walls until a composite picture of its destiny came to me. A map of America on the wall, a more detailed map of Arizona marked with pins and crosses plotted for attack. It took two days of deep concentration to assemble, to configure the layout of the desk; even the coffee stains were predetermined. Leave nothing to chance.

We took many trips to hardware stores around this period to gather supplies and provisions. It was on one such occasion that I realised I was being followed. This proved most disconcerting for there was the possibility of paranoid delusion on the horizon. One often worries that the world is out to get one. Sometimes one imagines that one is being followed. Far worse, I became convinced that I had seen my mother, twenty years in the grave. I really mean it, I saw my mother. I swear to God I saw her, and I saw her in Wal-Mart of all venues. She was investigating a red chemise. If I'm honest, it wasn't the first time and I doubted it would be the last. She could often be found perusing Macy's in the hope of ensnaring an off-season bargain. It was all too much. Threatening to derail my concentration, splintering perception and causing inner turmoil the likes of which I could not quantify, yet I felt it growing uncontrollably; fear. I felt a swell inside. I must focus. I was absolutely sure it was she because I spied on her for quite some time from behind the fixtures across the aisle, studying her contours. The protruding top lip that became even more protracted when she concentrated hard and nobody had a bottom quite so large for such a small woman. What vexed me most was that I could not bring my bewildered self to reveal my presence to her. The courage escaped me and made a break for the revolving doors. I was alone with flaccid spine. I didn't see her leave although I suspect she dissipated into ether as soon as my back was turned as I was temporarily sidetracked by the electronic corkscrews and remote-controlled cars. Woe is me. I should have lassoed her with $1.99 garden wire whilst I had the chance. Slippery as a bar of soap that one.

This is not entirely what one would consider normal and yet I knew it to be true. My instinct told me not to let Eugene know about my sightings at the outset. I heard that the first alien abductees had terrible trouble when they revealed themselves to the world, forever to be branded lunatics after divesting themselves of the news of their fateful visitation. It was unsettling. I intended to corner her the next time. I must ask her opinion on the Empire. She would have good ideas. My father's demise was her brainchild, although she needed me to execute it in practice. Mother really did have a morbid streak, deliciously morbid, even though she brilliantly covered it up in the guise of an old lady. The genius of that woman, she revealed it only to I.

Several weeks of homespun carpentry afforded us with an appealing enough residence to consider inviting people in.

Mother was the first new resident although she took many unauthorised vacations. She surprised me one day by arriving with two small leather cases she'd stolen from Neiman Marcus. I'd left my office for a couple of minutes to load up on supplies for another day of philosophising in my chair. There she was upon my return, laid out on the chaise longue, still in her coat and boots, complaining about the heat. I could do nothing to dissuade her from staying since the house in Virginia had been sold at auction long ago, so I had better get used to the dis–traction. No one offered us our west wing back. My official headquarters gleamed and glistened with dark red walls and stolen silverware. I had scavenged a throne-like chair from an unfortunate. The garden had been fitted with sprinklers and festooned with fine flowering cacti, an oasis in a world baron of all sense, a refuge. My office would show no signs of carnage, I had seen to that. Should it become necessary to evade the law, the walls were the colour of coagulated blood. They could take their DNA tests and shove them where the sun doesn't shine, for the walls had been brushed with kerosene. A lovely place it had become. Now it was high time to consult the files. I had them all arranged back when I was in high school, the sacred scrapbook, a list of invitees to my world of crazed righteous-ness. All of the rogues within those pages had provided me with so much happiness and kinship by proxy back in the day. Oh, there would be great stories to lament around the camp fire, first degree murder, arson, terror; *Full Fathom Five*! Even back then I knew they were waiting. They were waiting for someone like me to arrive so that the real fun could begin. I would be the catalyst, the reason and the rhyme, bringing all those loose ends together, those lost souls. I'd whip them up into a frenzy, then set them loose, whirling around all over the place leaving nothing in their wake but destruction; hurricane. Yes, whilst Eugene was cooking zucchini from his vegetable patch, I was in the study thinking about sex and annihilation. The place needed to see some action, thought I. He could not provide me with the stimulation I needed to exacerbate and coax out the mastermind within. To this end I had been having secret meetings with Mother. She didn't trust Eugene one iota and neither did I. She also felt that he did not take enough care over his appearance. That could prove to be a PR disaster which may undermine the Empire's image. He must be forced to wear a uniform of sorts. Although a romper suit was the most fitting garment that sprang to mind, she had insisted on something smarter in lemon. I was therefore in need of a seamstress. I insisted, *we* insisted on strict rules of dress and conduct.

Eugene began to suffer miserably under my gaze. He didn't seem able to find or accept his place in our two-man Empire. We must hail forth our comrades of tomorrow. I figured we could add some new recruits to the shortlist should we come across any favourable additions during our activities. The tormented ex-Iraq veteran who went crazy in the supermarket slashing and dicing shoppers because the government refused to accept the validity of Gulf War syndrome perchance. I had read about him in one of the nationals. Surely he would know how to load an assault rifle or rig up a ballistic missile or two. I had a gaping chasm in the scheme since I had never had the low down on dismantling and reassembling a gun or a war head. I had an opening for a bomb expert and you can't find one of those ambling around the aisles of Tower Records unless you have a keen eye. First we must take a trip to the rifle range and learn how to shoot straight, with even a modicum of precision. My aim was only true at point blank range. This was prone to coming adrift as I had found to my displeasure all those years ago. Physical co-ordination often let me down at such times as I had always been prone to accidents and falling, tripping over even the smallest of obstacles. I had nightmares of holding up the federal bank, only to be usurped by the troublesome doorstop on the way out with the bounty. I would be splayed out all over the street, dollar bills and bullion flying in all directions and then the sirens came. But those dreams were not nearly as troublesome as the sex dream I had about Eugene shortly before bolting out of bed, my heart beating so fast I could hardly draw breath. The horror!

I reasoned we shouldn't make life hard for ourselves. If there was only resource for one prison break, we should be mindful to bust out a couple of maximum security prisoners at once. In the event we couldn't have our selected fellows, we should just take whoever we could find to make up our quota.

My formulations were interrupted by a loud thudding at the door. Eugene was enraptured.

'Charles is here! Look Steves, look. So lifelike, so real. He was my closest confidant when I was a child. Welcome home, Charlie!'

I opened the door to a vision of such stupidity that I was not sure whether I was still slumped over my desk ensconced in some surreal dream state. Before me stood Eugene, next to him the Charles Bronson waxwork freshly delivered from his installation at Grauman's Chinese Theatre. His LA tenure over, Gene held the thing in a tight embrace.

'His nose got chipped during the flight but I can remedy that with a couple of melted candles and some modelling clay.'

What the hell did I do to deserve this, thought I.

At Gene's insistence, the wax Bronson was placed in the corner of my study. I agreed only to appease him until the comrades came but I resented Bronson's presence. Staring at me and watching my every move. At least there I could keep an eye on him. I would melt him with my cigar if he got up to any mischief. We eyed each other. Bronson won the staring competition but we would have a rematch some other day.

After taking receipt of Charles we made our way to the rifle range to shoot up some targets. It was the first of a full course of lessons. We progressed from failing to even negotiate the safety catch off without the aid of our instructor, to actually being able to strike the edge of the target board. We were blown backward onto the concrete simultaneously by the force of the shot. Eventually, we were able to hit the bullseye on at least fifty per cent of occasions. That was good enough for me. We spent a good deal of time on the floor holding our chests, shaking our heads and tending to our residue-covered broken fingers but it was all worthwhile in the end. We were like the A-Team by the time we'd finished, crack commandoes. But we would make doubly sure we didn't follow their convention of never actually killing anyone.

We spent those days fixing up the place some more and then some more again, shooting anything that moved. We booby trapped and electrified the parameter fence. All of this so that the emus could not get out and the public at large could not get in. Alas, we hadn't seen a living soul for miles in the three months we'd been setting up our homestead. I'd seen a dead person but I doubted a million volts would cause her much trouble. At last it was time. As the dusk set in one warm evening we poured over our endeavour, taking it all in. There we stood high on the hill, proud and tall surveying our achievement. A palatial compound of such gigantic proportion that even we were most taken aback by its splendour. The demesne spread before us, a retreat on the high desert plateau, north, looking down to Tucson. This would be where they would flock in their droves. Like the Pied Piper of Hamelin I shall draw them in thought I, fine zealot that I am. Welcome good friends, step inside the zealot's lair.

FOUR

Compound Growth

Nothing could have been simpler than the emancipation of our first comrade to the cause. She'd been toiling quietly in the local library since her arson conviction had been cut short. Granted early release for exemplary behaviour was she and for comprehensively sorting the library books into order from A to Z, eschewing the Dewey Decimal system. Having found her place amongst the piles of books and encyclopaedia at her disposal, her time was spent reading the greats. Wondering where she'd found the pyrotechnical will to burn her entire family to a crisp in their beds all those years ago. She'd had counselling but had forgone the lobotomy due to the lack of supporting evidence for its success. Always living frugally, in denial of her past, forever alone with her introspection, the lady never explained herself to anyone. She was secretive. Those that knew her viewed her as a studious bookworm for whom sex would be an impropriety. No one was more decent than she. Her mousy hair scraped back from her face, fashioned neatly at the nape of her neck. Her clothes covered her from her neck down to her ankles, always, much like a Victorian lady or a puritan might. Naked flame scared her witless. Nightmares of being consumed by a giant fireball invaded her thoughts nightly. Smoking isn't allowed in libraries, neither are candles or anything that might result in them being lit. She'd sit in the dark during a power out with only the glow of the moon to light the way. Only speaking in a whisper so low that one would have to crawl right up to her lips and press the ear to her mouth to hear. Raised voices aren't allowed in libraries so she was in her element. Her mind had retreated into the shadows, had lost resonance but in fact she was a sharp as a tack. Her days were spent making her own clothes and cooking for the homeless on Sundays. She was perfect for the Empire, a silent warrior with an inner demon that I had designs on unleashing at the crucial moment. Her nurturing streak would give temperance to our collective insanity once all of the acolytes were in place. A calming force she would be, a contrast.

I sent Eugene down in the car to collect her one evening as she locked up the library at closing time. I'd been watching her for a while; she was always in charge of the keys so she finished up last on the late shift. I figured my palpable manliness might frighten her away in the first instance so I should leave it to Eugene to make her feel sorry for him. He would visit on several occasions in those next few weeks. He'd roll up to the counter in his newly refurbished chair armed with his soft voice and very large smile and a thousand questions on Chaucer and Steinbeck. He would never mention *American Psycho*, never, in case it sent her running for the hills. He attended the workshop she organised on Wednesdays on the basics of Information Management and feigned interest in her favourite authors and pursuits. Good old Gene. She fell for his childlike charms. She even invited him to a cook-off at the local church in aid of the unfortunates which she won but donated her prize to the children's fund, no doubt in return for good karma. She had the kind of converted soul that makes lesser mortals feel sick, sheathed in a veil of silent sadness that makes a person wonder just what in the world has happened to this lost individual as she gazes at the floor. A million sorrows stirred behind those blue eyes. I think I have always loved the affectation of the kindred spirit, at one with the pain that never reveals or heals itself. Those soft lips that daren't share secrets for fear of falling to pieces once they are told . . . ahhhh!

Wait one god damn minute! I must collect myself at once thought I. What was I thinking. We had a pact Gene and I. It would be duly included in the constitution of the Empire. There must be no fornication between comrades. It causes confusion and divided loyalty that can only end in tears and tattered plans. I would not see the Empire dissolved by romantic infighting. No. We must show restraint and keep our hands to ourselves like good boys. Though I believed Gene's interest to be in view of companionship, my motives were more perverse. Besides, I promised Gene ladies and he would have them. I had delivered but I did not say he could fiddle with them. That is the truth of the matter. Perhaps I judged him by my own hypocritical standards, seeing catastrophe where there was none to be found but I wouldn't chance it. I shall strap my member to my thigh to avoid any uprisings thought I, but I didn't. I should have heeded my own superior advice.

Gene brought her back to the ranch on several occasions. We made fine hosts; we ate and drank merrily. We played some antiquated parlour games because neither of us knew what ladies liked to do. They took me ample time to master. Once I learned the ropes I gave my all and won with astonishing frequency, even if I had been cheating all along. She didn't seem to care, though Eugene was noticeably sore. She thought us civilised, which was the ultimate dupe as far as I was concerned. Eugene devoted much time and effort to conversation on world affairs and society talk that I couldn't be bothered to entertain. Therefore she bore me as the attractive, brooding friend. That was her spin I fancied. I would let her have it if she would join us with her sad eyes and her womanly ways.

'You don't get many New Yorkers round here.' It lent us some sort of legitimacy it seemed.

The lady was very much enjoying the tranquillity of our estate, so much more than her rented room. Gene showcased his herbaceous borders and our twee cockatiel roost. To me they were just sitting ducks waiting for a basting with orange sauce but Gene would have none of it, although I did offer to do the plucking myself. Her landlady back at the apartment was a domineering battleaxe. Our lady would shuffle around trying to avoid the harridan's wrath. Gene painted one of the spare rooms her favourite colour of dusky plum, adding cushions and throws in his inimitable way. She was only too eager to join us. She had no shred of doubt when we intimated we would need a woman's touch to soften the edges of our as yet, bachelor pad.

We collected her one night from the library, her small case in hand. She dropped the keys down a grate as she approached the car and waved them off on their trip to the sewer, a bold gesture of defiance against her old life. I half expected the place to go up in flames as we sped off. Besides, our library was much better stocked with many offerings from a certain author of great renown: T Steves. She could busy herself sorting those, who knew she might learn some new philosophies from those heaving volumes. I felt sure of it. We had her enchanted. Two cream teas and a homemade cobbler later, she was putty in our hands.

'Welcome home, Kathryn Monroe.' I waved her through with a waft of the hand and a wink. She blushed as the finest ladies do.

She fit like a glove; she really did add a new dynamic to the mix. I noticed that Eugene started to make some changes to his personal appearance. He shunned a second stack of pancakes for the first time in his life, even though I shoved the remnants almost in his face. Those appealing morsels; once he would have begged me for their heavenly presence in his cavernous mouth. Mother tipped me off that he'd skipped lunch the very next day. Something was afoot. Kathryn busied herself cutting patterns for Gene's new attire, a process that demanded many revisions since he was shrinking at steady pace. Within a month he considered life without his souped-up turbo chair for I had fitted an engine. The contraption was not as sleek and sophisticated as I would have liked. With rocket propulsion it chugged around the grounds suitably enough for him to complete a circuit of our acres in half the normal lap time. I could keep an eye on his whereabouts by following the plume of smoke which billowed from its exhaust. This meant that he could collect the vegetables and meats to cook us dinner.

I made plans. We had a rouge to catch, a loose cannon. We must keep to schedule. I had to see some action soon. The scene of domestic harmony pleased Eugene to the core of his soul but was a comfort I could not bear. Boredom was setting in. This wasn't part of my grand design. I slipped out in the night to strangle a cockatiel in pure frustration. The emus were far too fearsome for my liking and made an awful din when they feared death was upon them. Those bastards can run. Despite my nubile agility I couldn't keep up with them. I may as well have attempted to race a cheetah for all the good it was worth, those unassuming looking scoundrels. They faced me off with their bug eyes, hideous creations.

I concentrated all my efforts on the next recruit. I'd been on several reconnaissance missions trying to track the bastard down; Joe Derek Spangler. He escaped from prison during a wing wide siege. His compatriots camped out on the rooftop ripping up the slate and demanding safe passage to Mexico. How foolhardy. They must have known they would never get away with it. But hope springs eternal and will out those pessimistic realities. Who cares when a life behind bars is the only alternative. Once ushered back inside, the prison guards realised they were one Spangler short of the full compliment. He really should have been given the chair or the lethal injection. I wanted him for the Empire nonetheless, but in truth I think he probably deserved it. I don't think society could ever provide a justification for chopping anyone up into tiny pieces. It wouldn't have been my modus operandi, far too messy, although I do admire his flair for creativity.

He was on the run from the FBI of course, rated quite highly on their most wanted list. How appealing. I would not allow him to be the celebrity of the piece. He must know his place in the pecking order. I knew just where to find him. The homeless knew all too well that I wasn't 5-0. I had taken the liberty of tasking Kathryn with probing the bums in exchange for their meals at the chapel. I told her that Spangler was an old friend of mine, fallen on hard times. I wished to offer him shelter now that I was a man of means. It didn't hinder me any that I slipped them some meths to wash down their gumbo. As I had been consorting with the reprobates, all of which Kathryn found most benevolent of me, I had good opportunity to scope any other stand-out contenders ripe for the opportunity of joining the Empire. As we stood, a two-man army with our lady as mascot, we were not yet fully equipped to accost a wild man who may show incredible resistance to the recruitment process. In any case, one of us was quite severely disabled by several inches of blubber. There can be no nimbleness expressed in a fat suit. I would need brawn for this job, an extra man. He must be extremely strong and he must be extremely stupid, for only the stupid lend themselves acceptingly to taking instruction without question. It was fortunate that there should be so many examples to match this description down at the church. I was most spoilt for choice. After a couple of scouting missions, I singled out the best candidate. His unofficial interview was one moment of mind-boggling brainlessness that particularly captured my attentions. Dirk was only seventeen. His mother had been a big fan of *Battlestar Galactica* in her youth. Her first crush was Starbuck, that most handsome fellow. Giving birth at sixteen hadn't afforded her time to think long enough about suitable names for her offspring so she picked the first name she liked from the credits. He was truly saddled and he did not see the irony. Ugly, pimply, ruddy-cheeked and green as our well-irrigated pastures was he, but wide. He looked just as though he had been lifting SUVs for weights. My God, those biceps were wider than my thighs. Better still he appeared to idolise me. He would look up to me even though he was physically looking down and you could see it plainly on his plain face; admiration. Who could blame him. Such a stylish beast am I, with ingenuity, ambition and regal poise. Even he could see that.

Indeed, the lights were on but there was no one home. The occurrence that promoted him to first place on the wanted list took place one sunny afternoon as I was tapping some old boy for Spangler's whereabouts and slipping him Rohypnol. We were stirred from our huddle by an uproarious commotion of bellows from across the road. Dirk was being grappled by two leather clad Hells Angels intent on whipping his ass all the way to Tucson. He had mentioned that he admired their bikes before. Lines of black and chrome motorbikes parked across the street outside the diner, their usual haunt.

'Shiny.' He would say in a slow drawl and stare, he would point. 'Look at them . . . Shiny . . . ' as though he'd lost the thread of his sentence and was mesmerised by their gleaming beeswaxed exteriors.

He had clearly had a thought which must have come as a complete surprise to his empty head and decided to take matters into his own hands. He would seize one of those metal beast-bikes for his own without asking. He might just have got away with it if he had actually had the wherewithal to ride off into the sunset like any sensible thief would. But no, not Dirk. He revved up that engine to a thunderous roar holding the bike up with his arms like thighs. Most guys would only be able to lift it an inch before collapsing in exhaustion at their travail, but he was all beefcake and no steroids required. In due course, when the angels from hell heard the commotion, they came out to see what was afoot.

'Like the look of my beast, do ya boy?' Dirk glanced up from

123

his business and back to the bike, stroking its chrome petrol tank, he twisted the gears a little. 'Great piece of kit. She's my baby.' The hairy biker thought he had another adoring fan. He approached Dirk casually, his friend behind him wearing more leather than a full-grown bull. His boots landed heavy on the ground as he made it closer to the thief. We all stood in the church yard across the street, right under the sign 'Jesus Loves You!' illuminated overhead. We were slightly to the left of the Jesus Mobile, parked up front. We smirked. He wasn't really going to try it, was he? Had he been in possession of a brain, I would have thought it a brazen move. As it was, this was pure, uncalculated stupidity. We smirked on.

'Hey kid, you're fingering my high sheen. Took me all night to get it buffed up good for the tour so take a step back, keep your hands to yourself!'

'Yeah, you can look but don't touch sport. Just like a woman.' He laughed at his own inferior joke, but Dirk was concentrating so hard that he had failed to notice the change in attitude. He twisted the controls some more and made faces at himself in the reflection, screwing up the high sheen with his oil covered prints.

'I said get the fuck off of my baby, man!' The bikers started to gather pace. Heavy footsteps echoed across to the church's hallowed grounds where we stood, tarnishing its reputation. The neon flickered and the message turned over to 'Peace in our Time'.

'Little motherfucker!' they brayed.

Dirk had caught sight of those angry, hairy faces and took flight, running down the road with the bike at his side. He still didn't realise the obvious advantage that getting on the thing

124

would have afforded him. I doubt he could have mastered the controls at any rate. Buffoon!

'Come back here you lil' sack a shit. You're dead meat, boy. Dead!' We all stood in line, me and the old guys with their meths and their Rohypnol, drugged up and slurring.

'He's gonna get a kickin' Doug. I'm tellin' ya.'

'Hee, hee, hee, hee,' they cackled, raising their bottles.

'You better run.' Ike hollered. Doug chuckled. 'Hee, hee, hee.' He turned to me, his red nose covered in broken capilleries. 'I'll tell you somethin', that kid's got balls. Somebody call the nurse. Hee, hee.'

They were on him in no time and we did nothing to help. Jumping all over him and punching and kicking him all the way. Had he been anyone else he would have been minced meat. But Dirk swiped them off just like flies, swung round and thumped them so hard they crashed around like pins in a bowling alley. More followed from inside the diner hollering all the way. He'd bowl one crashing right into the others and they would all be falling around and getting back up for another swipe at the brain-dead behemoth. Smack, whack! Dirk held his own. He only took flight when the entire diner emptied, having seen the furore through the windows. Even he couldn't take on thirty Hells Angels all at once so he darted away, cast aside the vehicle and hid in an alley. They gave up the chase once they had recovered the bike, to return to the diner to top up their grit reserves and a healthy dose of bacon. I found him cowering behind a trash can nine hours later; the idiot. He exhibited a small amount of urine as I sneaked up behind him and shouted 'Boo!' at an alarmingly high pitch. He had sealed his fate, although he didn't know it. I wanted him in and I knew it would be as easy as taking candy from a baby. When he agreed to join us he near broke into tears of appreciation.

I half expected him to turn up with a knapsack, thorough-bred hick as he was, or in some kind of trailer truck with the American flag flying and a novelty hooter. He arrived on a manual scooter that had buckled in the centre owing to it being several times too small for his frame. He was not even approaching coolness. Nor was he homeless, but his mother had been wishing that she could get rid of her spawn and get back to the job of drinking herself into her grave. She had been only too eager to see him ejected from the nest. Now she just had to get rid of his brother Chuck and she would be free. Perhaps in a couple of years I could take him off her hands too. Dirk had no friends. The old reprobates at the church had been the only group with which he felt any kind of affiliation. The kids at school spent most of their formative years trying to climb him like a giant ladder so they could kick him in the head. Those little runts besieged him daily for the challenge. He was safe now and all too eager to please. As he was skilled with his hands, we set him to patching up the roof. When I showed him the mountain of tiles, he rubbed his hands together with glee.

'Huh, gimme two days.' He worked round the clock. The sun went down and came back up like time lapse photo-graphy and he was still up there toiling away. Gentle giant, cheer his servitude. He didn't give in until the last tile was in place at which point he promptly passed out. Kathryn developed a maternal streak and tucked him into bed of an evening whilst Eugene watched on with a strange cloudy look in his eyes that I had not seen before and I did not like the

126

look of. I needed Spangler and I needed him fast. Testosterone levels in the compound had taken a dive and must be topped up immediately. Bronson's presence did not help in this order at all and then there was Mother adding more ethereal oestrogen to the mix.

I heard that Spangler had been living under a bridge on Highway 79, erected some AstroTurf shield so that it perfectly blended in with the grassy knoll to evade the law. He hid behind it always, wearing a camouflage fatigue in desert sand. They were all he could lay his grubby hands on, but if he pressed himself low to the concrete you could hardly see his form. Some had seen him flitting from one side of the highway to the other dodging cars. Others had heard his distant calls to the wild dogs he called his friends, but none had met him face to face. A whisper in the night was he. His whereabouts could be documented not by studying stool samples but by following the empty cartridges he would leave in his wake, shooting up his supper or just for practice. But even when the end of the trail had been found he would have disappeared long ago. He had an arsenal behind there, behind the AstroTurf shelter. All manner of arms he had picked up from drug dealers and such criminals. He had wrung their necks with his bare hands utilising the element of surprise as his ally, and stashed the bounty for himself. What kind of a devious plan would one need to capture such an animal and what would we do with him once he was cornered, I mused. I doubted he would react cordially. Fight fire with fire! An ambush would be perfect; ensnare him with nets. Once we had him in our custody we would set to taming him. We would first throw him into the pond, then we should disrobe him with force if we must and scrub him to within an inch of his life. Free him from his swaddling crust. Holy sheep dip Batman! We shall not play host to lice in the Empire.

Ah, but this is for tomorrow. Today we must apprehend the creature, said I.

'Is everybody with me?' Silence. 'I thought so.' We would sniff him out, follow the cockroaches to his haven for he would be kindred to such creatures. He would not survive nuclear holocaust or the holocaust of the Empire unless he accepted the way of things. I could see the struggle ahead. We may have to restrain him for he would fight and gnash and scream like a raging beast. The nature of the hermit renders one oblivious to good manners and the rules of good social conduct. He would be a wild, hairy, bearded monster. He would have long forgotten he was once a gentleman and succumbed to the call of his basest biological urges. He would be rabid and deft in the art of camouflage, but his skills in this field would be welcomed by the Empire, an antidote to Eugene's beacon lemon jerkin in the night.

Personally, I had not seen any press about him since I snipped his cutting from the national all those years ago but I imagined this to be the case. I suspected he would still be agile for his age, surviving in the wilderness as he had been. His twenty-seven to my sixteen, all those years ago, now forty-six and still able to outrun a stallion should the occasion arise. He is Empire but he must be honed. He must be able to present himself as an acolyte to the Empires cause, otherwise how could we ever be taken seriously.

Kathryn set about crocheting some nets for our special

launching device with which to ensnare him. This was weighted at each corner with polished stones, lovingly lathed by Dirk, with small drilled holes to secure them to the netting. The thing was all pink and purple thread intertwined with a sparkly thread but then we never did tell our lady the real purpose of her mission. I allowed her to believe we would be capturing errant emus with the contraption so she had though it would never see the light of day and added her own creative touch. This would make us look gay for sure, but no matter. I forged a projectile device. I spent two weeks on that thing trying to get the correct forward thrust and Gene explored the best folding techniques to ensure its nets unfurled themselves in all their glory on ejection. We packed gas canisters in case silk thread could not contain the beast.

Meanwhile, I went to the library to garner some recordings on the call of wild dogs. If I could perfectly imitate the creatures I could communicate with Spangler via wolf and he would never know it was me. I specifically needed to isolate the call of the injured canine. I had no faith in its counterparts to come to a wounded brother's aid. Survival of the fittest and every dog for himself, but I figured Spangler would not be able to resist. I kept my subjects awake all night with my howling, for only when I had this art perfected could we set about implementing our plan. By the time I was done I had attracted every dog in the god damn country to the grounds, howling at the porch light like it was the moon. We lost many emus to their gnashing jaws in the process. I had mistakenly been practicing the mating call.

I was certainly building up my portfolio of new skills, all kinds of machinery and devices had been invented. It is amazing what you can learn from this internet. If I had known about that years ago I could have built myself a Cirrus plane and flown to some tax haven to live my life out in the style of a king on some golden beach. I could certainly survive now for a few weeks should I become marooned on a desert island. Necessity is the mother of invention after all.

Right! That was enough planning. We were a tight and sturdy ship. There is only so much preparatory work one can do before an overworked strategy becomes an exercise in procrastination. I hoped it would all go well. I needed a new pair of snakeskins. My leather soles were hanging on by a few threads and I worried that any slight scuffle might render me shoeless. I would cry for sure. I would mourn their passing so I was doubly cautious about the exercise. I presented my clipboard to demonstrate the plan for those flaky minds.

'Friends, we will drive close by the bridge and park up in a wooded area immediately adjacent to Spangler's encampment but on the river side of the trees. The river runs right along the road. Once there, we will position ourselves accordingly. I will entrench myself in some bushy outcrop, bed myself down and howl my head off until he presents his rabid self to my aid. Gene, you will fire the net gun.' I trusted him better than Dirk and he'd had training at the range. He would need only a pivotal spinning movement from a fixed position which would benefit him immensely by preventing him from hulking his girth after light-footed prey, but I kept my insults to myself for a change. 'Once deployed with supreme precision, Dirk will pounce from his cover and empty a canister of gas into Spangler's face. At this point I shall stop howling, having provided the perfect bait to lure the cretin. Mother will take on a supervisory role as always and alert me to any unsuspected developments that might require a quick-thinking change of plan.' This was a job to which she was entirely fit for purpose, considering her deviant credentials. Eyes rolled when I mentioned Mother.

'Great, we have an imaginary lookout,' mumbled Eugene but I ignored him.

'We shall then contain him and transport our human payload back to the ranch without incident. Gene, if he comes round too early you shall pin him down with your vast proportions.' That told them.

I lined up my men with Kathryn and Mother looking on and saluted them like a drill sergeant. They looked remarkably shipshape given their obvious flaws. We piled into the car. I made them sit in the rear seats since Mother always liked to ride up front. Gene was bemused at the seemingly empty seat.

'Can't I sit up front, Steves, like the second in command?'

'Mother is in transit!' I snapped, losing patience. 'You would crush her delicate frame. Besides, she's already belted up and ready to go.' The belt hung loosely down the side of the seat. He couldn't see Mother but she could see him, scolding him from her commanding position. The drive was only thirty minutes long and Mother wanted to stop at Taco Bell, but I wouldn't let her. Hopefully her rumbling belly would not give away our position in the undergrowth.

I took the appropriate left turn off the main road, the highway below us and stopped the engine dead at the top of the slope which ran down from off of the bridge above Spangler's lair. We free wheeled the car all the way down to the bottom of the hill. The Mustang's purr would have awakened him from any slumber for sure. We climbed out and pushed the car behind the trees, safe and out of sight. Eugene perspired as only a fat person can; with no apparent reason and patted his forehead with his ever present sidekick, the humble handkerchief.

Now to scope the hideouts; Eugene should take position behind a large tree. We had all dressed in brown to blend into the scenery; this was not a mission for my crimson lounge robe. I wore my houndstooth suit in a pleasant tan colourway. Mother wore red for no one could see her and Gene was saddened to leave his lemon jerkin behind. Dirk didn't give a shit, he just did what he was told. We huddled like a bunch of misfits pretending to be outlaws. Like the leftovers at school sport that nobody ever picked had banded together to form their own team. I motioned to Dirk to crouch in a bushel a few yards from my position. I exhibited a pounce gesture, we had practiced this before. He had been rather good at pouncing. If only there had been a vocation for that type of thing he could pounce professionally. When we were ready, I furtively got the thumbs up from all parties. Let the games begin.

I began with a low whimpering and gradually built up the performance into snarling and wailing. I had smoked twenty Marlboros before breakfast to lend a gravely quality to my barking. I would have believed it. Hollywood here I come! I say, do you have any vacancies for animal impersonators? This really is ludicrous thought I. Still, if we could bag ourselves another villain it would all be worth it in the end.

'Rrrrraaarrrggghhh . . . grrrrr . . . snarl.' I kept it up, making some dragging sounds as if paws were grappling at the ground, pulling along two wounded hind legs.

'Yelp! Aaaaoooooooooowww!!!'

A bush rustled.

'Snarl.'

I started to lose breath. Mother signalled me an OK with her fingers, right on target. What if he had a shotgun and just came to put the miserable hound out of its misery!? Don't think. Just bark. Whimper.

My whimper was met with a yelp from the approaching party. I still was not sure if it was Spangler as my line of sight was obscured. Another yelp from him. This man was an impostor; any mutt would have known it. That's the god damn mating call thought I and I was right as always and forever, no mistaking it. Oh please don't let him be partial to a spot of bestiality. My ass was prematurely sore and throbbed a touch. Again it came and I responded.

'Yoooouuuuwwwww.'

'Grrrrr.'

He was bearing down. My face to the floor, I could only move my eyes to see Mother through a parting in the leaves. She was giving me the execute plan gesture; OK fingers once again. I gave the boys the attack signal, which curiously came out as nervous wind. But they appreciated the time was right, even if a fart had not been the agreed signifier of action stations.

Gene fired like Clint Eastwood, excelling under pressure, his usual officious nature replaced with commando sniper skills worthy of Lee Harvey Oswald if we are to believe the official line and the pink sparkly net was flying through the air and wrapping its way around Spangler's neck within the blink of an eye. He was not down, nor was he out but the startling nature of the assault assured that he dropped his shotgun. His impaired vision would not allow him to relocate his firearm, at least not in good time to collect himself. For Dirk was pouncing in slow motion, flying through the air, arms flailing, legs wheeling, treading the air – ace triple jumper – champion of the pounce . . . and contact was achieved. Spangler was down. Dirk rolled off him on impact but clambered back on. They rolled around, rolling over and over down the river bank and into the shallows, thrashing as they went.

'Deploy the gas!' shrieked I in hot pursuit. Mom was clapping and whooping and jumping up and down, making out left and right hooks with her fists at the air. I ran to help but I kicked off my snakeskins first at the water's edge. Those legs were everywhere, both pairs. I was afraid Spangler might roundhouse me from his horizontal position, but I ducked in the nick of time as a leg thrust into my face. Water sprayed everywhere. Oh no, watermarked houndstooth! No attire for a gentleman of my stature but I pushed those thoughts to the back of my mind and grappled with Dirk's jeans in an attempt to free the canister. His wriggling made things doubly difficult to grasp. I whipped the can out of there in a trice and bore it down into Spangler's mouth. It went off surrounding us and a plume of noxious gas dissipated into the air before the can rolled into the water, poisoning everything in its wake downstream. We dove backward. Spangler was limp, face down in the water. A triumph indeed.

'My son!' Mother exclaimed and punched the ether again for added effect. We damn near killed him which was not our intention. Luckily his injuries were not fatal, well not quite. I do believe he flatlined for a moment before Eugene sat on his chest ejecting half a litre of sodden river bed from his failing lungs. Such weight would be enough to expulse anything within. He was only lucky the fat sot didn't squeeze out his intestines.

We dragged him up the slope and back to the car. I was barely exerting any energy, allowing Dirk to take the full weight of Spangler's limp body. I held on to his ankles with two fingers so as not to touch him and contaminate my greatness with his germs. We bundled the captive into the trunk, to adhere to the manner of celluloid conventions. It would contain him should he wake up before we were home. Besides Mother insisted on a trip to Taco Bell on the return leg of the journey as a reward for all her hard work and I couldn't have a scene over burritos. I hadn't planned a shootout at the fast food outlet, that's been overdone and would be cheap and unimaginative.

Back at the ranch we tentatively opened the trunk, fearing what we might find. Spangler was happily still out for the count, a pitiful sight, if the truth be told. Patches of clean pink skin shone out at us from the otherwise blackened face. Clods of mud hung from his beard, I was right about the beard for he had obviously been watching the movies too. This renegade looked positively ancient; a life of hard knocks had brought him to this. The army and then a life on the run, the stress and strain weighing on the conscience of a man who had hacked and sawed his way through many of his friends, leaving him alone to ponder his inadequacies. A man who could no more live with the people he loved than restrain his murderous urges to dispose of them. His hair was matted and black, his finger-nails long and cruddy. His fatigues reeked of oil and dirt and all manner of things that belong in the toilet. He was curled up in the foetal ball we had left him in, dribbling biliously. We dragged him into the pond. A good wash and haircut would do him justice. We could let no one see the man like this.

I left the boys to tie him to the bed, a restraint that would bide us time as I went back to philosophise about the Empire and the boys had a well-earned nap. It was four down, more to go. The potential collective was getting smaller every time I reviewed the files. Sure we, that is to say Mother and I, had Eugene, Dirk, Spangler and Kathryn. I was thankful every day for their attendance, if not dubious allegiance to the cause. I checked the files, some of the pages were missing; candidates had died or disappeared without a trace. Nathaniel Bartlett Junior had defected to practice the ancient art of Buddhism in the Nepalese mountain ranges without so much as a thought for the Empire's depleting numbers. I would issue him with a recall if only I could find his orange ass. He belonged to me, god damn him! Gilman had kicked the bucket. Damn them all. A little dedication to the cause wouldn't go amiss.

I must also set out the constitution to the cretins as I had my good acolyte Eugene. A points plan, much like the Rosetta Stone but not in code or perhaps more like the Ten Commandments, but equally not carved in stone, as my soft hands may become callused. Paper may not stand the test of time but was all I had. I set to, using my best fountain pen so as to send a worthy document into the annals of time and to secure our place in history. I fancied to write it in Latin but realised a document my followers could not understand would defeat the purpose of the exercise. It must be grammatically correct and an excellent example of English so as to be taken seriously by scholars the world over forever more, amen. The addition of hieroglyphs could also be beneficial to the scholarly overtures of the piece. I would like, I fancied, seeing my leather bound ramblings in a glass display cabinet at the Metropolitan Museum in New York. Alarmed and surrounded by disagreeable guards as other would-be despots would naturally try to steal my ideas and philosophies and pass them off as their own good work. A marketing strategy would be the first port of call. Disseminate the information to the masses with my own name attached in gold etching, of course, and perhaps a wax seal.

'The Last Bastian of Hope' would be the compound's name. It would be mounted above the doorway duly when I had figured out the Latin translation which would lend us more kudos and make us all look very intelligent in the future biography. This would not be duplicitous for my part but would certainly be a stretch for the cretins under my charge. This was good practice if the truth be told. I could not have any challenges to my authority or power; for there would be no Romulus and Remus type catastrophes in the Empire if I could help it. I had chosen my halfwit disciples with this in mind. I must garner some more minions to make up the numbers, although I had yet to form a plan as to how they might be controlled. I'll bet the government has some cunning device or other up its sleeve. How could they be forced to divest themselves of their trinkets? The Empire must be furnished technologically to the fullest capability, otherwise the CIA would stroll into the compound and blow us sky high. I had some of my own tricks up my sleeve though, I can tell you. I do believe they will have the utmost influence in years to come. They may even give me honours for my studies, those institutions. I would write it all down in the journals, of course. The library would be full within a few months and I would have my doctrine documented for posterity. I must polish up my ideas first though, thought I. They were not at publishable standard and if the truth be known and there was still an element of doubt as to whether they would work in practice.

Mind control; I had been researching some techniques. Margaret Singer's studies on the Branch Dividians had proved to be highly worthwhile and had given me some great ideas on how I might manipulate the troops. Kathryn would be my Patty Hearst.

Experiments; these would need to be carried out in order to ascertain the efficacy of my work. I would need to establish a lab. At the outset we were in the company of a Bunsen burner as our only piece of equipment. It was a lonely place, that lab of mine, for it was basically just a room with bare walls next to the kitchen. But we shall have test tubes, Petri dishes every-where, a centrifuge, all manner of things, thought I. We shall have computer simulations, which leads me to hacking.

Hacking; I would need to infiltrate government files so that we may use their own software against them in order to bring them down. I needed to know where their Achilles heel lay so that we may strike, I might also need to kidnap Bill Gates for this task. I would like to scramble all of the accounts in the federal bank, thought I. Localised robberies were not suffi-ciently large-scale operations to ensure our place in America's conscious. I would plan to break into the Oval office in the White house and move things round when the President was in the bathroom or playing golf. To really screw him up when he came back and saw his table and chairs all piled up on top of one another; cum on his seat, that kind of thing. All would be well as the operation rested in the hands of my divinity. I saluted myself. I had visions of desecrating my father's grave; him lying there rotten in death as he was in life, laughing at me from down below. I would take his bones to Atlantic City, he always hated it there.

I holed myself up in the operational hub that was my study for days and nights passing without relevance in time and space, plotting revenge. I could glance out of the window and see the charges going about their chores. I could hear Spangler wailing. Kathryn administered his tranquilisers at my behest. The only way of getting him to conform would be to wear down his will to live. Let him give up in his mind; to relinquish himself to our whim and righteous instruction. Break him.

Eugene attended to commands in my absence. He had come on in spades under my tutelage. I had him reciting the constitution of the Empire without persuasion and he had noted several amendments to my satisfaction and in accordance with my doctrine. I was doubly impressed by his ability to conform for it was his own particular brand of adaptation. A sovereign pupil, he sucked it up with gay abandon. He had found a cause celebre to sink his teeth into as though it were a twelve-pound steak. He seemed pleasured and full of direction. He had garnered new respect from allegiance to my cause. I actually saw Dirk salute him that morning as I returned from the kitchen with breakfast. A feeling of wellbeing descended from the heavens. A great commander was he, a sturdy and forthright follower of the book. I had taken away his autonomy and self-respect but he'd had it restored by the other cretins.

'Surrender to me!' I told him, 'and they will surrender to you.'

It was fortunate that this be the way of things as I do not believe I could ever have the time to concoct plans and implement systems at the same time. He was fierce in his own reserved way. The new found power had gone to his head like a surging tsunami. He could see he was not up to the top job and so he took it in his stride. Knowing his place and receiving direction as though it were a gift. He had made the post his own, personalising his position by sporting that lemon-coloured jerkin as his signature piece. One might call it his self-elected uniform, but by force, an emblem of social escalation; grand scheme.

I left him to it save for brief excursions into the field to check the imperial subjects. I couldn't be bothered with the paperwork. Eugene brought me reports. I never asked him to document his movements but I was pleasured by his efforts all the same. They were comprehensive and colour-coded, pink defined this, green defined that. Black customarily defined tasks of high importance, completed with victory. Large red crosses depicted errors of all fashions, quickly followed up with a confidence building gold star, once the blundered task was righted. Dirk's report was always plastered in red. Gene should have worked for the state department. He should have been a school teacher or a bank clerk. Instead, he was the First Officer of a subterranean sect. In defiance of all laws he knew to be good and righteous and true. Natural law, I told him, is our yardstick. He didn't fully understand the implications but took my word for it as he would if he was a fully-fledged employee of the Bank of America, with full benefits and private health care package; ticking and stamping and documenting. It was his way.

'The world needs clerks,' I told him, just as long as the clerk isn't me.

So Eugene made doubly sure Spangler couldn't get free just like I said. He realised the necessity of the purpose, that the man was delivered to the Empire to be rehabilitated. The treatment was his medicine, Kathryn his devoted and loving nurse. He wailed for weeks on end, tied down in his bed. He refused his refreshments until dehydration set in. Once we took his gag off, he had nothing more constructive to say than to snarl expletives and mutter something about our destiny with a kitchen knife.

'Gonna hacksaw ya!' he spluttered. 'Yank out your tongue and slice it like baloney.'

Kathryn stuffed bread rolls into his mouth to shut him up but he just spat them out, 'I'll cut off yer ass!' he choked.

He must admonish himself of such thoughts and come to identify with his captors as any good victim should, thought I. Lengthy waiting ensued for Stockholm syndrome to assert itself. It took longer than I thought it might. I visited him every day on my rounds to ensure that all jobs had been completed to my satisfaction by the comrades.

With every sunset and every new dawn the shrieking became less and less until nothing at all. He had lost muscle tone. He had lost faith in almost everything but not in me. I would deliver him. I was here to save his life. If he stayed with his new family he would come to no harm and he would be respected in the new collective where all could have a life that would be impossible outside our ideological fortress. Did he really want to go back to the instability of an existence alone with only dogs as friends and no safety net to soften his fall? After all, all any of these people wanted was companionship, a family; love. How foolish. Something to hold on to that they never ever had. I was here to give it to them all. Applause. They would be nothing but a bunch of lonely losers eking out their half lives if it weren't for me. They should be grateful and if they weren't, well, I would make sure they learned the hard way, for no one dared set upon me. You cannot kill a god. Dissent against divinity would be paid for in blood. Nobody can assail the wrath of Steves for everybody is scared of the indefinable quality, of something that they don't understand, the fascination with and the fear of the enigma; my defence.

I never socialised with them, for maintaining distance is the key to securing the power balance between the general and his troops. I am not one of them. I am a leader not a foot soldier, just like Mother said. So I would go to bed alone, to work on my persona amongst other things, I fancied myself an English country gent, a royal. I sighed to myself; alone just as I liked it but with no one to attest to my hard day's labour as a great philosopher, no credit, no plaudits, no pats on the back. I could theorise my life away and they would never acknowledge my contribution to humanity because naturally they are heathens and I cannot countenance the proletarian hordes. During the day I seldom surfaced unless they were all gone on some tour of duty or other. I simply sent them out into the fields. Since by their own volition they would sit and tell stories around small fires that I did not give them permission to light or clamour and roar together like a rabble of animals no doubt. But they were worse than our four legged cousins for they were without industry unless directed. They simply waited for me to augment their vacuous lives; wastrels, directionless cretins. I should have poisoned their meals for they deserved no better.

Spangler and Dirk were the worst. I felt they were having an adverse effect on the more cultured Eugene. Even though he had become my official mouthpiece, he was very willing to fit into the crowd when he thought I wasn't paying attention and when Kathryn had turned in for the night. Gone were the soliloquies and in with the baying. I have always hated the instinct of the human race; its willingness to conform to whatever new fad or clique had surfaced from the depths of human insecurity, to give them a sense of identity. Mules, donkeys! I must rein him in.

We reluctantly freed Spangler after four whole weeks of captivity, but he was still no gentleman. However, he had been tamed after a fashion. I would give him some Oscar Wilde to read if I thought he were literate. I held him in particularly low esteem. I believed him to be most unhygienic. I wouldn't let him touch me, I may contract scabies, thought I. But he had guns and we were in the market for those so he set about stocking our armoury. This resided in the basement. Out he would go to our truck, saluting at us and performing some kind of peculiar march I certainly had not taught him. The empty flatbed would leave a dusty trail down the road and not two hours later half the US gun amnesty would be straining the suspension back up the hill. Spangler was resourceful if nothing else, for he had found the warehouse where the authorities kept stocks of illegal guns handed over by criminals in a fit of conscience. Good old boy! We would be armoured to our armpits when we led the final assault and we may need some bayonets to defend our honour when we bust Jim out of jail. This was his redemption in my mind; that matted hair, the bearded, dirt-encrusted villain. He had not yet tried to kill any of us. I told Mother he had been fully rehabilitated, that he had turned his back on his rabid ways. The broken will would not allow him to bite back at the hand that fed. But I knew those latent urges would resurface at some point and wondered inwardly whether or not I had made a mistake with this recruit although I would never admit it, ever. I never turned my back to him. I never let him out of my sight.

As for Kathryn and Eugene, I had noticed some sinister new developments in their behaviours. I felt quite sure that our ex-arsonist was making overtures of love toward my fine steed Eugene. I was safe for the moment as he hadn't quite plucked up the courage to nurture this new and amorous development. Should I catch her coming within arm's length of my benefactor with passion in her eyes, there would be trouble the likes of which she could never imagine. Once a loyal, committed and welcome member of the Empire, I feared she may be turning retrograde in a selfish bid to circumvent his virginal mind with thoughts of a carnal nature. I must first rule out any chance that this could be paranoia on my part, but if not . . . Oh, I felt quite sure that she could not be trusted. I should tell Eugene so at every available opportunity so as to cloud his judgement first and turn him against her. If she saw fit to make illicit advances, with my influence over Gene, she would be rebuffed. Then she would bear witness to him packing her bags and waving her off without regard, like a child bidding farewell to a departing grandmother on Boxing Day. It was unbearable to see the sordid nature of the affair. Mother said so and I do believe that Charles Bronson would have agreed if

I hadn't turned him to face the wall. Yes, he was watching me too in my office, my only place to relax, a place where I didn't have to hold court all the time and there he was behind me scrutinising my every move. I saw Eugene sneak in and whisper in his ear and I forbade him entry ever after, wretch. It felt sullied in there after his breach. It was as though someone had rifled through my smalls drawer and studied my crotches. I battened down the hatches, four locks should do it. I would even lock myself *in* when I didn't want to be disturbed, which was always. It became mine and mother's conference room. Locks couldn't prevent her entry since naturally she could pass through walls.

Fears aside, the acolytes were fostering a wonderful homestead. I didn't agree with any of their attitudes but nevertheless, on an operational front we were all set. There were rotas for cooking and cleaning. All of the plumbing, electrics and structural defects had been fixed. We had a pond with Koi Carp now, a veritable farm with livestock ripe for slaughter coming out of our ears. The grounds were tended well. The digging and hoeing had melted one hundred pounds clear off Eugene's frame and he now walked with a stick rather than riding his chair. There was a rosy glow about the place, Kathryn had fixed the lighting just so, just as she liked it. It was very welcoming. A games room had revealed itself although I never bothered with it as I am too intelligent to indulge in such trifling fare. The armoury was bursting at the seams. Some guns hung on the walls, some in glass cabinets; trophy pieces, others, less fine specimens, piled into wooden boxes and ammunition for all brimmed from a tall cabinet of drawers. There were knives too and swords. Spangler had dipped his fingers into the community centre's martial arts equipment room. They had been left without regalia the night before they were slated to hold a grand performance at the cultural centre in Tucson I hear; pilfered, all. I read it in the local news only to stumble into the basement to find those commemorative pieces displayed fanlike on our walls and hung crossed above the fireplace in the sitting room. We had furniture, carpets; pilfered paintings and adornments, linens, a range stove, garden ornaments, opulent mirrors, stockpiled non-perishable foods to be used in the event of a siege, even a family dog. One day Eugene brought back a brand new pair of snakeskins, also pilfered. I hated that he was trying to get into my good books with gifts of material offering. But new snakeskins were the order of the day and I hugged him, his eyes gleamed. No sooner had I done it than I felt sickened by my spontaneous show of affection and kicked him up the butt as he left the room. I couldn't have him thinking he had my approval for he could become complacent. Damn! Never show cracks in the armour, never show weakness. They were wonderful though, sigh.

By this time I had finished the final draft of the constitution and it was time to lay my cards on the table. I gathered the troops in the great hall one day. It was the first time I had purposefully run into any of them in weeks, such a revered figure was I. I would have a musical accompaniment to my majestic entrance. Eugene played the bongos and Kathryn supplemented his paltry efforts with a drum roll on what seemed to me to be the smallest drum in the land. I had also laid on some recorded mood music for extra atmospheric impact. I would wear my tin hat just in case any of the acolytes took exception to my proposals and lobbed any available missile in my direction. Right; tin hat, lounge robe, snakeskins, cigar, manifesto; I am ready for my audience now, thought I. I swept in with a flourish of thrusting dynamism.

'Greetings acolytes, fine comrades, friends and loyal keepers of our peace . . . ' I threw my arms up like Christ on the cross or an enthusiastic conductor might. My robe spread out in crimson excellence, cardinal of the highest order, so regal it made me look twice my normal size and ten times as grand.

'I trust my fine acolyte Eugene has bestowed upon you the reasons for your being here before me this splendid summer's morn. I am most proud to see you in your finest glory and humble deference.' I placed my fist on my chest. 'Whilst we have been parted, all of which has pained me more than words can ever convey, I have been setting out our future, ensuring our continued success. This has culminated in the constitution that shall govern us and keep us safe and in solidarity for the rest of our jubilant days, from dawn till dusk. Now hear this!' I pointed, for it is important to point. It is assertive, confidence-boosting and ensures my leadership credentials above the swine before me. I hastily stood on the podium that Eugene had arranged for me. I had forgotten to do that when I arrived.

'It must be followed to the letter. Deviation will lead only to our ruin. We cannot be party to that lest we orchestrate our own demise. I haven't thought of a name for it as yet, so for now we will refer to it as the constitution and by God we shall do everything by its conventions from here on in.'

I wafted the document about my head. I would frame it and display a copy in every room so there could be no excuse to ignore its directives; thus:

- Treason – Against Steves, punishable by death, the mode of which will be Steves' choice, assuming he is not dead already.
- Religion (Other) – No person shall practice any religion other than the religion of the Empire's teachings.
- Any reference to God shall be replaced by Steves, for example: 'Steves Almighty, that's huge,' just to be contrary, Steves might also replace God.
- Trial and Punishment – To be determined by the highest member ie Steves: judge, jury and executioner. Punishments will vary according to Steves' mood.
- Judicial Limits – None.
- Choosing the presiding member – This shall be conducted by Steves who will naturally choose himself. No person shall hold office in the Empire except Theodore Steves (Sir). Should holder of office die, he will elect a replacement before said travesty. This shall be Mother since she is now immortal.
- There are no term limits.
- No person shall be allowed to harbour, instigate or commit acts of a sexual nature with any other member of the Empire.
- No contact with the outside world unless this is part of a directive issued by Steves, ie a murderous mission. No cell phones or subversive communications equipment of any kind allowed.
- Steves has right of veto over all constitutional issues ie he may change his mind and contradict himself on any number of occasions.
- There shall be no elections for this is essentially a dictatorship (let's not pretend.)
- Civilian power over military (or any other) order – None.

- Each member shall honour all others with respect to personal welfare.
- Right to bear (vast quantities of) arms.
- Any member found to be in breach of any of the terms of the constitution shall be extradited to Atlantic City or killed. If he has committed an act of severe depravity he will be killed in Atlantic City.
- Amendments – There are likely to be many, all of which will be made arbitrarily at Steves' whim and fancy.

'Now friends, place your hands to your bosom and do most solemnly swear that you will live and die heretofore, by no other authority than the authority before you; embodied in I, the helmsman extraordinaire of the Empire of Steves.' They looked onward and upward to me and clasped their fists.

'What are we?'

'Empire!' Ah, a chorus! What joy! But I wanted to hear it louder, more fervently. I needed to hear the dedication in their voices, conviction that did not falter, that believed.

'I said what the hell are we?!!!' I bellowed, I boomed, I resounded like I said I would one day, for the hall had fantastic acoustics. Yes, just like I knew I would. Just like James Earl Jones. I pounded my fist to the lectern.

'Empire!' they erupted, 'Em–pire! Em–pire! Em–pire! Em-pire!!!' in surround sound!

My time had come. It had arrived. I had become myself. I looked on at them, those brutes, finely honed and trained to peak performance. There they stood tall and proud, soldiers of fortune. Good Lord, it was the culmination of all my efforts, a sight to make any grown man weep and wail and possibly throw himself about the place for a few precious moments of self-indulgence. The joy, the pride, the feat, everything I had ever wanted and all there stood before me, in my honour. The tears were flowing down my cheeks but for once I didn't care for the momentary loss of masculinity. With a chest bursting with pride, I pressed my hand to my temple and saluted them; the new order of the Empire of Steves.

In a moment I was gone, swooped off the podium in my cape like a superhero, premier don. I threw myself into my throne locking the study door behind me. They were still stood there for a good while. They eyed each other sideways without turning their heads, unsure if they were allowed to move, still saluting, still believing. I don't know if it was a sense of belonging or a sense of ownership that I felt, but I have never felt such happiness in the world and I never will again.

FIVE

Deliverance

Onward to fix the Jim problem, for it had been taxing my brain for some time. I longed to leave him to rot in prison. It would be a far simpler course of action for I. Alas, no, Mother would not hear of it. He must be liberated. She could be a pest sometimes but I knew she was right and our numbers would grow as a result of our benevolence. I should be canonised. I would have to write a letter to the Vatican to let them know of my good deeds. I felt the acolytes were finally ready for action. I had drawn up a plan and would need the services of my comrades to gather together the necessary equipment and to rehearse their parts in the scheme. It would be like this; we would bust Jim out of jail and we would do it like the show-men we were, with props and costumes; disguises. We would steal in there in the middle of the day just to be brazen. We would swoop in and swoop out like the secret service, scoop him up and deliver him to freedom. The debt repaid; sweet redemption.

I wondered what state of mind Jim might be in after all this leisure time in the state penitentiary. After all, he had been incarcerated for twenty years as a direct result of my short-comings. I expected him to be a little miffed to say the least. I reasoned that sentiment would fall away once we had orches-trated his return to freedom. He should thank us but most importantly, he would thank me. I harboured notions that this exercise would exonerate my previous poor form. Perhaps we would have a tiff or two about my lack of responsibility. I should learn to take the consequences of my actions with good grace, etcetera. There may be a tear. Perhaps I would say that I had learned my lesson and that if only I could take it all back, live life over again, I wouldn't have vaulted the fence and left him to his fate. In essence, I would lie. There was no malice intended, just oversight. I could not have predicted the cops wouldn't believe his protestation. There was no one to fight his corner after I fled, poor boy and Mother certainly wouldn't have pointed the finger at me, even if she wasn't dead. Even today she thanks me for her liberation and she is every bit grateful to Jim for taking the fall. That is why we had to set him free, she said. He had done me service and without reciprocity I would be in for a karmic thrashing for sure. I had no wish to feel the lash of its all-encompassing whip on my soft attractive cheek.

Feeling ready for the assault we admired our silhouettes in vast mirrors. We looked beautiful in our day dresses. The most beautiful collection of ladies you have ever seen, thought I. We were shaven and rouged; I had applied a mole with brown pencil in the Marilyn Monroe style. It looked divine with my pearl necklace and floral ensemble. I must say being a lady is a welcome departure from the usual bland palette. I would not forgo the snakeskins, even if it meant imminent capture, I would not remove them from my feet for they were my lucky charms. Surprisingly Eugene cut the finest figure; my shoulders were too broad, my jaw line too square, Spangler was too haggard and Dirk too tall. Nevertheless we persevered, a four-man travelling drag show. Yes, we persevered until we pulled out of the driveway. We hastily turned back after being hailed by a passing bunch of hicks hollering 'Look it's RuPaul!' and laughing off into the distance. Pah! This is no disguise! We'd be in the cells before you could say lady-boy. Better head back, curse it all! I thought Eugene looked rather fetching in his ladies hat and smock dress. The hues perfectly complimented each other in a rusty orange. He had clear lost one hundred and fifty pounds by now. His disguise no longer even pretended to follow his curvy lines, that old dress had been quite snug not a couple of months earlier when we had our dress rehearsal. I wondered how a guy with the metabolism of a sloth got so thin in two short months. I'd only tightened up my belt one notch; he was now using his as a skipping rope. Subsistence farming and an absence of meatball subs had heralded vast payoffs and in his new manifestation as a woman, I found myself taking quite a fancy to him. Soon he would sport the figure of a prima ballerina; I must sneak some lard in to his gruel to subvert my transgender fantasy. Ahem.

Feeling ready for the assault take two! We admired our silhouettes in police uniform. This was a much better formulated plan. We were the fittest and most able collection of police officers America had ever glimpsed. The owners of these fine outfits were tied to beds back at the ranch being lovingly tended to by our lady. Great ruse! We would have them all outwitted in a trice! We piled into the truck for we had a squad car to apprehend, grand theft auto. Who could be so bold! We were on fire. Mother was quick to point out that we were vulnerable to capture, impersonating police officers being a federal offence and all. One would look mighty foolish to be captured en route to the bust for an unrelated offence. We sat low and removed our patrol hats. Eugene's outfit fit perfectly. Fat cops are de rigour and they do not run as fast as the more athletic breed who managed to dodge our ambushes by wriggling free and breaking for the border. We were drowned in our strides. No matter, hopefully the squad car would house some lithe types.

We had driven not a couple of miles before we caught sight of the first prospective police vehicle for our acquisition, parked up outside a diner. I was hoping they were fresh from a drugs bust, ten pounds of cocaine on the backseat that I could later sell and make my fortune just like the old days back in New York. We disembarked and probed the scene to find those fools taking a post-breakfast nap. Surely they deserved to be robbed, those idle cretins. How would it be if the criminals practiced such indolence? Good grief. Let's show them what a man is made of . . . I sent in Dirk. He seized them by the hair and pulled them from the vehicle, dragging the driver across the passenger seat and near scalping them both in the process. They wailed as he dragged them behind the diner and knocked their heads together, putting them both out for the count. Their ordeal was over in seconds. Nobody in the diner had noticed the fuss, drowned out by the sounds of the bad juke box and sloppy chewing from their loose jaws. Just one lone face witnessed their demise, a teenager resting on his pushbike with his arms crossed defiantly as teenagers do, chewing on a large ball of gum and smirking tauntingly throughout. He tipped his imaginary hat to us, smiling wryly as we burned on out of there in our new wheels, the naked police officers groaning and half-conscious. Ha! Haaaaaa! Let us play some Meatloaf for it was all those inbreds had as a musical offering. We blasted out the music as we blasted down the highway, like a bat out of hell.

Assholes! We'd be twenty miles over the state line and they would still be counting the cartoon stars swirling round their heads. This would be the penance to pay for ripping my favourite shirt at the airport, those heavy-handed louts. No coke though, just candy wrappers. We burned down the highway singing *Day Dream Believer* and other assorted classics. Mother still rode up front so there wasn't much room in the back for the boys. We would require another vehicle for our return journey otherwise we would have to dump Jim in the trunk and I do not believe that would be ideal considering his stature as our guest of honour.

How inconsiderate of our judicial system to put Jim in jail so far away from our compound. There was a considerable way to go. We would cross three county lines before we got out of state and then we would have a squillion more to go. I couldn't remember the last time I had spent so long in the company of other human beings, if you could call these cretins that. I felt like a tiger might feel in San Diego zoo. Eugene needed to pee frequently as his rolls of fat still pressed into his bladder when sitting and Dirk kept on asking questions like kids do.

'Is it far to go now? Let's count how many red cars we can see on the way, the one with the most wins. Could we slow down to get a better look at those girls' legs?'

We settled on I Spy for an hour or so. Mine kept them guessing for ages . . . something beginning with 'm'. Well, of course they couldn't get it, they couldn't see Mother. We had a prolonged argument about it which spilled over into dinner time conversation. Gene said I was mad. I 'high-fived' Mother, she thought me supremely clever in my efforts. They saw me slapping the air above the passenger seat and rolled their eyes.

I will brush over the obligatory motel stop as nothing impressive enough for comment occurred there, except for Gene's snoring which kept us all awake for the duration. I had time alone to reflect on how fortunate we had been to keep getting away with felonies left and right. It occurred to me that if you imbue law enforcement with less than contempt as they surely deserve, you will then see them in their clearest light and take your chances, toying with their feeble minds and winning with one hundred per cent frequency. The law of averages suggest that quite naturally at some point one will encounter one of the sharp variety, as thin on the ground as they are prone to be. Probably working alone so as to remain unhindered by the stupidity of their compatriots, but as yet the law was on our side.

A couple of days later, we arrived in Virginia. It took me back some, I felt sixteen again. I felt as though I could do anything. Bust Jim out of jail you say? All in a day's work for me, just like killing your parents; easy. We camped out at a dive bar in our civvies, swigging whiskey and huddled so close that no one could hear. I produced the plans of the State Penitentiary, every last air duct, every corridor, every possible escape route documented; the grounds, the exercise yard, the leisure times, the community service rota. Everything like clockwork all the time, all scheduled, all measured. I even knew what they served for dinner on any given day of the week because I had been studying every day for the last four months in my office. What the hell did they think I had been doing in there, twiddling my thumbs? Secretive creature that I am, I had them all surprised. My authority was restored if ever I felt it slipping away. I had clawed it back by the skin of its miserable teeth. I spread the plans out all over the table like they do in war films. The barman peered over to see what we were up to so we huddled even closer to create a human shield.

'Planning an armed robbery!' I shouted over to him. He snorted patronisingly from behind the bar and continued drying his glasses with a towel as though we were a bunch of drunks without the brains necessary to steal our whiskey glasses, never mind clear out the post office safe. Still, I prefer people to underestimate me, it only means I can surprise them when they are least expecting it.

'Fellows, this is Operation Phoenix Rising,' I told them, whispering and keeping low to the counter, how inventive. I had Jim's cell marked out on the maps with a smiley face sticker. They nodded their heads approvingly.

'We're going to stroll in there boys. Going to stroll right on in there, pick up the "package" and leave. But we're going to need a stooge. You see it will be like this; a straight swap. We deliver our criminal, whoever the hell he is, into custody and we take Jim with us, and everything's going to be sweet and smooth because they won't know he's gone until it's too damned late. I've got a spare uniform for our friend.'

'What if they count the cops?' asked Dirk. 'What if they count the cops and they realise we got an extra boss. One, two, three, four . . . wait a god damned minute, there's five!' He looked perplexed as though counting to five had blown a connection in his brain. 'Now that ain't right now, is it?'

'And whoever heard of five cops dropping a tax dodger. He'd have to be a high priority felon, a murderer or something. We'd have to find ourselves an Ed Gein.'

'Precisely. Gene, you got it right there on the nose, good man. He would have to be on death row because we have to get *into* the high security wing to get Jim *out* of the high security wing. Oh, why do I bother? Jim's been commuted for good behaviour but that doesn't mean they let him roam around the grounds free reign. He may not be getting the chair but he's still Class A. He did murder two people after all.' I winked but they didn't know why.

'Couldn't we just walk in there and blow everything up? I got a couple bombs in the trunk and some tear gas. Let's go for an all out assault! Yahoo! it'll be like Nam!!! Spangler had excited himself. Everyone else ignored him. 'Aw, come on guys.'

'Listen up, we have to use our brains here and I can clearly see they are running in short supply. I don't know about you but I intend to survive this foray. Practically speaking, this is the best way to ensure our legacy. What is the good of a god if he is dead? Then he was never a god at all.'

'Besides Spangler, you never were in Nam, you asshole.' Dirk pointed out the obvious which surprised me.

'Was too.'

'Was not.'

'Was too.'

'Weren't.'

'I'll slit your throat and pulverise your kidneys with my bare hands, eeedjot, just try asking my illegitimate son Hu Jun, if I ain't, weren't, never in Nam, you ninny.'

'Quiet!!!' I loved to chastise. They were really testing my godly patience and besides I was the only person Spangler seemed content to listen to, incompliant being that he was.

'There is such a thing as subtlety you know and it will take you far my sweet gentlemen, refine yourselves at once. We'll blow their brains out as a last resort, should it come to that. I'd like to save the Armageddon for our final assault; here we must content ourselves with a stylish, clean sweep. The fireworks are on the way, so you can stop the histrionics right there.'

'Steves . . . '

'Gene, that includes you.' I brushed him off.

'But Steves.' Insolence. 'Steves! The damn map's upside down.'

'Oh, ah, yes, just testing. I see you have your eye to the task. Commendations, you have passed with both an ace and a gold star.' Ass!! Why must I always undermine myself in such spectacular fashion . . .

'Right, listen up. The penitentiary is designed in a circular formation. One might call it a rotunda just to be flash. We must hasten ourselves to this point here. I have flagged up the drop point with a red spot. On recreation the yard will be brimming with convicts hither and thither but let us not forget that those blaggards are neither scholars nor gentlemen so keep what wits you can muster about you. Jim works in the office, filing and such. He should be in there when we deliver our prisoner. Now, the scoop is this; one Mr Henry Baker has been sentenced to life and will be trundling his way to prison by unmarked vehicle this very afternoon. All the evidence is piled up against him. He hasn't got a chance of walking free so it's assured. I have been following the case. It is at this point,' I furtively looked for the coffee stained road map of the county. Aha! 'It is at this point here,' I pointed, 'that we hijack the vehicle like highwaymen and continue our journey as rightful custodians of the lifer. We drop him off, filling out all of the necessary paperwork and smuggle Jim back into the vehicle unnoticed before taking flight. We shall be in the office, Jim shall be in the office also. Dirk, you will cause a fracas, a distraction, whatever that may be and Gene and I will usher him out amongst the commotion. Spangler, you are back up and will stay with the vehicle but keep your machine gun handy in case anything goes awry. We will make back to our car which should be exactly where we left it earlier and continue back as such. Mother has agreed to allow Jim her seat so as not to convolute plans with more vehicular theft than is absolutely necessary. She has other business in Virginia to attend to. Does this seem an exemplary plan? I thought so and any man who ruins this exercise shall see his ear lopped off as punishment, you hear?' They saluted, good sports.

'Well, I ain't so sure about all this ya know. I ain't been hidin' out all these years just to get blown to smithereens by some half ass prison guard. I'll do it. I'll do it just like I said I would but if I have to make my way into the war, I'm gonna go out all guns a blazin'. I ain't seen no carnage for years,' said Spangler, licking his cracked lips.

'Must you always use double negatives man! I'll have to put you on an eloquence programme, to fast track your degenerate mind toward a more gentlemanly disposition.' Spangler looked confused. I doubt he understood the implication of my offer in any case. 'All will be well. If anyone has any gripes he had better speak up now or forever hold his peace.'

'Oh, I'll be holding my piece alright sir, see if that ain't not right.'

'Well, that's a fine thing my dears because I shall set Mother on you otherwise. She is sat to my right flank as we speak, listening to your disclaimers. She is very disheartened too, I don't mind telling you. Carry on like this and you'll all amount to nothing. Gene?'

'Yes, I suppose so.' He offered half-heartedly, 'I suppose we've come this far and I wouldn't want to let anyone down, I suppose.' He looked at his feet, a novelty as he could now see his toes over his belly. He wriggled them just to be sure they were his.

'Dirk?'

'Hell yeah! You can count on me boss!'

'That's God. You can count on me, God.'

'Ye-aa-hh.' He looked perplexed. 'Anyway God, I'm all in. What else would I be doin' if I weren't doin' this? This is so cool. We're gonna be famous!'

'Correction squire, I am going to be famous.' But every star needs his hangers on, thought I.

'Then we'll go home to see Kathryn? She must be so lonely on her own in that big house,' snivelled Gene.

'She is not alone Gene. She has representatives of the law keeping her company. Florence Nightingale of the Empire that she is. Good sort. We had better get ready. Bartend! We must pay up for we have a robbery to perform!' The barman grunted and we paid up leaving a tiny tip so as to buy his silence.

We ran out of there with the wind at our heels, back to the

car to change into our uniforms. I turned my back to them as I shimmied into my pants. I could have sworn I caught Eugene glancing at my proud buttocks, perhaps it was a competitive thing. I doubted Kathryn would prefer his to mine. He would have some way to go before he achieved my stature as Adonis.

I predicted the police van would roll by our position at 15.19 precisely. I had calculated the time taken from base after factoring in traffic lights and illicit cigarette breaks. Right on time Newton; at 15:19:20 it tore by us at a steady clip. They were due at the penitentiary at 15:30 but had a good twenty minute drive on their hands to make it and then there would be the vehicle handover time to include. We would have to radio in reporting a flat tyre or some such obstacle to good time keeping. We ripped out of the car park and followed right behind for about five minutes or so. We would need them to halt the vehicle so that we may pounce. We must make spontaneous, opportunist decisions since developments from here on in were out of the boundaries of calculus and could not be anticipated. We must react to any eventuality with nimble body and mind. Several blocks down the road and it was looking highly unlikely we would be able to apply our ingenuity alone to halt the vehicle, so we would have to go about things in a more heavy-handed manner. We were going to have to intercept them. I slung the light onto the roof of the car and started the sirens, building up good speed so as to demonstrate the necessity of our purpose. The van began to slow down and why not indeed, we were clearly trustworthy members of the establishment. It came to a halt at the roadside and we pulled up in front.

'Now just take it easy ladies. Let me do the talking.'

I stepped out of the patrol car with a firm footing, snake-skins first. They did not match my uniform at all. Behind us both prison officers clambered out of the van. What fortune, imbeciles, everyone knows the protocol; one officer always stays with the vehicle just in case some hapless bunch of deviants try to pull a fast one. Idiots to think we would have some camaraderie based on the premise of our job description. They all make it so very, very easy.

'Morning, gentlemen.' I saluted them.

'Good day, you got a problem, boys?'

'Yes indeed sir. I have narcissistic personality disorder and Spangler here has paranoid schizophrenia.' They paused looking confused.

'Just playing with you now,' I toyed. 'No, our business here is of a much more practical nature.'

'You radio back-up?' one of the officers asked the other.

'No Jack, I ain't done that.'

'You get a call from control?' Jack asked me. 'We ain't asked for an escort. This crim is doped up to the eyeballs. Caused quite a scene at the court house you see. So we don't need no help, it ain't gonna wear off for an hour or so I guess.'

'Well that's just dandy but we didn't get a call from control, you see, we will be needing to confiscate this vehicle as a matter of highest security. I cannot divulge the reasoning behind it since this is a top secret matter.'

'You don't look FBI to me, friend.'

'No, we're just highway patrol but I've got this authorisation, you might call it outsourcing. Take a look at this.' I produced a document from my top pocket. Jack took it and started to read it out loud.

'Burlesque dancers . . . strip tease . . . eight pm . . . Wednesday at Bunny's . . . Hey! This ain't no . . . '

'Donkey!' I biffed him with my balled-up fist in the solar plexus. He let out a shrill scream which lost timbre as all of the air left his lungs in swift exhalation due to intense visceral pain. Winded and done, he went down on his knees like a lead balloon.

'Hey!!!' yelled the remaining officer and bolted back to the passenger side of the vehicle for what I could only imagine to be the gun he left behind. Before I could react, Spangler had taken aim. He fired two shots at the officer's heels, as precise as any I have ever seen. Two tiny bullet holes in the back of his shoes, a fine spray of blood emitted and he was down too, screaming and writhing around on the floor grappling at his feet in agony. Spangler advanced and put the barrel of his gun in the guy's mouth.

'Now you ain't gonna squeal, are ya boy?'

The officer's eyes were almost popping out of his head on stalks. The whites of his eyes all lit up in terror, nodding his head from side to side with tears rolling down his face. For a moment I thought Spangler was going to give it to him. We all did. Instead he kicked the guy I'd busted in the face, twirled round and made his peculiar march to the vehicle. He sat in the middle seat humming the theme tune from *Sesame Street*; the unpredictable freak.

Gene dutifully backed the car into a shallow ditch behind me. He slipped down into the seat like a child, looking on at the insanity he had by now grown to accept as the shape of things to come. As he always had before he grew more and more accustomed to turning his cheek. Dirk smiled as though this were all just some game with no consequences. I was buoyed and filled with love by the way each accepted their mission, my mission, just because I said so. Spangler, oh dear God, he was certifiable, with our band only for the opportunity to see some real action once again, for the thrill he thrived on.

I climbed into the van at the wheel next to Spangler but not so close that I touched him. He had digressed to humming the *Friends* theme tune. Dirk bounded in like a puppy, all energy and enthusiasm. Eugene hoisted himself up, stepping over the wounded cop as he did so, as though he were just some piece of driftwood shored up on a beach and not a person anymore at all. He ripped the security pass from round his neck, met with a sob from below and kicked him into the ditch along with his pal. He sat with his head down and his arms limply at his side. Dirk jiggled along to Spangler's musical accompaniment. I slipped out of neutral and joined the road, all was clear.

'Control?' I accessed the frequency to radio in with our fantasy tale of engine trouble. 'Control, Jack here. Radio on ahead and let the big house know we're running ten minutes behind schedule. Engine overheated but it's all under control now.'

'All right Jack, will do, we'll let them know you're on your way, out.'

We pulled up to the security gate. I flashed the pass and we were waived in. There was no time for fooling around. We were all stoic, knowing what needed to be done. Dirk and I had to drag the captive from the back of the van; he was still out for the count, the wiry little sod. We hooked one of his arms over each shoulder and hauled him through the double steel doors.

'Got one for ya'll.' I feigned a terribly witless country accent so I could really get into the role of being Jack, who was still writhing around by the roadside.

'OK, we'll take it from here,' a pot-bellied officer approached us followed by two guards and lugged the guy along the corridor banging his feet on every door frame as they went.

'Just need to fill out this darned paperwork and we'll be done for the day,' a cheery voice trilled from the office. 'Come in, come in, it'll only take a second.' Ass! I had forgotten the form; it must be in the van somewhere, probably in the glove compartment or under the sun visor. I sent Gene rushing out to get it, as quickly as he could with his tiny little steps. I grinned widely and surveyed the office. Mr Sunshine here was the only person in the room.

'So, you here on your lonesome?' I enquired. Really my mind was screaming out, where the fuck is Jim!!! Arse, damn you!! Cursed hindrance! Arrggh!!! Urrggh!!

'Oh, I got the afternoon shift. Vladimir is in the back filing. Nothing much happens on the noon shift. The prisoners are all in the yard so it's pretty quiet up here.'

Gene rushed in with the form. Mr Sunshine took it and looked very pleased with himself.

'All in order, fill out these release forms if you will and I'll be done with ya.'

Gene took his fountain pen from his top pocket and began to read through the documents slowly. We had to stall and he was on to it. The others hadn't managed to fully corrode his intellect as yet.

'Dyslexia,' he told him smiling innocently, 'They employ

me as part of the force's equal opportunities initiative, won't be long.'

'You mind if I piss?' said I.

'Oh sure, no problem, it's out back just behind there. It doesn't flush properly so don't turd.'

I passed through the office and out into the back room. I had memorised the layout of the building so I was ready to go for a reconnaissance assessment operation. Jim was scheduled for work from twelve until four. I knew this because I had infiltrated their computer systems with self-taught hacking techniques. Genius of the electronic age. I would surf through the Pentagon's files with consummate ease. Yes, I had gathered up all the loose ends so that this kind of tomfoolery would be a figment of my doom-ridden imagination. There was simply no room for this kind of distraction. The plan would have to undergo swift modification. The fool cops we had busted earlier were sure to be up and running soon and calling in to report us. Good thing I had the genius to shoot out the radio before we left. I guessed that the best bet would be Jim had gone for a stretch in the yard along with his brethren but I had to check the can first, just in case he was in there causing another blockage. I stepped through the back door into a small room. I almost tripped over whom I presumed to be Vladimir the clerk whose head was buried in a filing cabinet, his legs stretched out all over the floor like some trip wire. I slammed the can door behind me and took the longest piss in the universe. The whiskey and rum had gone right through.

OK, thought I, think! I'll steal out of the side door unseen. I had noted it on the way in, just to the left of the toilet. Secret operatives always take care to note potential escape routes on entrance. I would just bolt out; besides, the clerk was more interested in his papers than in some cop snooping round. I guessed officers passed through there all the time and didn't so much as give the poor fucker a second glance; menial swine. I would say that I had got lost and use a good dose of the old Steves charm to throw them off my stinking scent. I flushed the putrid bowl but it just churned up the crud even more than before, someone had clearly eaten a poisoned meal. The effluence! The very essence of putrescence! I was about to exit when a voice came from the other side of the door. Gods! Don't let the cops have radioed mayday already. Was I to have my last moments of freedom in the john, surrounded by stinking faeces?! Say it isn't so, thought I. Great people have met their downfall in such a humiliating circumstances, just ask Elvis; the King and the God brought to their knees in the toilet. The shame of it. I pressed my ear to the door.

'Vlad you asswipe! Release papers in the wooden cabinet, acquisition papers in the grey cabinet. How many times do I have to tell you. Git!' Slap. 'Just git outta here!'

'Sorry Jim, sorry I get confused.'

'Git!'

Jim? I chinked open the door a touch and peeped round the corner. It was him alright, tall and skinny as he always was but with less hair. I stuck my arm out and yanked him into the can.

'What the fuuucccckkkk . . . '

He struggled, limbs asunder, flapping all over. The light was off so I yanked the chain whilst trying to keep his flying limbs from making contact with the face. We were illuminated suddenly. It was as though he had seen a ghost. He ceased flailing and stared right into my eyes and I into his, inches apart in the tiny, reeking cubicle. His mouth fell wide open but no words came out. He just stared at me like the last time I had seen him twenty years ago but our bodies were transposed onto a new scene, taller, broader and more haggard by time and trial. He squinted and looked closer, pressing his nose right up to mine, studying my face.

'St . . . Steves . . . Theodore Steves?'

'Praise be, Jim! It is I! Come to liber . . . Aarrrgghhh.'

He lunged for my throat, grappling and squeezing and choking me. Gurgle.

'Can't breathe.' Gurgle.

'You son of a bitch. I'll kill you! I'm going to fucking kill you!!! Then I'll really have a reason to be in here, you motherfucker!'

'Arrrrgghhh, gurgle.' We tussled around the stinking pit, sliding around the sticky walls. My hat toppled off into a stagnant pool of urine on the floor. He had me leaning backward against the wall, his right foot bolstering him from behind for extra strength. His fingers pressed up in my Adam's apple causing untold pain, compression of the larynx and cutting off my oxygen supply. The little shit had certainly gained in strength what he conversely lacked in forgiveness. Blood collected in my head and my supraorbital vein rose up through the skin and pulsed. He forced me down, lurching to the right, applying the pressure harder and harder. Oh good Lord, not the can! Anything but the can! He pushed me closer to the bowl. The stench rose up and little black spots appeared in front of my eyes. I summoned a knee to his groin in a desperate attempt to escape the clutches of death. I applied it short and sharp, it was all I could muster as a defence. He went crashing backward into the wall, doubling over. I gasped for breath as his hands released, refilling my lungs with the sweet elixir of life. I drew it in, weakened. We both slid down the walls to rest, our knees together, we panted with fatigue and grasped our assaulted areas just like the play fights we had as kids.

'I'm here to get you out, you asshole,' I panted, a wheezing tone croaking out, still holding my neck.

'Gee thanks.' He replied wiping his eyes, his face still contorted, gripping his swollen balls.

'We can have this out when we get out of here.' I groaned. 'Right now you need to put these on, there's not much time.'

I tugged at the uniform I had stuffed into my jacket. I had left his hat behind so he'd have to have my moist offering to cover his face. That should obscure the tears rolling freely down his cheeks.

'How could you do it to me, man? I loved you, man. I trusted you and you fucked me over.' He emoted but he wasn't getting an answer and he knew it, not now. He pushed himself up the wall with his legs and started getting dressed, slowly, still crying from both frustration and testicular pain.

We collected ourselves, aching but recuperated enough to make the short journey back to the van where Spangler waited outside. Out through the back room and into the office. Two cops, an ordinary sight, two cops strolling out of the office, except Jim was limping and slightly bent over. Two cops getting into their vehicle, routine, nothing to worry about, nothing to see here. As we brushed by I saw Eugene, his head buried in a flurry of papers with the officer. Mr Sunshine was reading out the text to him so that he could understand.

'Oh that's wonderful. Thank you so much. I didn't realise

that signature meant I put my name on it. I can do that now that I've learned to write it and not just put a cross. That's Jethro Peterson,' he said slowly as he wrote. 'That's my name, it sure is, says so right here on my pass.' He beamed widely.

'Clever boy,' said Mr Sunshine patting Gene's shiny head as though he were five and not thirty-five.

We made it out to the van unhindered, our journey slow and measured so as not to draw unwanted attention. I signalled Jim into the back as there wasn't enough room upfront for all of us. I didn't feel much like talking but Spangler wouldn't shut up. Anyone would have thought he had been sat alone waiting for us for hours, not fifteen minutes, with the way he was going on. I blocked him from my mind and sat at the wheel waiting for Gene and Dirk to surface. A couple of minutes later they emerged and assumed their places up front.

'What a job we did on those goons. I feel like an award-winning actor in a Hollywood blockbuster. I had them all fooled. Did you see Steves? Did you see me?' enthused Eugene.

I ignored him.

'I didn't even get to do my part. You stole my job, man. I just had to stand there lookin' like a spare part. I was all ready to knock over someone's coffee or break somethin'. That ain't fair.'

'I didn't get to blow anyone's head off so you can quit your bitchin'.' Spangler shot back at Dirk.

'Oh you jester,' muttered Eugene.

I pulled out through the gates without a problem. We would have to ditch the van as soon as possible. I could hear Jim rolling around in the back at every sharp turn. I made sure he had a bumpy ride, the ungrateful bastard.

'I'm glad you put him in the back, Steves. I'm not sure I feel comfortable being cooped up with a double murderer. What are we going to do with him once we get home?'

I still wasn't speaking, stupid sot. There he was worrying himself over some small town kid, grown up, who never did anything to anybody in his life except cop a feel of some airhead at school. All the while he's sat there next to a guy who chopped up his family and most of his friends, some strangers too for good measure and left them spread out all over the southern states. Of course I never told them about Spangler. I knew they wouldn't take him into their confidence had I laid out all the facts. Spangler smiled to himself, fully aware of the dupe. I could almost see what he was thinking. He was thinking what Gene would look like carved up into pieces, a limbless torso. Dreaming about sawing through his fat neck, he squinted at the point where his fantasy hacksaw got to the spine and crunched right through to the other side. I didn't speak for a good ten minutes, I couldn't help thinking about Jim; emotional blackmailer extraordinaire. Why the fuck did he have to cry? I hoped he'd collected himself by the time we got back to the ranch. I didn't want him blowing my cover, Gene would never understand.

'We're going to have to find another vehicle, sweethearts, there's probably an APB out on this pile of crap and they'll have impounded the patrol car by now. There's a mall coming up ahead. Let's pull in there and bag ourselves a beamer.'

We all stood in the parking lot like a bunch of male strippers. Our civvies were in the trunk of the patrol car, probably undergoing DNA tests in some government lab. Some tech removing strands of hair and dried fluids, CSI, what sport. We were wearing our leather police issue gloves so there would be no prints to examine. My lab results would be a revelation.

'We've never seen anything like this, the structure, it cannot be human, it must be the product of a higher being,' they would say and I would defy the laws of chemistry forever.

Now, what shall we have today, thought I. I was most disinterested in most of the examples before me. I strolled around for two minutes and forty three seconds and settled on a rather stylish Cadillac.

'Come on my dears, your carriage awaits.'

They clambered in whilst Dirk hotwired the engine. I kept guard like a hawk. I smiled politely and waved at passers by. It was getting dark now and we had the cover afforded by our uniform. Nobody would suspect that we were not on police business here. I even helped one struggling shopper load her bags into her car. I liked to think she fancied me with my devastating charms and famed charisma. We ripped out of the parking lot. All I wanted to do was to get home and I was prepared to drive all week if I had to. If we stopped for rest, I felt sure Jim would try to abscond. What good it would do him was anyone's guess for he was now a fugitive on the run and his face would be plastered all over the papers and the TV by the morning. How brilliant.

Jim was quiet all the way. He didn't speak for days. He stared at me through the rear view mirror but he could not bug me out. I pretended I hadn't noticed his passive aggression. When I did take a glance just to be sure the swiftly approaching headlights from the rear weren't the real cops, I managed to wink at him and smile pleasantly as though I wasn't really angry as hell that he had tried to choke me half to death for doing him a good turn. His face showed no emotion. I couldn't tell what was going on in his mind and I did not like that much at all. I was accustomed to the omniscience of seeing deeply into people's souls. Still, what could the hometown boy do? He didn't seem to have been corrupted by his spell in the slammer. You don't catch the jail house hard nut doing extra hours in the office. Not unless that was his cover and he was really messing up their systems. Secretly dealing contraband cigarettes, booze, narcotics and doing a black trade in illegal kidneys as a sideline; selling them to the highest bidder on ebay when he got half a chance. But I reckoned that might be my imagination running away with me as always.

We pulled up the driveway just as day began to break. The guys were all asleep, Gene snoring up front. I was the only one awake for one of two reasons, not least that I happened to be the designated driver but more so because I feared that either Spangler or Jim might try to knock me off if I took my eye off the ball. Today I would sleep in my office with the door locked four times from the inside. I might even barricade the door with the waxwork Bronson to ward off bad spirit and bad feeling. This was all adversely affecting my Chi. Mother had taken herself off on another one of her vacations. I hadn't seen her for days, not since we had left the motel. She always said she would have liked to have taken a cruise, but Dad never let her go because she had to make sure I didn't blow up the school whilst she was away. Maybe she was doing a little catch up in the Bahamas or maybe she just decided to go home. Whatever, she seemed to trust me enough to perform the bust by myself so that was all just perfect. That woman, that dear, dear woman, she was always right about everything. Bless her.

I woke them all by honking unnecessarily on the horn several times. They shuddered and groaned, rubbing their bleary eyes. Spangler awoke with a fit, flailing about and yelling 'You'll never take me alive!' before he realised where he was and what good company he was keeping. Kathryn came to meet us at the door, all ready with my lounge robe. She helped me into it over my uniform before ushering the boys in and warmly greeting Jim who looked as though he had no comprehension of his surrounding or what in the hell was going on.

'Welcome to the castle,' I told the disoriented boy.

Everyone got to doing their thing. We were all worn out and wanted nothing more than to collapse on fresh linens but our beds were occupied by the kidnapped cops. There was one residing in each of our pits, bound and gagged just where we left them. I was not going to sleep on those sweat sodden sheets, all bedsores and open wounds where their ties had dug in, tied too tight to allow any wriggling victim their only mode of expression. It was their own fault, they should have laid still. Kathryn had rubbed their wounds with salt as any good nurse would if she had madness in her heart. That woman, I wondered if she hadn't been taking lessons from Mother.

The boys decided on breakfast whilst Dirk removed the hostages to one of the outhouses and Eugene changed the sheets. I retired to my study for some R and R. Jim wasn't going anywhere. I turned on the TV, which was in my office purely for business matters, news and documentaries only, you understand. There he was, staring out at me from the screen. Folks better look out because there was a murderer on the loose, the anchor explained gravely. Baton down the doors and windows and stay inside. I couldn't believe it. I laughed to

175

myself until I felt bilious. The reprobates, they will believe anything they are told so long as they are told it in a credible manner; sinister indeed. That is precisely the reason that I decided to turn my back on a world too obtuse to recognise and applaud my genius. No one ever took me seriously.

I lounged in my throne. I was nodding off when Mother decided to put in an appearance. She seemed vexed. She told me she had been in the process of taking breakfast in the motel diner when we abruptly left. Now she had missed all the fun and games. However, she had amused herself by making a swift visit to my father's grave to pelt his headstone with missiles so as to render it to a pile of rocks. She reportedly also pissed on it but I was not entirely convinced that ghosts went to the toilet so I just went right ahead and agreed with her. We needed to have a summit at any rate for I had to decide the best course of action in handling Jim. He seemed bemused, confused and subdued by the events of the last couple of days. Once he had time to collect himself I was sure he would be more responsive, so I would have let him rest for the moment.

'Why is Steves talking to himself?' said Jim on the other side of the door as Gene passed by my office en route to the laundry room with the soiled sheets. My hearing was finely attuned. God is all-knowing.

'Oh, he's probably talking to Charles Bronson. It can be quite therapeutic. He always listens to you and he never answers back.'

Jim shook his head. It was beginning to dawn on him that he had entered a terrifying madhouse where everything most definitely wasn't as it seemed and he was going to have to get used to it if he didn't want to end up on Death Row.

'Chair or injection?' chided Gene on the way back. 'Just playing now, you hear.' He had stolen my sense of humour, the guttersnipe.

On the other side Mother sat with me and patted my leg. I had done a good job. I had aced that shit but our mission had only just begun. It had been great for her to get out and see home again. She had visited the house and all her flowers had gone and someone with dubious taste had replaced them with hideous garden ornaments, all different animals and little wheelbarrows so she had desecrated those as well. Mother hadn't wanted to stick around with Kathryn taking over, so she rubbed the cops' wounds with salt and poisoned them with a little sprinkling of arsenic so that Kathryn would have to spend the weekend cleaning up their vomit. Kathryn had not mentioned this at all. Good soul. Perhaps Mother's jealousy was natural. After all, I had developed a small soft spot for our lady but that was probably because she was the only woman around after Mother and you can't be interested in your Mother because that is just about as disgusting as it gets. Isn't it? I forget.

'We have to get rid of her, son. She is corrupting poor little Gene. He isn't aware of the carnal minefield. She'll steal his mind and use it against you. I'm telling you son, she ain't to be trusted. If she gets her claws into him, he will be lost to us. He might even decide to keep this place for himself. It is his name on the deeds after all. Never forget that. I'm sure he hasn't.'

'Mother, calm yourself please,' said I. 'Eugene is nothing more than a baby trapped inside a huge body. Even if he skipped a thousand lunches he would never be the lady's choice. I can confirm that.'

'But what if she isn't after him for his beauty or character? What if she only wants his money?'

'No, she wouldn't,' I pondered. Could Mother be right? Could I really be surrounded by con artists without my knowledge? No! For I am divine and I would have noticed it. How perplexing, perhaps Kathryn really was an iron fist hidden inside a silk glove. Should that be the case I would need stratagem. I would need to be ready on guard; overthrown, a coup no less, mutiny! I must find out what their brief was before it became too late! What about Jim and Spangler? Oh God, the only person I trusted anymore was Mother because I knew Dirk would go with the prevailing wind whatever the suggestion, by whomever it was suggested. Good grief. I wished I'd never bothered speaking to her now, she was making me paranoid. However much she had unsettled my spirit, I still needed to keep her counsel. She was always working for the good of the Steves family name and I, being the only remaining member meant I had her unequivocally onside. I must restore respect to the household. She expected me to make my mark, to put things back in their rightful place where she and my father had failed most miserably at every turn.

'You are the way,' she told me, 'the last vestige. The Steves name dies with you son. You have the power and you will have the glory.' Well amen. I liked that kind of talk. Together we would do some strong work indeed.

'Don't worry yourself, Mom,' I assured her. 'I shan't let any person conspire against us. Not Gene, not Kathryn, not anyone.'

Besides, the wheels had already been set in motion, they could not stop the juggernaut now. If they tried to intervene I would destroy the lot, everything that I had built around myself, my empire. If I cannot have it for myself thought I, I shall destroy it along with those stinking rats. They could go down with the ship whilst I paddled away on the dingy of opportunity. After all, failure is just a missing rung on the ladder of success; it only means that you have to take a bigger leap to ascend to the summit.

'Climb that greasy pole Steves,' I would say and he shot up it like a ferret. 'Commendations supreme master of madness, I salute myself.' Mother nodded approvingly.

'But what about Jim?' I pondered it. 'Talking to him will be tantamount to taking a swim in concrete boots. I wouldn't call him a soldier of fortune. Perhaps he could be a kitchen hand or some such minion. He is fit for nothing except to remind me of days I'd rather forget. I never think about Dad anymore. Looking at Jim is like taking a most unpleasant stroll down memory lane and being ambushed by the fourth horseman of the Apocalypse. Like flicking through the pages of some long-forgotten college yearbook with all the faces scratched out. There are no fond memories for me. My time has come and he isn't part of it.' She patted my leg again. 'You made me free him.' I snapped back at her rare yet touching gesture. 'I would have been more than happy to let the bastard rot in jail. Are you sure we did the right thing?'

'It clears my conscience,' said Mother as reflective as I have ever seen her.

'That's funny, I wasn't aware you had one,' said I 'Besides, conscience is dangerous, it'll kill you, far simpler and less arduous to bury your head in the sand. Whoever invented that conscience shit should be strung up and de-balled. Who was it? Neitschze? The asshole, if I had a time machine I'd go back and teach him a lesson.'

'Just talk to him. You'll work it out, I know you will.' And with that pearl of sickening wisdom, she disappeared once again into the ether.

Good Lord, I was more scared of having a conversation with Jim than I would be were I mounting a cavalry charge on the White House because that bastard would try and make me feel guilty. He would do everything in his power to pull at my heart strings. They were locked away behind an impenetrable force-field but he knew there's always an Achilles heel. Bastard! Bastard! I would prevent him from weaselling his way in. I would kill him before I would allow him to get to me. I would rather destroy it all than show emotion because I am indestructible. Destroy him instead, rip his heart out first. That is the way, the way of the winner, either that or don't talk to him at all, don't give him the chance because I know deep down that I wronged him badly and I won't accept it. I won't! I will not! Running away from confrontation is cowardice and I am a fighter, a rebel and a leader. A great leader no more runs away from his failures than he does his successes. All the same, I reckoned I'd leave it a while to give myself some time to regroup. A nice nap should help. A cup of black coffee and a cookie, yes, that will make things better and the bottle of whiskey I downed wouldn't hurt either.

Before I knew it I was out for the count, dreaming of shedding Kathryn's large and unnecessary garments, thus releasing her from fabric imprisonment. Nimble disrober and robber of a fine woman's dignities that I am. You know she calls out to me in my dreams as she would not dare to when awake. It must be the fear of rejection that is stifling her amour. She would never be subjected to a humiliating dose of that at the hands of Eugene. Perhaps that is comforting, the safety of being accepted, even if she is constantly looking over her shoulder at my perfection; always so aloof and brooding, so as to be unobtainable. I am doing myself no favours in the romance department, even so I am convinced her Puritan loins are stirring beneath those pesky robes. In my dreams she is wearing a transparent diaphanous gown and she is beckoning me with her little finger. When she looks into my eyes, her pupils dilate like black holes sucking me in. She wants me. I know she does and if she isn't careful, she's going to get it.

I awoke from my pleasurable sleep with a glad heart. I stretched and issued Bronson a morning greeting. I usually kicked him up the ass or in the legs, so he was happy too. This was a day for good tidings as my manly desires had been sated in slumber. That was more than enough for me for the time being. I felt contented to have the memories in my mind. Besides, I had almost forgotten how to differentiate between delusion and reality, they merged and how fortunate since most of my greatest work goes on in my head. What's more, I had slept right through the day and the following night no less, reinvigorated and ready for anything. I had an idea that today would be a big day, one for the journals. My intuition was working on its highest plane. Yes, if nothing else I would have to have my one to one with Jim and that was sure to be a memorable exchange. I was right for sure, as always and for-ever. Tuesday 19 August would be a memorable day indeed. Let's call it 'Steves day' for posterity; if I had known then what I know now, I would have stayed in bed.

I sashayed into the lounge, twirling as I went. Still in my police uniform, lounge robe and snakeskins. The smoke from my cigar trailed behind me as I drew the toasty inhalations into my tormented lungs. All that fresh country air can't be good for a person anyway, dirt stimulates the immune system.

'Good morning friends,' I twirled into the kitchen where Gene and Kathryn were sitting together at the dining table in deep conversation. They looked surprised to see me so early and stopped their conversation midway to stare. Granted, I wasn't usually so chipper at any hour of the day but I managed to suck my cynicism inside for a few moments before it came spewing forth once again.

'Are my ears burning, dears?'

'I shouldn't think so,' said Eugene.

'And what are you mulling over? I hope it's all good stuff, remember, there'll be a trip to Atlantic City if you're up to no good.' Gene rolled his eyes.

'I'd like to go to Atlantic City. I ain't been there before.' Dirk butted in as he slouched into the kitchen with a half-eaten ham sandwich.

'Have you not been listening all this time, boy?' I pointed vigorously toward the framed constitution hanging by the door. 'Can't you read? Atlantic City is a bad place, it is purgatory.'

'Oh,' said Dirk scratching his head, 'actually I can't read but if you say so I won't go there.'

'You may not have a choice, dullard,' said I.

I wouldn't let them ruin my exuberance. Kathryn fixed me a piece of toast. I hadn't eaten more than a cookie in two days and I was ravenous so I stole Gene's breakfast from under his nose.

'Hey! That's my low-fat granola!' he protested.

'Oh really, is it now. On a diet are we squire? Why might that be, dearest?'

'Nothing,' he muttered and shuffled out sulking. Kathryn smiled weakly.

'And how is our lady?' I sat next to her so close she slid away from me an inch or two and clasped her hands together, her elbows resting on the table.

'Well, I'm just fine,' she whispered amenably.

'WHAT'S THAT?' I put my hand to my ear. 'I CAN'T HEAR YOU! We shall have to buy you a megaphone. That should make you just about audible,' joked I. There's nothing like mirth to get a woman onside.

'Have you seen Jim this morning?'

'He hasn't come out of his room yet. I've barely seen him. He's very quiet. He said he doesn't want to speak to anyone until he's had words with you. Still, he seems like a nice man, very distant, and if you don't mind my saying, he doesn't seem capable of murder but then I guess we have all made mistakes haven't we.'

'Yes you have, my dear,' I riposted. She looked into the distance, an inferno in her mind. 'No need to rub it in though is there, a clean slate good lady, we shall all have one of those.'

'Quite right,' she agreed. 'Who did he kill? Why did he do it? Surely he must have said something to you.'

'Two old-timers, nothing to worry about. He did them a favour by all accounts, put them out of their misery, you might call it euthanasia. He's not so bad, I'm sure you understand.' I put my hand on hers.

'Oh more than you know,' she replied. Then she got up and began clearing the plates away. I didn't let on that I knew what she had done in her shady past. I preferred the subtle approach.

She would offer the information when the time was right, although I suspected Gene might not be so forgiving. A fine currency that, I could certainly use it against her should she turn on me. Always keep something back for insurance. If only Gene knew that he was surrounded by the biggest bunch of murderers on the planet, all under one roof, he would expire on the spot. Genius; I was the only one who knew it all and I revelled in it. History would reveal our crazed brilliance.

Now that I had managed to clear the kitchen by virtue of my very presence, I decided to go and tick someone else off so I headed upstairs to find Jim. It had to be done and this time was as good a time as any. I passed the landing window to see Spangler battering the wall of the outhouse and goading the cops within.

'I'm a-coming to get you girls. I'm just going to get my knives,' laughing hysterically. He was under strict order not to kill anyone so I hoped he was only jesting. If he did take the plunge he would have to bury them himself. I wouldn't be getting my hands dirty.

I found Jim curled up in bed with a pillow over his head. No doubt to drown out Spangler's taunts. I poked his leg and he drew the thing from his face.

'That guy's insane,' he pronounced. It seemed as though he'd had enough of it all already, there was a certain despondency in his tone.

'He's just having some fun,' said I. 'Come into my office, we need to have a chat.' He got up and followed me down the stairs.

'You're insane too,' he muttered from behind.

'Thank you.'

I ushered him in and plopped into my throne. I had selected

a particularly uncomfortable stool for him to sit on and I set it in the middle of the room in the first stroke of psychological warfare.

'Have you met Charles Bronson?' Jim looked over at the waxed Bronson, all hideously deformed in the ass and legs where I kicked him every morning because I resented his presence and because it made me feel better. He did not respond. Never mind.

'Before we commence I would like to welcome you to our home, "The Last Bastian of Hope". I do hope you are enjoying the comfortable ambience and the run of its vestibules. Have a cigar.' I offered him a Cuban but the bastard had no guilty pleasures to satisfy so I proceeded to blow my smoke into his face. That should get a rise.

'How was your good long rest at your country's pleasure? You don't look to have been troubled by your service.'

'You really have got the nerve Steves, in fact, you've gone mad. You always were an arrogant asshole but you're warped, man, totally fucked. You ruined my life. You took it away and crapped all over it and you have the temerity to ask me how I'm doing!'

'Ah, temerity, a fine word, I'm as audacious as the fox and twice as . . . ' He cut me off.

'And what's with the fucking Shakespeare talk, man? You ain't no fucking bard, you ain't no regal king, you're a fucking asshole from Virginia who took too much LSD or whatever you've been shovelling down your throat. Hanging around with losers too scared to tell you how fucked you are.'

The insolence, his lack of respect would be commendable were it directed at somebody else. I felt a swell inside.

'I got you out of that stinking hole and don't you forget it. You never even said so much as a thank you, you ungrateful little swine.'

'You put me in there!'

'You put yourself in there, you little shit. You wouldn't have caught me doing time for someone else's crime because I'm not that fucking brainless. You only had to open your mouth and say it wasn't you but no, no, you just pissed yourself and didn't say jack until it was too late. Come on, we've both seen the movies. I'll bet you picked up the fucking gun didn't you, you asshole. Never pick up the gun. Did Columbo teach you nothing?'

'This ain't the movies man, this is my life.'

'You could have squealed.'

'I did! They didn't believe me. The school told them you hadn't turned up for class in weeks and nobody had seen you for days, at least. The home helper said you were nowhere to be found. You hadn't been looking after your mom properly. When they came the place was a hell hole. There was trash everywhere and your mom had been eating cat food out of tins with her hands and they were all cut up and infected. There was a month's worth of mail behind the front door. Everyone thought you'd disappeared long ago. You were supposed to be looking after her, Steves, your own fucking mother. No wonder she went crazy but then I guess that's in the genes.'

That was enough; he didn't know what it was like for me. I was just sixteen years old, I wasn't ready. I never asked for that shit and nobody ever did anything for me except treat me like a piece of crap. What I did was the only way to end it, the *only* way.

'And you know something else? Your dad was gonna put her in rehab and when she got out he was going to take her on that cruise she'd always wanted to go on. He'd already booked it, arranged it all so she'd have something to get better for and what did you do? You blew her brains out before she could get help and go on her vacation. You remember that Steves, you remember how much she wanted that? She would have got better for that and you know it.'

'Shut up, shut the fuck up.' I clasped my hands over my ears.

'You hear that Steves, she was going to have revolutionary treatment at the military base. She was going to be OK.'

'I'm not listening, I'm not listening. I can't hear you.'

'You killed her for nothing!'

Think of nice things.

'She's not dead! She is here with me every day. Now she lives forever. I saw her yesterday, she seemed happy enough to me.'

'You think you've seen your mother,' he laughed. 'Now I know you're insane. You're fucking nuts. If she's alive, why don't you ask her to come in here right now.'

'She's invisible. Only I can see her. She only comes to me because I am her saviour.'

Jim stood up and advanced toward me. He had been on the edge of that damned stool the whole time.

'You killed her in cold blood!' he said, pressing his face up to mine and pointing at my head. 'You selfish, cold-hearted, murdering psychopath.'

He leant over me. I was fit to burst. I was boiling over with rage. My head ached, my lips pursed, my eyes squeezed into slits. I ground my teeth together. He was staring at me, his eyes swirling. I stood up bolt upright which made him flinch, I saw it. My teeth still grated together so I thought they would splinter in my mouth. My lips curled up into a sneer, contorted. I stared at one spot right ahead of me, focused. I kept it together. I walked slowly out of my office, never looking back because if I looked back I would rip his head off with my bare hands. As I reached the door I turned round but did not look at him.

'Get out,' I told him, my voice so low it growled. 'If I ever see you again, I'll kill you.'

I continued walking out into the grounds and over the hill. I had to control the boiling anger in the pit of my stomach. I had to force it down. I had only felt rage like this once before. This wasn't like shooting a cop in the leg or running over some stranger that I didn't care about. This was personal. I knew that if I allowed the feeling to prevail and the pressure inside to rise I would do something rash. I would lose my cool to the nth degree and blow up like a volcano, destroying everything in my path. I always knew it; keep the lid on, nail it down because there is anger and venom in there so tangible that even I didn't have the strength to fight it. I walked for miles, only getting back to the ranch before sundown. I had to put that old crap back in its place, back in the box. I didn't want anyone to see me like this, weak and out of control. I hated Jim. I was glad he had gone.

I paused at the back door and took some deep breaths before I entered. I prepared to go on stage with my fixed smile like a thespian. I spread out my arms and looked upward to the sky breathing long and deep. No one had to know about this small setback and I certainly wouldn't be telling Mother about the cruise that never was but could have been. That made-up shit

Jim had concocted to make me feel bad. I would not be privy to those mind games. It was all crap, it was all fucking lies. I returned myself to my office, kicking that stool clear to the other side. Where's the whiskey? I could knock back a whole crate and it still wouldn't be enough. I could hear laughing from upstairs, winding its way down and along the corridor to goad me. Are those bastards laughing at me? How dare they have fun. I watched a documentary and drank and fell asleep.

Before I knew it, hours had passed and I was stood in a pool of blood, staggering around. It was everywhere, smeared all over my hands and I was laughing to myself so loud they could have heard me in Tucson. How did that get there? I felt light-headed, elated, on another plane. I looked down at my clothes. My officer's garb all muddy and ripped and fucked up and literally soaked with blood and water and clods of clay hung on it all over. My robe was stained. It looked watermarked because it was crimson already and provided no contrast to the fluid that saturated it, but I quickly realised it must have been blood if the rest of my appearance was anything to go by. My snake-skins were ruined. I never would have inflicted any harm on them voluntarily. Who did this to me? Was it Jim? How badly was I hurt? I checked my body for wounds, deep gashes or anything at all. There were none that would cause fatality. It must be coming from somewhere else. I staggered over to the mirror to see if I'd had half my head blown off whilst I was asleep and the adrenaline had flooded my system and made me so numb and high that it had spared me the pain. I didn't want to look. I was too scared but I forced myself.

Oh shit, I'm fucked.

SIX

The Empire Implodes

Rewind.

It's time to retrace those steps, young man. How did we come to this? There were gaps in memory, chasms in semblance of mind; a loss of consciousness perhaps; a loss of control, definitely. Set yourself on the road to regaining clarity. Come on Steves, hold on to the thread. Something had snapped.

'If I ever see you again,' said I, 'I'll kill you.'

And the darkness parted and Steves said 'Let there be light' and there was and it shone down only for me.

In balmy heat I basked and revelled in the beauty of what I had created, what I had destroyed. I remembered the pleasure as well as the pain flooding back; the sweet beauty in destruction. I decide, always, it is my choice and that is my virtue. I walked out of the room slamming the door behind me. I smashed it so hard it almost ripped off its hinges. The strength gained from adversity. I was fired up, a super human ball of hellfire, measured, only as long as I could keep it inside. Rushing up and swallowed back down. I needed space but those bastards wouldn't let me have it because they were in my head, closing in on me, they were laughing. Poke the monkey, make it dance, see how long it takes before it turns demented. I was almost at the back door but something made me turn back. My body started to climb the stairs as my mind climbed the walls. I was as stealthy as the most thriving predator; natural selection would keep me on top of the pile. Creeping and listening to the deception carried on the wind and funnelling down the staircase, just like Mom warned me. I would wrest the mantle from the hands of their shameful deceit. I would wrestle them for it and I would crush them with it.

A catalogue of errors brought me to this ideological place and I had been intrinsic in compiling it unawares. I had turned my cheek for too long, in denial of Mother's reason. Who but she could have foreseen such madness come into being, could have predicted such unscrupulous duplicity toward a fellow man if he weren't listening at the door as Mother had? Who on Earth could be so bold and so snakelike so as to turn like the proverbial worm, vile and dirt-ridden creatures of the soil that they are. My question was rhetorical for I knew with the totality of my conviction that the unmentionable had become the inescapable truth. Eugene had betrayed my unwavering trust in his mind. He had betrayed my nurture, my generosity and bitten the hand that fed with the rabidity of a drooling and gnashing dog and he wasn't the only one. Did he not see that I can and will bite harder and with less restraint; that I will bite down to the bone and scrape the skin back with clenched jaws as I pull away. I will skin those digits in vengeance. I will exact the might of the Empire on the Man because the Empire is all that I am, the Empire is nobody but Steves. I know that now and I accept it. I would end him and his little lady. There could be nothing to deter me, only vitriol to spurn me onward. Enmity. I resolved myself to cut and dice and scratch and tear. No revenge can grip a soul as mine can. I would part the seven seas if I had to in order to right this wrong, for no cauldron can mix a potion as potent as my fury and no man on Earth can escape its reach whilst losing everything in the vain attempt. If he had learned just one thing by now, he had learned of my omnipotence. Trying to escape it is the fight of a man on the edge of reason. I absolve myself of all responsibility for what I am about to do, thought I and I did.

There they came, faint whisperings in the distance. Where do they come from you ask, from behind Eugene's bedroom door, no less. I crouched down and listened. Muttering and the television turned up louder than usual, just like the Strauss used to be. I could make out two voices but not their words. I could hear the jingle of the evening news. A floorboard creaked as I skulked so I suspected my presence had been noted. I pushed open the door and there were Kathryn and Eugene in an embrace staring at the mugshot of Jim beaming out of the TV. They parted quicker than a ho's thighs for a hundred dollar bill. They jumped up and caught their breath for they had been discovered, touching. It was against the constitution and everything they had been taught was right and fair and just. They trembled together and stared at me. I had been too god damn quick for their trundling thought processes to even begin to outwit. I had been most cunning. I expect that they feared the wrath would come immediately but I prefer to deliver my retribution stone cold. I needed some time to ponder which parts of their disgusting anatomies to remove first with my rusty blade. Those rabbits in the headlights before me, Eugene regained his composure and his shallow breath. I figured if they were going to jump ship it would come soon enough, now that they had two enemies to fear; the law and the God himself. He pointed a chubby digit at the TV.

'The cops are coming for us Steves. It's all over the news. How long do you think it will take them to find us here?'

How long before you abandon me more like, thought I. He was as transparent as that whore's knickers but slightly less transparent than her soul.

'I would give them a couple of days, more or less. I assume they have collected stray hairs and secretions from the car by now. I don't think they have anything on me but they've got your genetics all mapped out in the system, remember. Fingerprints and semen samples and you were sat under that camera in the jail office for quite a while. They probably have your inside leg measurements and everything else by now. Still, at least you're thin enough to run now, give or take. You had better get your sneakers on, boy. There's no hope for you.'

'Oh good God! We have to leave, Steves. We have to go right away. If we stay here they'll find us. Let's go back to New York. It's safer there if we don't leave the house or go out in the dark or make any noise or bump into any crazies.'

'Or breathe.' I paused for effect. 'Anyway Gene, the anonymity of the city won't save you,' said I wagging my finger. 'If they come looking for me I'll lead them straight to you. The kiddy-fiddler and the arsonist did it, I shall inform them. I shall set them straight and then melt away into the night.'

'Who's an arsonist?' said Eugene.

'Who's a kiddy-fiddler?' said Kathryn.

They looked at each other with nervous unease.

'Just playing!' said I jovially. Like hell I was.

There was Jim on the screen again. How dare he garner such fame. I felt a secret streak of jealousy pass through my thoughts and settle again for future festering; the nebulous of another

193

bitterness, no doubt. I would add it to the collection. He did look quite handsome for a convict. I should have been quite pleasured were I him, to have such a stunning mugshot displayed to the masses. He must have ingratiated himself to the prison photographer.

'No word of a lead as yet ladies,' said I after listening to the pointlessly un-newsworthy report. It is unlikely they would hand us useful information on a silver platter. I suspect we should leave tonight.

'Yes Steves.' Eugene saluted me but he could not win me over that easily.

'Well, what are we waiting for? Set to it. Pack some weapons too. I need some time to formulate an escape plan. Can I at least trust you with that task?'

'Yes, sir.'

'You'll delegate?'

'Affirmative.'

'Strong work, soldier.'

I swivelled around on my heels in the customary fashion and left them alone, once again unsure of what I was about to do, whether or not I was lying about their transgressions, whether they should clasp each other behind my back or if I was going to come charging back at them with a pick axe and murderous intent. I can confirm the latter.

There had been a tear in the very fabric of the universe because it transpired that Kathryn fancied Eugene and not I. How could this be??! I had cast it aside as a ridiculous conspiracy. A smokescreen for his true endeavour, to restore the Steadman ranch to its pitiful standing as a homestead and retain its wholesome legacy alone with her, ergo, without me. I mused. I stomped back down those stairs with a growing fury. Then I fumed some more on the way out back. I paced the porch, first sitting, then standing, then sitting again and standing up some more. I had no idea what to do with my body and my mind wouldn't leave me alone. Nausea had me in its grip and a feeling that all was in flux. Evil forces of good were at work here. Steves, we must obliterate them. We must crush good intention and cast it back onto the sea of hopelessness from which it ran aground. *Pace*. I hoped Jim was far away by now, far away running lonely along some dusty dirt track to avoid the highways and imminent capture. Running for his life as the county sherriff spotted his sorry ass and chased him in his squad car, only for him to stumble and fall and crash out under its spinning wheels. I hoped they would give him the chair. I hoped they would bring back hanging. A hot poker for you boy, then quartered and boiled. I hoped they would gauge out his eyes and then scoop out his balls. I wished it all for him, the bastard of hell. How dare he. How dare he show such disrespect. How dare he tell me I killed Mother for nothing at all. How dare he say I hurt her! Arrrrrrgggggghhhh-hhhhhhhhhhhhh!!! I would never hurt her. You hear me, never!

My legs carried me hurriedly across the grounds, out past the emus with their sinister faces and ways. I hurdled over the parameter fence leaving the green and luscious land behind me to head into the desert. I had never felt so focused in my life. I pressed on, spurned and purposeful, although I did not know where I was going so it was all an illusion. There I was ripping along in my police officer's outfit, lounge robe and snakeskins, a misfit, in mismatched costume looking like a runaway from the loony bin. I caught myself mumbling something or other. I wasn't sure what it was and who cared, no one could hear me. My hands were flapping about at my sides.

Back at the ranch everyone was rushing around with their own agendas firmly in mind. Spangler taunting the police with a cattle prod reserved for wanton emus. Dirk munching jerky and playing with the dog out back by the pond, kicking up dust and shooting cacti with an air rifle meant for target practice. He never got any better. His limbs were too long for coordination of any functional value, his centre of gravity too far from the ground. Kathryn and Eugene were busy ignoring my orders and packing up their own belongings ready to flee before I returned. I guess they felt if they couldn't have the place to themselves to bring up the Steadman offspring they may just as well cut their losses and leave before I could further tarnish their already stained characters. Better that than rotting in some prison cell in the western hemisphere. Get back East where it all makes sense and hope they don't draft in the FBI to come hunt you down. Maybe, let's not wait to find out.

I steamed on ahead. Steaming and frothing at the mouth. I stopped on a rocky outcrop and screamed at the top of my lungs into the dry air. Baron land surrounded me as I frightened the prairie dogs back into their holes. I considered jumping off the edge for a moment. I considered it for 6.9 seconds. Then it occurred to me that with this amount of failing luck on my side, I might just as easily end up a paraplegic in a wheelchair than a tragic hero of the downtrodden. Then I would have some poor sap wiping my ass and scraping food off of my face for the rest of my pitiful days. So I walked up right to the edge, gave it two fingers and rolled back off down the hill, backwards. I pissed on a scorpion once I finished my descent. I righted myself and I pissed. Every time it moved I stemmed the flow and started right back up again once I had a good enough aim at the target. I blasted it a few feet before I ran dry.

Mother was nowhere to be found as always when I really needed her. I called out to her loudly but she was ignoring my pleas. I may just as well have thought it, she lived in my head after all. She had gone off somewhere again, typical. Maybe she found out about the cruise and hated me now. Maybe she realised how much she had fucked me up with her crazy shit. She thinks I don't remember that. Now I needed to rest. Thoughts can be so tiring. They make you want to curl up in a ball because they are arduous and too prolific not to send you nuts, shooting about all over the place, out of control. I felt like I had run cross country in stack heels carrying a sperm whale and never stopped for rest, food or water. The thoughts still traversed the mind. If one were to pull them from my head like a string it would be possible, I believe, to wrap them round the Earth three times and still have enough left to make it to Uranus. But that isn't scientifically proven, just speculation. Tension builds up in my brow, that is why I have so many lines.

I began to saunter, losing speed. I had been walking around at pace for over an hour. My Timex could confirm that. The heat was so persistent that I was soaking with sweat. Up ahead I spotted a shack. I had seen it before although it did not belong to our estate. It looked empty and uninviting, which is why I hadn't bothered to explore it earlier but it was a shield from the sun and I could surely do with one of those suckers. I eyed it from behind some trees. It did not seem to be in use but then we all know appearances can be deceiving. Never trust, shoot first and ask questions later. I took my gun out of its holster.

Good thing I was a lazy bastard and hadn't removed my police disguise, otherwise I would be defending myself with hair pulling or some other lame, girl's fighting style. I tied my hair up with some off-cut of string I found on the ground. I would need to see the panorama should anyone attack from the side. All was quiet.

I rushed up to the window and ducked beneath it, furtively glancing. I crept sideways toward the door under the sill on my haunches, pushing myself along with my back leg. The door was slightly ajar so I poked the butt of my gun inside and teased it open, not a sound. Should I rush them thought I, perhaps it would be best, wild west style. I peered through with one big eye squinting, remembering that they could be behind me, those assailants. I flicked my head from side to side. Fuck it; I'll rush them after all. I jumped in, in a flash, robe flying and caught under foot. Ass! I tumbled in there, the door rattling as I went barrelling in, everything everywhere. I crashed out in a heap in the middle of the dusty floor. I cut my head above the brow, it hurt. I landed head first and full pelt onto an old nail sticking up out of the floorboard. Ass, butt cheeks and balls! Not the face for Christ's sake. It would need to be intact for my televised debut. I lay for a moment bewildered, like Christ himself on a horizontal cross, nails embedded into head instead of hands. From my rodent view I could see machinery of all sorts looming up around me. Aged, rusted, no longer used and huge relative to my ground level stature. All balanced against the walls, forks, hoes and chainsaws. Dust covered it all and I had dislodged it with my bumbling fall. It settled back down onto my bleeding forehead and formed a convenient seal on my wound. Nothing organic of note in this place, just me, except for an ant scurried past my nose and disappeared down a crack between the floorboards. It looked huge in my immediate line of vision, like an ant from Mars. I tried to crush it with the butt of my perceptively giant gun but it was too fast. My head hurt. I pulled myself up slowly, onto one foot and then the other. Ah, a chair in the corner. I thanked the god of carpentry for his foresight. I would sit in it and recuperate. My head was so full and my body ached, I needed a rest. I flopped down and it held, just. I really should have checked that first, thought I. No matter, it had proved steadfast. My mouth was as dry as a bone but there were no supplies. I would have to drink from my special little travel ration. I would drink my own body weight in whisky upon my return to the ranch for it would help to temper the loss of my steed and his hideous little henchwoman. I sat there swigging tiny sips, my legs laid out before me, arms resting on the arms of the chair. I felt my head, reopening the wound and blood trickled into my eye. Crying blood like the virgin herself, was I. Every divine soul must have his moment of arduous toil, his humble moment of clarity so that he may feel at one with his philosophies, his innermost thoughts and visions. I had visions too, of fame, of infamy and grand adulation. I had visions swirling. I took a long hard swig and gulped down hard. Just as always I had visions, visitations in the night; visions of Mother.

I felt weak and sick; the sickness in my heart and in my head. Thoughts turned to bewilderment. I blocked it. I started to go blind with the stress, everything goes a little lighter and a weakness comes at the nape of the neck. Block it. A tear rolled down my cheek. Blood, sweat and tears, the world had had it all from me. I wished to throw those memories onto Satan's pyre. Nobody can make them go away, ever. No matter what happens the pain is stuck firm inside me, impossible to extricate, to exorcise. Seeping and creeping up to the surface without warning. The tension in the pit of the stomach, disbelief, why me? It made me what I am today. It is a part of me so perhaps it has served its purpose. You are cordially invited to participate in its insanity. It reigns, I fight it and it wins. I am a servant to its all encompassing supremacy but I have learned to live with its omnipotence and its mischief, whereas others have not and never will because they will be dead. I blame it all on that which has gone before because it is not my fault. I absolve myself once again for what I have done and for that which I am about to do and I did.

As those flashbacks rallied through my head I grasped onto the arms of the chair so hard that wood splintered up into my fingers but I did not care. I laughed it off. Nothing can hurt me anymore. I will avenge the wrongs. I shall make them pay, all of them. Everyone who I fear is about to hurt me, I shall hurt them first. I shall never let anyone get the best of Theodore Steves. I shall go about my own twisted business happily in my twilight world, bearing as it does no resemblance to any reality but my own. I make it so. I am no longer scared. Yes Steves, retreat to crazy land and make up some excuses for yourself that only you can give credence to. I don't need anyone's seal of approval. I have the Steves approval rating and I must mention I have scored very highly and the system works fine. And consequences damn them, what are those? I have no time for them at all. Yes, Mr Larkin, this indeed be the verse and I have blood on my hands and hydrochloric acid in my heart. Bring some hand wash for the eternally stained. I'll order a truckload and bring me some booze, squire, my ration is running dry, just like my patience.

I saw Mother again. I was sat in the chair as though bound to it, clasping tightly and Mother was not there but she was inside *here*. I am small and she is large and she is leaning over me in the dark with a bullet in her head and Father is at war. I closed my eyes and the movie plays over and over again.

At once I am roused, pulled out of my nightmare by the sound. It seemed to emanate from the corner of the shack, the electronic ring tone of a cell phone. The sort of devious contraption fools carry with them everywhere so they never need to be alone to indulge their solitude. I shifted, turning my head to pinpoint its location. The outside world once again impinging on my private time, distracting me from morbid thoughts conjured up by the past. I stood up and followed it. Just like stepping out off the sidewalk to find the traffic lights change the moment your foot hits the road, no sooner had I moved myself to investigation, the bastard stopped. It was somewhere over in the corner, of that I was certain. There it came again. This time I had it. I pulled up some old sheeting draped over a small dresser. Aha! A sports bag, not dusty, brand new. Someone had been there very recently. I unzipped the side pocket and searched within, pulling out some garments, a police uniform no less. Jim, it had to be. The cell still rung out but I did not recognise the caller. Where in the hell did he get that from, the unscrupulous little reprobate? He must have had it in prison, the deviant. In direct contravention of the constitution which quite adequately dictates that cell phones are banned and damned and so are snivelling little fuck holes. I would rip his head off. Still cowering under Mother's shadow I made off. I would kill him. I smashed the thing on the ground. I stamped on it again and again and again in rage so that its innards spilled out all over the floor in tiny fragments. Its circuitry sprang out all over and there was silence and I boiled and Mother touched me. I lost the thread.

My vision tunnelled. I felt a blockage in my throat and this time I didn't swallow it back down hard. My eyes were red and my pupils as small as pinpricks, furrowed brow. Dizzy and not fighting the demon inside anymore I climbed onto its back and rode roughshod out amongst the rocks and the small withered trees. I pounded. A contorted face of pure anger and hatred, snarling: something had taken over me. I staggered on, every feature of my face pinched. My hands wanted to lash out so I struck at everything that I passed. I kicked rocks and barely rooted plants that sprung up with dust and earth with every blow from the snakeskins. I felt fire in my stomach ignite. I was letting out low growls of animalistic extraction, head down; the eyes looking upward and forward with purpose. I came to the top of a rise and peered below, grunting and growling still. Every touch from Mother's hands pushed me onward. She was right behind me, willing me on. There I saw him, the tiny figure crouching by the dried up old river beneath. I knew it was him though I couldn't make a precise identification. I didn't care. Whoever that bastard was, he was dead. The beast within demanded that he die. I skidded on my backside down the hill, tumbling from time to time as I lost my footing on loose rocks. I stretched out my arms as counterbalance. Every little move and I snagged my uniform and my robe, ripping and tearing and dusty as the moon. It was in my mouth so I swallowed it down with what spittle I had. I bore down upon him. He only became aware of my presence when it was too late to flee. The wind on the plane howled round his ears drowning out the sound of the predator's encroachment. He had his back to me. The innocent had not even learned to look over his shoulder to this very day, a practice I had had drilled into me as a very young boy. Either of my parents could have been behind me.

He twisted around as I gained footing on horizontal ground. His body twisted but his legs remained facing forward, his hands in front of him like a zombie. He's burying something. No wait, he's digging something up. There was a spade in his hands, procured from the shack no doubt. He caught sight of me advancing toward him and his mouth fell open. Lost and found by the beast man from the deep. My visage etched with perverted determination. I lurched for him smiling madly and baring my teeth, arms stretched outward to him, beckoning him with my fingers into my cobra grasp. Once I had hold of him he would be done for. The sinewy weakling would stand no chance just as before. I had no fear. In my mind I told him 'Come to me my friend, give me a nice big brotherly hug,' and I would squeeze the life out of him and shatter his skeleton to a fine powder. All would go limp in my arms, held together only by his thin skin. All contained but with no interconnected bone and cartilage to keep him vertical and down he would go, a skin coloured pile of jello. Come hither my dear. Come on, I know you want to. I beckoned him again, still lurching at pace and sweating and covered in dirt. The whites of my teeth and the whites of my staring eyes breaking clear through. I gnashed them and bit them together as I might once I sunk them into his arm or his thigh. King Henry VIII will dine tonight on Jim's carcass and blood will run freely down his chin.

I flew at him. He tried to scramble up and away but it was no use, a pitiful attempt and a futile one at that. I launched aiming myself at his legs so that he could not retreat as he had planned. He went down trying for all his might to batter me with the spade but he fell onto his front and couldn't get his arm round far enough behind him to make any impression on me. He kept hitting it down on the ground beside me missing my head every time and straining his arm and losing precious power. I got one hand on the waistband of his pants and lying on him, I clawed my way up his legs squirming my way up to his middle. I raised my head backward full tilt; his thrashing had revealed the small of his back and his side, plump and juicy. The skin revealed to me. His arms continued to flail. I got my neck right back as far as it would go and snapped it back down, lips peeled back. I lunged at the skin on his right side. His legs were crushed by my body weight and he could not move. I bit down so hard that it hurt my gums. He screamed but I did not deviate, it was music to my ears. I bit harder and harder as a fighting dog would if it were set free to do what it had always been taught and it were fighting to its rabid end. I felt the liquid enter my mouth. I tasted iron and salt. When I could clench down no more I came back up and went in for another bite of the cherry. This time I pivoted my head so I had the whole circumference of my mouth impregnated on his fleshy side. The wounds joined to form a ring. The first hit had gone deep but the second was even deeper because this time I could get more purchase. There was no longer a flat and even surface to negotiate. It was soft and mushy and it had some give to it. I clamped my teeth and unlike before, my jaws started squeezing further and further together. I went at it until I thought my jaw muscles might spontaneously combust. I chewed; serrated, gnashed. Now it had the consistency of tenderised beef. It wasn't long before it was more like meat for a patty. Jim wailed and screamed so shrilly that it might have broken glass were there any around to shatter; they reverberated from the cliff haunt-ingly. Soon he could not even manage that. He no longer formed cohesive words. His brain had circumvented the facility for speech, in such intense pain was he. His body became rigid, his limbs limp and unable. He shuddered and trembled against the pain. I grunted and growled as before, deranged, until I felt a small piece break away and a new texture under tooth. Then the whole thing came away in my mouth leaving a red raw wound two inches in circumference. I felt it there in my mouth. I let it rest on my tongue for a moment and then I rolled it around a little and flipped it over. I spat it out onto the ground, laughing and wiped my face on his shirt. Then I began to claw my way up his back to his collar.

Lumbering up his body my belt buckle caught the mulch wound and snagged it causing blood to course out freely. Jim let out another yelp, yet ostensibly he was now crying the tears of a desperate child. I knew them well. I covered his mouth with my hand as I reached up to his head. There was no protest.

'Shhh,' I whispered in his ear. 'Quiet.' I stroked his cheek and rested mine on his.

'Who killed Mother now?' said I.

'You did, you m . . . m . . . mother . . . fucker,' he knew he was a goner anyway.

'That's what I thought you would say. You always were a pathetic little cunt.' I exhaled and closed my eyes.

Uncovering his mouth, my fingers lingered on his lips for a moment. Just a short moment before I plunged my fingers up into his eye sockets. One finger for one eye; one each. I plunged in as far as anatomy would allow. He nearly deafened me for my ears rang with the first signs of tinnitus. So shrill as though his lungs put out so much they would burst. I continued to gouge inside feeling for his brain if only to prove that he had one. I curled them up inside. Blood was everywhere. All over my face and running out down my fingers, down my arm and onto the ground. I would say that I had never seen so much but of course that would be a lie. He screamed for a while and then he turned silent. I was still going for it, plunging back and forth, up and down; soft, squishy, mushy and aqueous; the humour, so very satisfying when it all ended. No more was he. The accusations would end here and now. Revenge had been delivered. Dead was the man who decimated my family, I would say and the skeletons would stay in their closet under lock and key. The vilification dies with him. His lifeless body lay under me, so quiet, so peaceful, so very calming.

I slid out my fingertips and rolled off of him, his head lolled away from me. I lay there and stared up at the sky, the sun grilling me beneath. It was all blue save for a few fluffy clouds passing by quickly, blown on by the rapidity of the wind. I held up my arm. Blood had trickled down to my elbow and beyond. I traced its tracks on the arm inquisitively. The tension was gone. All was good and right in this moment as the devil had begun to recede and lose his hold over me. My furrows ironed themselves out. I giddily giggled to myself in awe of the beautiful sky above and this beatific land I lay in. Breath came back freely once more but my ears continued to ring and spoil the peace and quiet as the screams ebbed away. With arms tucked behind my neck and my legs crossed at the ankles, I rested a while. What blissful relaxation for a hard-working boy. I rolled over onto my side to face Jim and moved closer. I hooked an arm around him, cuddled up and took a well-earned nap.

I supposed around an hour later that I should really move on. Basking in the afterglow is all good and well but I hadn't finished my work yet and the sun was no longer high. I swigged the last of my ration for extra strength, I would need it. I stood above Jim's body, towering over him as I contemplated the best method of transportation. Perhaps the fire fighter's lift would be the optimum technique. I had never moved a dead weight before. I can report that when the object in question has no capacity to jump into your arms and help out in the endeavour, it is very difficult indeed. I raised one of his arms and dragged him up. Christ! I got him half way, conjuring all the power the good Lord had given me. I bent over so his torso rested over my left shoulder and wrenched him up and over. I stumbled slightly, tipping backward, saving myself in the nick of time. I was stooped. I must walk like this for miles unless I could find something to aid my travail. The journey up the rise proved the most trying. Like the first men who walked on the moon weighed down by heavy suits and apparatus, I was wearing one Mr Jim from Shitsville and he was heavier than a truckload of manure with a ton weight balanced on top. I had descended so quickly and I made it back up so very slowly. At times I had to let go of Jim's leg and grasp at rocks hoping to retain balance so he stayed on my shoulder and didn't roll off back down the hill on his lonesome. I trudged, hardly able to bend my legs, doing some sort of side to side special shuffle that I had developed half way to base camp. I finally reached the shack. There I leant forward and dispatched my charge onto the floor. He crashed down, landing heavily but it no longer mattered. His arm stuck up at an odd angle, I think I had just broken it.

What to do, what to do; ideas man, let them come thick and fast. I felt compelled to haul Jim back to his rightful place in the Empire as I had designed it. I would not let him squirm out of his obligations even in death. I spun round. I kicked him in the face but it didn't aid my quest. I needed pressure. I flipped up against the wall of the shack, balancing on my head. The blood seeped down, the veins filled and within moments I had it all figured. I ran back to the Empire. All two miles of the journey I had steamed a few hours earlier. I vaulted that fence and made it to the furthermost outhouse from the ranch. Therein I found Gene's redundant turbo chair just as he had left it a couple of months earlier when his legs had found the courage to support his shrinking body and that was courage indeed. Yes, that chair would be a fine thing, the doctor had ordered it. Gene stowed it away in the outermost reaches so that he could forget the necessity of its purpose, for he had reinvented himself as a portly connoisseur of the finest cuisine and denied its use in the past as an aid to an early grave; a punishment for allowing himself to become so very inadequate. I rode it through the gate. I could not be dynamic and jump the parameter under the circumstances. I rode it full throttle. It spluttered a little at first and then kicked into action for its calling. I nearly upended it on a couple of occasions, up onto two wheels and slamming back down; Gumball rally, mark two.

Do you know that by the time I got back to the shack that bastard was starting to go stiff on me. Now I had to break more bones as though I hadn't done him enough damage already. This really had become more trouble than it was worth. I should have finished him in my office. I would have some cleaning to do but that would be all. I could brush him under the carpet. I got him more or less into the turbo chair. The arm still jutted out at an odd angle. The legs positioned sideways as a woman might sit had she been to finishing school. His ass wasn't seated though. I feared that any small bump would dislodge him and I would be doing the same thing over and over again, picking him up and putting him back in. Waste of time, that nonsense. I got a foot onto his groin and held his shoulders in place, hopping for best position. Then I cracked his pelvis as hard as I could. I certainly broke his hips but at least he was comfortably seated. Then I rooted around for some wire or string to tie him into the chair with. I bound him tightly. All set! I rolled him out and programmed the chair to a medium speed, jogging alongside. We were having some great conversation. For once he was answering all my questions just as I liked. Never had he been as amenable as when I made up his side of the conversation for him. I could get used to that sort of thing, always being right because it's a nasty old business that, being wrong. I suddenly liked him a whole lot better.

Along we went, him and I; I and he. I told him of my intentions. How one day I would have myself surrounded by adoring followers. They would join me at the ranch. We would build a monumental extension onto it because for all its rooms and grandeur it still wouldn't be large enough to accommodate all comers. So what if Eugene was not among them. Soon I would forget him anyway. I wouldn't dwell on the loss. What loss, said I and if Jim wanted to stay, well that would be grand. He could sit in the corner and watch on as the Empire unfurled itself in all its glory. Oh, watch on indeed, that was my gag with myself as he appeared to have two large cavernous holes where his eyeballs used to be. I would never tire of my own jokes. We were on sound terrain and the chair chugged on. I embellished upon my dreams that were now mushrooming to Manson-esque proportion and more. I had settled on a plan to do away with the ailing psychiatrist who meddled with my mother and had a fair stab at infiltrating my guarded mind. I would perhaps develop a celebrity following, appearing on late night chat shows and opening various establishments of note. I would have attracted quite a coterie of adoring girls, all snapping at my heels but I would not indulge them, for that would be crass. There would be an anti-establishment under-current. I would not affiliate myself to any existing political party or persuasion for I would mount my own presidential campaign. Jim wondered how a murderer might sign up potential voters but I assured him that to date, and he really should have known this, nobody had discovered my perversions. My genius would ensure that they never would. In any case, if anybody exposed me, I would merely do away with them as well. The simple plans work best. Find a formula and don't fuck with it. Mother would be my press campaigner and she would have great product to work with. I would ensure I looked sharp at all times, especially when the cameras were rolling. They would never see me in this state, my people. A vision of chiselled handsomeness I would be. It always goes down well with the public. Besides, I would be in good company with those politicians. There is no greater corruption to be found in the world than that in the corridors of power. I would keep their secrets and they could keep mine; quid pro quo. From this standpoint I could mount war against whomsoever I pleased. Hell, it never stopped them before. I would fit right in and moreover, I would not have to do any of the dirty work myself. I could send some poor people out to do it because that is what they are for. Yes, that is the way it works when you are in charge and I for one concur. But that is for later. I would start with the Empire on a small scale and build it up to other worldly proportion. By the time the Empire Party was firmly established and ahead of the race, I would be eating steak every day, screwing my secretary and dictating orders from my sports coupe. I really got into the dream.

Before I knew it we were within eyeshot of the ranch, jogging along still. I fiddled around for the controls. Jim's arm protruded over the control pad on the arm of the chair as I tried to keep an eye on ahead, jog in time and harness the brake. The parameter fence was getting closer and closer and Jim's stiff elbow was preventing me from shutting the thing off. Oh dear. Oh dear, dear. We were upon it. I had done all I could to prevent a collision. I halted a few metres from the fence for I knew it was electrified and did not want to be too close to that pile of metal when it made contact. I winced. Sparks flew as though firecrackers had been set off at Chinese New Year. I found myself temporarily blinded by the light display. I shielded my face from the heat and from the hideous sight of burning and sizzling and juddering as the current went through his body. He remained stuck to the fence, drawn in by its power; frying. After a time his body parted with the chair and he toppled onto his back, away from the electricity and the indignity. He was still as stiff as a board. His arms and legs were raised from the ground in horrible contortion, blackened, charred and smoking he lay. Now I had seen it all and it disgusted me and that is not easy.

I left him to smoke for a few minutes until he cooled. The last thing I wanted to do was to burn my fingertips or to have his melted skin adhering to my person. I wondered how long it would take to solidify. I had no accurate measurement to make comparison. When my father melted himself I made myself scarce. I should have stuck around and studied it more thoroughly. I stood above him for a couple of minutes hand on hip, fingers to lips, moving around him and contemplating how I would go about touching him just as Jackson Pollock would have, were he producing his genius art. But this was no paint-splattered masterpiece I was dealing with here; nothing remotely aesthetically pleasing about my creation. I cringed. When I tried to handle him on the first few attempts my body naturally recoiled in disgust. Something might break off. Although burnt and blackened, he had not gone so far as to be entirely carbonised, so I eventually plucked up the courage to move him. Nothing came adrift thankfully. I praised Vulcan the god of fire and metalwork for that. I hauled him into the wheelie chair with sooty hands. It was still warm but the rubber handles protected my palms from the heat so I could push it. The power surge had robbed it of its electronic capabilities. There was Jim stuck out all over the place, with no eyes and burned to a crisp. I wheeled him into the compound. Even the emus darted for cover from the macabre sight. I trundled him along until we reached the porch. There was nobody around. I hooked it under the armpits and dragged the thing into my office and kicked the door closed behind me. I had decided en route that I could not possibly view this monstrosity as a person any more, although it was vaguely person-shaped. I had seen this sort of thing in films, kept me stockpiled with nightmares for years. It was a good thing Bronson was facing the wall. This would have given him nightmares too and he was just wax. I sat in my chair and pondered how I could get out of this predicament. There is more than one way to skin a cat. The cops would have been searching for him but I doubted he would match their profile now. Should I dump the carcass, let's say in a ravine, they would take their photo-fit picture out of their pockets, place it beside his head and say 'That's not the guy we're looking for, no way, no how, no siree.' On account of the fact that he had no eyes, no hair and perhaps no teeth because I may just as well knock those out to avoid identification. 'No, that's not him. Next!'

None of the acolytes had witnessed events so I could just be really quiet about it and get on with the packing and keep my mouth shut. I had ordered him to leave so they would probably just think he had run away to Oakie. But that would remove my need to kill them from the equation. I could sit back and relax if I so desired, take it easy; get some well-earned shut-eye. We could all run away together, if they hadn't done so already.

Of course I hadn't taken the time to check yet. Despite the relative ease of this plan, despite the fact that this would make my life a hell of a lot easier, it just didn't appeal. I had to kill them because I needed to kill them, because I wanted to and I relished the thought of it. I couldn't get it out of my head. Eugene had to pay; there isn't a thing in this world that comes for free. Money doesn't grow on trees and neither does the dignity they had taken away from me with their appalling deception. I couldn't simply go and pluck some more from thin air. It is not infinite; once it has been taken it is eternally gone and can only be replaced by the sacrifice of their souls. They could not substitute another to pay their debts. They must pay up with their own blood.

I rubbed my palms together. Oh yes. The devious plans were beginning to form in the dark recesses of my mind. I continued watching the documentary. I must have damaged my prefrontal cortex because I was about as socialised as a rogue elephant, rampaging everywhere with wild crazed eyes and indiscriminate violent thoughts. With these acting as a lullaby, I drifted off to sleep for what seemed like days. I awoke to the closing credits and couldn't remember a god damn thing. A blank canvas, black, nothing, void.

Fast forward.

Blood and dirt was everywhere, all over and disorientation was the order of the day. What had happened to me during my slumber, wondered I. One minute I was resting in the comfort of my leather throne, the next I awoke feeling as though a juggernaut had run me over twice. I scratched my head. I rolled

214

it round my shoulders stretching the ligaments. I staggered up and around. The robes, the snakeskins destroyed and in tatters, without explanation and no pain. I spun around and around. The room started to blur into a kaleidoscopic whirl. I stood in the middle, in the vortex, the eye of the storm, spinning, sucked in. The colours, the colour red in various shades, the colour of blood all around me; they were spinning round and round. If I reached out into it I could dip my hands into the mass and my palms came out red with blood dripping all over. I became lost in it. I must escape the swirling madness that held me captive. The swirling madness of my mind.

I dove out of the funnel to save myself. I dove right out with a burst of energy that only a man besieged could harness. I fell onto my knees. There was no orientation. I staggered up but I couldn't see anything before me because everything merged into one, still spinning furiously. I lurched as one would on-board a boat on a stormy sea. My vision had tunnelled. Everything still appeared red like the walls. But the blood on my hands did not come from the vortex at all because it was all over me and most of it was dried, except for that on my face. I could feel its scarlet wetness running down my neck. I needed to see from where it was omitting. Who had hurt me whilst I was unable to resist? Some spineless freak. Why was I unable to feel pain or fear and why did I feel so powerful, so omnipotent, like a god?

The room began to slow after time so that I could just make out a path. I stumbled aiming for the mirror behind the door. I must steady myself along the way, on the fireplace, on the table, on the waxed Bronson. He gave me a helping hand. I could only see those things as I was right upon them. Crawling along the walls I went. Objects began to come into focus for the first time. I rested myself up against the wall with one hand, the other checking my head for wounds. At first there were several versions of myself stood before me, peering out of that mirror. Several deities moved about the place becoming fewer and fewer, blending into one another, then finally blended into one. There was I, as clear as day.

Oh shit, I'm fucked.

I was wounded and not by short measure. The blood that I felt trickling down my neck appeared to be oozing out of my mouth. Oh my God! It's coursing down my neck. Everyone knows that when blood emits from the mouth you're a dead man. It signifies internal bleeding, rising up from the lungs filling with the stuff and then you drown in your own personal juices. But wait. I am fully mobile and I can breathe with ease, thought I. No, that's not it, that's not it at all. I put a finger in my mouth feeling softly inside. Ahhh! That hurt. My God, several teeth were missing. I got in closer to the mirror, my nose right up to the glass. Some of them had broken off into razor sharp shards poking out of my gums, which were hellish swollen, surrounded by blood and all manner of cruddy detritus. How shall I French kiss the ladies now! God damn it. Everything was fucked. My eyes were bright red where the whites once gleamed and twinkled like a globetrotting playboy. They weren't bloodshot. The blood had seeped in as though some large and very important vein had burst behind them, both of them. The blood had pooled inside. This is indicative of head trauma. Now I would be in need of my brightening drops for sure and by the gallon. I had been assaulted beyond comprehension. How could I not have awoken mid-thrashing. My skin was blackened as though I had been blowtorched and was sensitive to the touch as though sunburned. Yet it was approaching dusk and I was covered in crud of the non-faecal variety. As I touched my face I could see that my hand was ripped to shreds, the nails half torn off and the cuticles were pulled back. I simply stared at myself, at this horrible, disgusting sight before me. It was I, of that there can be no doubt but it was no version of myself that I had ever met before. Something had changed; some wild look in the eye, the stare. Those boyish good looks erased. Spangler looked less feral when we pulled him from the wild and obscurity. I was a beast. The possessed. I was fucked but not as fucked as what I saw next. I inspected my injuries up and down, from the brow to the neck and from ear to ear, ensuring both were still attached to my person. As I strained to see, the damage assessment exercise completed, I caught a glimpse of something behind me in the reflection.

Oh shit, I'm fucked. The TV career is over. Someone has taken a hatchet to my handsomeness!

No. Wait. What is this? He's more fucked than I am. I should think myself lucky. In all of God's creation how could this have gone so wrong? I turned to face it slowly, very, very slowly. It might move and I would be five miles away within a milli-second. The hairs tried in vain to prick up in horror and stand to attention but they had been singed off by my ordeal. This looked like some genetic mutation, the cast off of a human

217

experiment gone catastrophically wrong. What is it? But more pertinently, who is it? Is it a person or some Halloween dummy? No, it's only August, can't be. Don't take your eye off the game Steves, it might ambush when the mind is wandering, I reprimanded myself. I eyed it suspiciously and craned to see in more detail. As I approached its repulsiveness some flashes etched my mind. Although I could not collect them all into one cohesive strand, I knew I had done it. This was my handiwork and I knew that this was indeed my good friend of yesteryear and trusty scapegoat Jim, mutilated with my very hands and that now I could not be saved. There is no rehabilitation for this kind of perversion. I had mastered my art, cornered the market. I had become the high priest. No longer the apprentice was I, for this was the final rung on the ladder to madness. A shooting for example is an initiation ceremony for rookies and for tests to prove one's manly credentials in the face of naysayers, much like drinking games. I had scaled those heady heights and taken the national trophy, if not the world cup. Champ. I could only be worse if I ate him. After all he was already cooked but I would save that for later. Should it be possible to lose one's mind to any higher degree, then I would come back for supper. Maybe, but I wasn't convinced. I saluted myself and I imagined him saluting me in return. I couldn't possibly let my new skills go to waste. The triumphant vanquisher must forge forth and apply his craft with relentless and fastidious study. A man's determination to learn and improve himself is an odyssey without end, the eternal pursuit of intellect. I salute myself again for gratuitous profundity; most brilliant of fiends. I may as well relinquish myself of the burden of denial, for I had sinned in the most abhorrent of natures.

Where once I fancied this to be somehow nefarious, I must admit I found it all rather agreeable once I had let go of the guilt, fleeting as it was. I was liberated. Limitless possibilities engulfed my mind. I still couldn't embrace cannibalism though, no, I couldn't even bear to eat veal. No, responsibility will kill you just like your conscience so I shall once again exonerate myself but this time without the option to return to sanity. Like Jekyll turned into Hyde I just got stuck in the crazy place and forgot I was there.

SEVEN

The Empire Explodes

'Let's go Mr Hyde for we have much work to do.'

With focus and calm reminiscent of my dear deceased father and an unusual spring in my step, I took myself off down to the armoury. I had barely spent any time there in the preceding months for it was Spangler's domain. Inside there was a treasure trove. Guns gleamed in every corner, all of them attended to the highest specification. They were polished so well that I could see my face in them as I walked by, stroking their barrels; a fairground mirror effect, my reflection mutated as I went. There were handguns, shot guns, machine guns, knives, swords, clubs and batons. All were kept in order of calibre or size and under each wrung was a small case filled with the appropriate ammunition. Nothing in Spangler's life or mind was as organised or tidy as this showcase. His medals hung on the wall. Maybe the man had some wit after all. There stood chests of used weaponry on the floor ready to be reconditioned, to be sold on or deployed in the fight. I perused the selection, deciding upon my weapon of choice. I took a sword from the fan-shaped display on the wall, a ceremonial piece with a beautiful carved bone handle and a glimmering silver sheath. It was as majestic and graceful as it was deadly, much like myself. As I unleashed the blade there came the sound of metal on metal. I wafted it about my head. It was supremely heavy but I summoned super human strength and brandished it as capably as any cavalier. I returned it to its scabbard, strapped it to my belt and continued my search for a firearm. If an American has learned anything from the Civil War to this day, it is that you cannot win a fight without a gun. Just ask some Indians if you can find any. I rest my case. You can call it cowardice if you must; I call it the only way to survive. I reasoned that I would need a handgun for backup and I resolved to take one of the shotguns too. I sat on a stool and loaded the weapons, then filled my pockets with extra rounds. There, I was tooled up and ready for the final assault, the revised plan that did not require world domination, the truncated edition. No matter, one should always salute the small victories, for they are milestones on the path to glory that ends in nirvana. I pottered up the stairs from the basement and back to the office with my bounty. I strolled, taking in the serenity of the moment, the victor awaiting his prize of delayed gratification. I slugged a third of a bottle of rum and felt it burn all the way down my throat, stinging my wounds and anaesthetising the pain as it welled in the gummy holes where teeth used to be. I did not think about anything much at all for I was God and what I decided was final. I did not think about the lives that were to be lost or tomorrow's children that would now never be. I did not dwell upon the hopes and dreams that would shatter and die when I pulled the trigger or swung the blade. It was of no consequence to me. The pain of past traumas and disappointments that mean so much to others and are nothing to anyone else; futile emotions carried on the wind. Those personal feelings, the loves lost or unrequited, so

221

all-consuming to their owners, a memento from the battle field imbuing a wisdom that can only come from experience and that I would wipe out of existence without a flicker of recognition. I did not have a care in the world for them because I cared only for myself. Someone had to and if I was to be the only one, well, there could be no room for anyone else. I must compensate for my neglect, nay, I must overcompensate. For the truth of the matter is that I had no mind for anyone because I was crying for the boy trapped inside me. The boy wanted revenge and he wanted it immediately. He did not care from where it came or who paid the debt. And even though I knew all of this, I still did not care at all. An unholy empty space sat inside my heart where childhood dreams used to be. They were stolen by people who should have known better. That is why I could never blame myself for anything at all. I was beyond reproach. I was lost. You won't like me now, if you ever did, for I have no remorse and I don't care about that either.

I poured a small amount of rum into a glass for Jim and placed it by his side and one for Bronson too, hell, why not. I invited them to toast me and I toasted them. Then I checked my weapons; hand gun, check; shotgun, check; samurai sword, check. I used the sword as a walking stick and bid the boys farewell.

Strolling out of the office, I poked my head round by the laundry room. It was empty so I went on through into the sitting room with a jaunty step. I clicked my heels dragging the sword behind me now. The sound resonated around the empty room with its high ceilings. On through to the kitchen, Dirk sat at the table. He was playing chess by himself, paying no attention to the rules. He broke off from his concentration and looked up at me, his lips pursed in a puzzled fashion. He saluted. I returned it. Then he made an illegal move with the bishop. He didn't even notice my bloodied appearance or the fact that I was carrying around an arsenal. I suppose he thought that was the kind of nuts things I might ordinarily be inclined to do to pass the time. Then there is the small point of his stunning stupidity to factor into the equation. I passed right by him, still dragging the sword, making an awful noise and took out one of his pawns with the invisible player's queen. That would screw his strategy up for sure and keep him occupied for hours, trying to think of a comeback. He raised an eyebrow in deferential acceptance and continued to plot his next ridiculous move. Out onto the back porch I went and round the side of the ranch to the outhouse. There was no sign of Spangler but the outhouse door was open and the cops were gone. I stuck my head round that door too, it was empty. A trail ran out through the grounds and into the bushes as though something large had been dragged along leaving its imprint in the dust. All clear then. I would have to find someone to kill before I lost the urge. I would look upstairs and if there was nothing to slay up there I might just as well make do with the idiot Dirk as consolation.

I ascended as only a deity can, floating up the stairs as though carried in levitation on the air. I was silent and calm and contented in myself but ready to fight my evil foes with fearsome aggression and unwavering resolve at the flick of an internal switch. There would be no absolution gifted to them with a delicate hand. The degradation of their mortality was complete. I must restore the delicate balance of the universe by putting those cretins out of their misery. Now where were they hiding, wondered I. Where were they keeping their despicable bodies, intertwined no doubt in disgusting human affection, embracing, joined together as one. I felt the bile rise up into my mouth. I must teach them a lesson, those dirty, sullied, indecent monsters beyond redemption; those reprehensible, immoral beings with animalistic temperaments without the acumen to rise above their primal instincts. I had not surrendered myself to such base compulsions. I am made of richer materials, honour, integrity and the virtue in godliness and saintliness all rolled into one higher conscious. I existed beyond the binds of human craving, misinformed as it so regularly is. I am not bitter, I am righteous. I am justified. I am correct to the finest minute detail. Where are the shameful sots?! I scurried along the corridor for I knew the last place they would be hiding was in Gene's room. I scampered between the rooms along the corridor thrusting open the doors one by one. Each banged as I threw it open and peeped inside with my shotgun, pistol and sword hidden behind me.

'Eugene,' I sung in a high pitched voice like a choir girl. 'I say, Eugene, come hither, I am prepared to leave. Won't you join me?'

I smashed open the next door.

'Here Genie, Genie, Genie. If I rub the magic lamp will you come out and play? Can we all have a wish?'

I scurried behind the door and hid out, just in case he was in the adjoining bathroom. I crept toward the door.

'Do you know what my wish would be, were you to be so kind as to grant me one?' I crept. 'My wish would be for you to *die!*'

I leaped into the bathroom, stopping abruptly at the edge of the bath and ripped back the shower curtain. Nothing! My face contorted. This was a tiresome game. No. Be nice Steves, be nice. You cannot attract the attentions of others with rage for they will run away. I regained my jaunty composure begrudgingly, grunting in bass tones and then restoring my angelic voice. From Angel to Satan, serenading high pitch taunts and then issuing guttural grunts in time, eyes like slits, head thrust forward, shoulders hunched.

The next room was empty and the next. I pursed my lips and my nose twitched with growing anger. As I tried to conceal it in my voice, so it revealed itself upon my face. The blood was caked and dry now. It no longer oozed from my mouth but sat congealed on my chin and up my cheeks. I must not let him see my personage before I cornered him or the ruse would be up for sure. Why was he hiding from me anyway? What did he think I was going to do, kill him? I smirked to myself, for there was no one else to smirk at.

Room by room I went until I had seen them all and each one was as empty as the next. My temper was heated to a rolling boil. I sneered. Then I smirked. I would find those insolents if it were my last task on Earth before I rose up to the heavens. I got down onto my knees to sniff the trail but my senses had been compromised by too much rum and tobacco. They had rendered my sinuses incapable of snorting even the finest line of cocaine, much less sniffing out the human scent. I winced, the smell of sodden bodies, bloated and dripping with per-spiration through ungodly acts; I, nauseated. All the while there was some commotion going on outside. The emus were unsettled. Perhaps there was a twister on the way. I peeped out of the window as I descended the stairs. The sky was swelling with grey and ominous clouds but they were here for me. A signal that I must execute the job, that a higher power had sanctioned it, that higher power was me.

'Tuck, tuck, tuck, tuck, tuck.' I smacked my tongue against the top of my mouth like Mom used to do when she wanted the cat to come inside and as Dirk did to round up the chickens. I paid him a visit in the kitchen as I walked on through to the east wing since it was the only wing we had. Eugene had not been summoned by my animal coaxing methods. Strangely neither had Spangler.

'Boy?'

'Yes God?'

'Have you seen Spangler or Eugene?'

'Nah, I ain't, sir. I've been sat 'ere losing this 'ere game o' chess. Can't figure out what a person should do with this queen. It sure is easier when you're only playin' with yourself and you can cheat and everythang.'

'A wonder your mother didn't name you Dimwit instead of Dirk. I expect the meaning of the word would be lost on her as well.' Dirk looked confused, it was his natural state. I scowled at him and spun around to leave.

'Oh, wait a minute. I did see Spangler a while ago. He was headin' out to the coop, came in for a paring knife, said somethin' about cookin' a nice plump chicken for dinner before we leave. He looked a bit crazy but then he always looks crazy, don't he.'

Had the degenerate no eyes? I was covered in death and he didn't even notice, yet he thought Spangler to be insane. My God. It occurred to me that my brainwashing techniques had worked on somebody! I was elated inside. I stared at him madly right up to his nose, I stuck out my tongue. He acted as though this was normal. Brilliant work squire, there was no way I could kill him now. He was too stupid to be bluffing, yet he had just bought himself a passport to the rest of his life, in servitude to me admittedly but a life all the same. He didn't even know it. Perhaps I could come to regard his stupidity as an aptitude. This had certainly brightened up the proceedings. I was full of vim and vigour for slaying once again. My attitude had been restored to its former wonder and cheerful abundance. This man had some brilliantly camouflaged feathers in his cap. It would only add to my hubris. Oh joy and elation. Thunder clattered outside and quite unseasonable rain began to thrash down from the bubbling clouds above thus creating a thick electrified atmosphere that made me feel free and alive. Something 'other' was at work. The conditions were right for Armageddon.

'Do you like my toys, Dirk?' said I, sweeping aside my robe and revealing my sword to him. He was back to concentrating on his game. He looked up only with his eyes. He nodded as though a crazy man stood before him with a colossal sword was not a threat at all. He smiled innocently.

'And what about Eugene, have you seen him? Have you seen Kathryn? Have you seen them together?'

'Mmmm . . . nope. Haven't seen 'em for hours. Last time I saw the fat man he was tryin' to get into your office. Think there was somethin' in there he wanted. I'm not sure. I don't want to get him into no trouble or nuthin.'

'Don't you fear about that my little friend. Why would Eugene be in trouble? Has he done anything to be in trouble for?'

'Ummm . . . Dunno.' Now he looked uneasy.

'Did you mean to say that he was trying to leave, without actually saying it? Did you see him trying to get away without saying goodbye? There'll be a reward in it for you if you tell me. What would you like?'

'I'd like a horse,' he smiled, 'and I'd like a tropical fish . . . and a tank . . . with some plastic coral in it . . . and one of those lil' chests.'

'Why, I could go out right away and buy you a thousand of those. Now, tell me what Eugene has been doing whilst I have been away.'

'Shouldn't really . . . '

'Oh, come on. We'll play it like it's a guessing game shall we, to make it more fun. Like the car games.'

'OK.' He cheered a touch. Damn retards and their inhibited brains. I might be here forever with this ludicrous pastime.

'Can I have a puppy too?'

'Yes, yes, yes, you can have whatever you like.'

'And a new scoot?'

'Oh for Christ's sake, yes, boy. You can have them all. You are starting to make God angry and you know what happens then, don't you.'

'It thunders.'

'Well it might begin with thunder . . . '

'But it's already thundering.'

I sighed deeply. I wished to strangle him to death and broil his bones but I managed to keep it down. It was hard work indeed. My face was showing the strain of keeping the anger inside.

'Was Gene touching Kathryn?' I said it firmly and slowly because it conjured up the vilest of imagery.

'Might've.'

'Was Gene packing all of his things into the truck so that he could run away from us?'

'Might've.'

For Christ's sake.

'Was Gene trying to kidnap Charles Bronson?'

'Might've.'

'Did you actually see *anything* or are you using this ruse as leverage for material gain? You are in danger of forfeiting the fish if you don't tell me what you know, boy. I know damn well the fish is your first choice so you may as well speak up. The clock is ticking and you're running out of time.'

'Need the fish. I'll rat. He was touchin' Kathryn, in fact he was touchin' her whilst he was packin' the things and he was trying to steal Bronson whilst he was packin', whilst he was touchin' Kathryn. He was doin' all those things at once, yes, sir. Can I have two fish now or they'll get lonely?'

'OK, two fish. If they eat each other don't blame me.'

'But what I always wanted was an aquarium tank like in the zoo so I can feed 'em and work on the flyin' fish pool so I can see them soar and everybody will be amazed how great my fish are. So, I'm gonna tell you what else he was a doin'.'

'There's more treachery. Could there possibly be more?' I leaned in. 'Unburden yourself, boy.' I commanded it.

'He went out with a spade just as soon as you done got home. He was watchin' you come back in but it was dark see, so he couldn't really see anythang but he knew it was you alright. Kathryn gave him the all clear. Anyways, as soon as you got in your office there, he took a torch and set out. I dunno where he went but he came back all wet with a big dirty package and took it straight to the great hall where he done been hidin' out 'til he bolts it. He's been runnin' round the house avoidin' you since you came a lookin' for him. As soon as you went out the kitchen door he comes runnin' through, when you comes back in he goes runnin' out again. Every time havin' a go at that lock on your office door. Put me off my game. I guess Bronson means a lot to him, don't he?'

I thought hard. I though long, I though hard and long. Jim was trying to dig something up when I extricated him from his ruinous existence. It had to be a drop, maybe drugs and Eugene went to finish off the job. I had forgotten all about it in my haste. No, for that would mean that they were all working together, in cahoots, apart from Dirk and Spangler that is. I wouldn't trust those loose cannons either. This one was spilling the beans all over the place for a fucking fish. My, my, my, the betrayal ran deeper than I had ever thought feasible in a millions years of skulduggery. I had underestimated his fraudulence as he had underestimated my fortitude. I would scalp the man and after I had scalped him I would dine with his lady on his entrails. Now I had a payload to collect as well as a bevy of would-be defectors to kill. I must seize what was rightfully mine and let it be cocaine I prayed again, this time to the god of narcotics. I would only indulge in one snifter before I sold the rest on for three times its usual street value on the promise of life-prolonging properties, an elixir of youth with a stiff little kick. I would go back to New York and sell it to society types or to aging film stars in LA I would make trillions.

I digressed in my flight of fancy for a short time but pulled myself back from dream land. The weight of duty was upon my shoulders, the harsh reality of the situation kicked in and goaded me into action; the finality with which justice must be dealt with a strong hand and a polished sword. I stroked my metal instrument of vengeance. I adored it. We would go places together and we would be accompanied by several pounds of the finest white powder Columbia could bestow. Now my sword was my only friend, the only thing on which I could rely apart from my wit and cunning. Mother was nowhere, so I had even counted her out of my entourage. Whether she would present herself in future was anyone's guess. I was not willing to rely on life's ambiguities, what ifs or maybes.

Good thing I had upped the ante and locked my door seventeen times instead of four. Gene would never get in even if he charged at it using his body as a battering ram. The only way in was the conventional route and I had the keys in my underpants. Fat sot of hell and damnation, he was still physically repulsive. Our lady was blatantly scraping the bottom of the barrel with this one. Dirk was staring at me awaiting a response. I decided not to give him any because this allowed me to have power over him and showed him I was the boss.

'Right boy, I have a job for you and it carries with it much responsibility. Do you think you are capable of that?'

'Oh sure, God.'

'Good sport. Now, I will need you to go and sit in the truck. I will need you to keep guard. If anyone, and I mean anyone comes anywhere near it, I want you to shoot them with your air rifle but let me make one thing crystal clear; this directive does not include me. Do you understand?'

'Yup, got my gun, gonna take my chess too.'

'Do not leave the vehicle, no matter what happens. Do you

hear me? Otherwise you will incur my wrath and that is a bad thing. We don't want Eugene getting away.'

Dirk saluted and gathered his chess from the kitchen table. Walking slowly and surely so as not to disturb any of the pieces balancing on the board, it took him at least a minute just to reach the kitchen door. His tongue stuck out the side of his mouth in concentration and his eyes flickered up and down, the brain groaning under the arduous toil as he tried to harness elusive spatial perception. This guy was never going to be able to take anyone out with his pretend gun, not even from close quarters. I couldn't believe I was about to trust this retard with anything at all but at present it was the only choice I had, my not being able to be in two places at once and that he appeared to be the only acolyte who knew his place in the pecking order.

I waited five whole minutes for him to reach the truck. I predicted that his balancing act would make the forty-seven second journey approximately six and a half times as long as it should have been, and it did. As soon as I heard the driver's door bang shut, I swivelled on those snakeskins and made like fury to the great hall with my arsenal at hand and a heart heaving with vitriol. Ready for the fight with my fat disloyal foe was I; my pasty rival, I would gut him. I was a one-man stampede on a mission. Now where was that fool. He couldn't hide himself away for long in his glowing lemon jerkin. I would see him coming a mile away, his garment emitting a radiant glow from dark corners of the hall. Yes, he would be cowering in a crevice for sure. He hadn't the gumption to do anything other than run away. He would never admit his treachery. He would merely pretend it didn't exist. Only committing random acts of unfaithfulness behind my back, worse still, he would send a woman to do his dirty work. I would crown him!

I made it to the heavy oak doors of the hall and collected my anger into one seething ball. Like a superhero does as he is getting ready to launch his personal power onto the villain in spectacular fashion, so I allowed mine to amass inside. I felt huge again. I felt empowered. I felt like God. Prepare for the deity Steves to arrive, my expectant masses. He is here in his most evil incarnation. Come hither friends for I am lying in wait and any moment now I shall pounce. Run for your lives! I heard canned applause in my head.

I stood for a moment, one hand on each door and blew them open with such force that they almost came back to take me clean out for the count but I was fast as a gazelle and jumped back in the nick of time. That would have foiled me for certain. Taken out by a moment of foolishness; my pride would never have recovered from that. All was silent within. All was dark and eerie. I went for the light switches but none of them worked. Gene had cut the wires. Devious brute, concocting plans of his own accord, how dare he. Some shafts of light cast down from the stained glass windows above. It was all I had to work with so I attuned my eyes to the best night vision I could muster. My mother always told me to eat my carrots and yet again she was right. I feared a surprise attack. He had obviously made contingency for my arrival. Yet, perhaps on the flip side, I had caught him unawares. Who knew, I would soon find out. I went low. It's the best tactic unless the fiend had rigged up tripwires, then I'd be screwed. I couldn't see a thing. I unsheathed my sword. Perhaps if I could catch the shafts of light on its blade I could reflect them in front of me and light my way. The same premise as burning bugs with the sun rays reflected through a magnifying glass, as we did as boys. I shuffled around on the floor. Gene's belongings were stacked high ready to be loaded into the truck. If he wasn't loading up and he wasn't in here, he certainly hadn't gained entry to my office, then where the hell was he? No sooner had I thought it than my question was answered. The doors came open slowly and in he crept, followed by his odious girlfriend. I shuffled quietly behind his haul of belongings. The bastard had packed up my golfing irons, I could see them poking from the pile. This enraged me even though I had never used them and had no intention of doing so. In he came with more bounty.

'OK. I think that's everything,' came the whisper from the dissenter. 'We should go while Steves isn't around. He'll be back soon wherever he is and I don't want to be around for that. Crazy son of a bitch.'

Motherfucker! I'd never heard the man swear in his life. He had clearly been storing up his lifetime supply of cussing out for me. His disloyalty became more serious by the second. I wanted to pounce but I had to bite my lip and bide my time. I wanted to catch him from behind. This was not indicative of cowardice you understand, for even I cannot fight two able persons at once. The greatest minds of all have made the astute observation; that the knowing of one's limitations and the working of them to the best advantage is the key to success. That is the kind of man that wins the war. Not the freaking idiot who cries 'charge' as he bolts it over the trenches and gets shot to smithereens.

'OK, hold me for a moment,' Kathryn whispered. They embraced. How vile. I signalled the puking gesture even though no one was there to appreciate it.

'You take these light things. I'll take the trunks, one at a time. Make sure you don't make any noise now, my darling, quiet as a mouse does it and soon we will be free. Back to New York, I can't wait.'

'Have you got the package, Gene?'

'Yes I have it, sweetness. It's safely tucked into my belt.'

'What about Bronson?'

'I'll have to go in through the window. I think he's barricaded the door.'

Had Eugene possessed even a speck of guile he would have armed himself to the hilt for my return, but as history had proved time and time again, he had not the courage of his own conviction. I should have been sat braced with my back into a corner and a loaded cannon between my thighs, pointed directly at the door, were I him. I would have been ready. I would have seen me coming before I even had the genesis of the thought myself. His anal organisation had led him to run overtime with this pernickety packing and all of this covert skulking around was a pitiful sight to behold. What the hell was he going to do when he ran into me with his hands full with a trunk of kitchenware? I felt so sorry for him that I almost wanted to give him a head start but if he got outside I'd only have to deal with Dirk swinging into action shooting ball bearings all over the place. He'd probably take out one of my eyes. Besides, two dimwits were more than enough for my patience to handle at any one time. Anyway, it would screw up his chess. I watched them leave the room and gave out my most fervent sigh. I was just about to emerge from my hideout when Gene came back in, padding tentatively. He was obviously looking for something forgotten and absolutely necessary for the first load. That would be the keys to the truck then, no doubt. As he slipped back into the room on his lonesome, I quietly slipped behind him and dropped the metal bar into the lock position. Clunk. I guess he knew his big plans had been scotched now. I stood by the door, a centurion, bearing my sword in the half light.

'Good evening squire.' I said it drawn and slow, deep earthy tones given resonance by the great hall's lofty height. Gene daren't even turn around, frozen mid-scamper.

'Going somewhere, are we? Looks like the game is up, old boy. You didn't think you could outwit me did you, poor soul, poor, poor misguided soul. Bless you, lady.'

There I stood obscuring his only exit route. My legs spread wide; robe spread wider, my sword gleaming, shotgun in hand pointed right at the back of his dome-like head. He couldn't see me yet for he was too scared to move but he could see me in his mind and the reality was much more sinister. I walked back and forth by the door, at my post. A whimper omitted from his quivering lips. He shook uncontrollably like a wet puppy left out in the cold. Bless that man for he made me feel as strong as an ox. His meekness spurned me to even greater heights of ego and arrogance. I had peaked at the summit of my hubris and felt dizzy with superiority. Nothing could break my illusion for I was riding high on the crest of power, rising up before him. I put away my gun for I would not be in need of it immediately. He would not challenge me. Look at this wretch, thought I. He couldn't bruise a soft fruit much less make any impression on my person. Fool. I watched him shrivel before my very eyes and I relished every moment of it with sheer delight. To toss him a crumb of promise I assumed a jovial attitude. I would toy with him for it would make superb entertainment and I had been without merriment for some time.

'So my good steed, make yourself comfortable for we have much to discuss, not least your impending departure. I do believe you were about to forget to say goodbye to me, were you not?'

Gene stood up straight and turned to face me slowly. I could see the pearls of sweat glistening in beads on his big fat furrowed brow. He presented his hankerchief and began to blot the moisture. He squinted and bent forward, presumably to get a better look at my fucked up face.

'Good God. What happened to you?'

'A tussle with Jim, nothing more.' I wafted my hand in a gesture of flippancy. 'I might ask you the same for you appear to be covered in muck. How might that have happened? Did you fall into a flower bed perchance?'

'It's nothing to bother yourself with Steves. Will you let me go?'

'I think we need to have a chat to clear the air you might say before you abandon our cause like a big dirty rat jumping from a stinking ship. Relax yourself.'

He leaned back on the pile of his belongings and eyed me like a hawk. I took a step forward. He shirked backward as far his crud would allow.

'Is that a sword?'

'Ah!' I unfurled it and brandished it thus. 'Yes Gene, this is my new best friend. Say hello to him. I have named him Herman.'

'You have named your sword?'

'Of course, doesn't every man name his sword?'

Gene tutted. I must always bring everything down to its basest element condescended his inner voice. I could hear his thoughts without the need for utterance.

'What are you planning on doing with it?' he gulped.

'Oh, this and that. I thought I might dress up in regalia for your leaving parade, make a show of it. You know me, always a showman.'

I could see his fears melting away. Ha ha. See him under-estimating the Steves for the hundredth time. It would serve me well.

'You wouldn't do anything with it anyway. Look at the mess you've got us into. All your promises have come to nothing. This place is a sham and you've spent all our money on guns and emus and security systems that we didn't need in the first place. Spangler brought me the bill for the armoury. A rocket launcher that I've never even seen let alone used cost me ten thousand dollars. You've bankrupted me Steves!'

'Man, they don't depreciate like Hyundais. We can sell it on.'

'Who to?! Who do you know that's in urgent need of a rocket launcher . . . for the love of . . . There's not exactly a ready-made market for it! Anyway, what the hell were you planning to use it for?'

'Alien invasion.'

He was speechless. However, should the extraterrestrials come, we would be well able to take them to task.

'And . . . and . . . I don't even understand you anymore. You talk funny and you're insane. Nothing makes sense any more. You're more dangerous than New York ever was 'cause you nearly got us caught for busting out a criminal and he's a murderer too! We're going to do life for this Steves and now you're holding us up. Even the dog ran away already 'cause he had more sense than you and the cops are going to be here any moment and we'll all get put on death row but you'll get to go to a mental home 'cause you're nuts! And we'll all be dead. And it'll be your fault.' He gasped for breath.

'You're breaking my heart Gene, you really are.' I mused in a fashion of pure nonchalance, shaking my head. 'Besides, I am above the law. Very strange that you should say that though my friend, for that's just the kind of monologue Jim foisted upon me without my permission. You two haven't been colluding have you? Hmmm . . . putting your heads together behind my back, making secret plans. A pact perhaps?'

Gene shook his head furiously. No he would never do that.

'That's fortunate because were that the case, I would certainly have to kill you and your arsonist girlfriend. Did she tell you about her murky past, Gene? Well, did she? She likes to play with matches you know.'

'I know about it Steves. I know it all and I'll tell you something. I'll never let you come between us, never. She's paid her dues. She told me about prison, how it almost killed her. We have no secrets.'

'And what about those innocents, lying in their beds, sweet dreams running through their heads and all of a sudden BOOM!!! Their skins flayed off and they're winging their way up to heaven.'

Gene shuddered and looked at the floor.

'That was a long time ago, people change.'

'Do they now, do they indeed? Then there's no need to be afraid of Jim then, is there? Or Spangler.'

'I'm not afraid of Spangler. He's just an old eccentric.'

'Oh, you stupid oaf.' I grinned. 'Spangler's wanted in three states for mutilating his victims, for actually chopping them up into tiny pieces and dumping them in trash cans from here to Timbuktu. He's a serial killer, you asshole. At one time I do believe they thought he might be the Original Night Stalker but that's just hearsay.'

Gene's eyes widened.

'You let me sit in the car with him, eat from the same table as him, sleep in the room next to him! He could've hurt Kathryn. He could have done anything. He could have had a go at you! You're still just flesh and bones like the rest of us Steves, you're not immortal. You're the craziest son of a god damn bitch I've ever met! Apart from Spangler maybe. You put all our lives at risk, for what? So you could have a power trip and pretend you're God.'

'Kathryn could have combusted you whilst you were asleep. You didn't seem to be too concerned about that. Oh and I can assure you one hundred per cent, there is no pretence involved in my claims to godliness.'

Gene looked to the ceiling in despair.

'Sanctimonious prick,' he muttered it under his breath. He would lose an ear for that.

'So, will you be leaving presently or would you like to say goodbye to Jim. He is languishing in my office.'

Gene looked confused. He didn't know that I knew about their little deal to steal the stash and run away without me, so he was puzzled as to my claims about cosy drinks with Jim.

'Yes, we were having a little toast before you all leave. I think you should join us. Come, come, let's go.'

A small light bulb flickered on in his mind and I knew it. He wouldn't struggle or try to make a run for it. This was the perfect ruse for him to gain entry to my office where Bronson still stood facing the wall. Once again my wit was of an infinitely higher caste than his. I was aware of his determination to steal Bronson and he didn't know that I knew that either and I wasn't about to tell him.

Outside the great hall Kathryn had started knocking rather politely at the door; afraid to test my famously short patience for fear that I might take retribution upon Gene. I ushered him out hurriedly, my sword on full display, leaving our lady feverish and useless in our wake and recoiled at the full horror of my disfigured visage.

'Remain in your current position Kathryn.' I instructed, 'For I, I mean, *we,* shall return.' I skipped off down the corridor prodding Gene with my sheathed sword along the way.

We remained at my office door for a few moments as I foraged in my undergarments for the hefty bunch of keys.

'I'll have it in a flash,' said I. Gene didn't take his eyes off me. Feigning courage now was he. He would see the error of his ways. We gained access to the hub after I had negotiated all seventeen locks.

'Close your eyes Gene. I have a surprise for you.'

He did as he was told. Compliance was the only way for him to ensure entry without a scuffle. I guided him in and set him directly in front of Jim, placing a shot of rum in the old boy's hand for our toast. I poured myself some and shone my most brilliant smile.

'You may look now.'

He dropped his drink in terror. Glass shattered all over the floor but I kept wearing my best smile all the same.

'Do you like my art? It's a piece from my black period. Actually I'm quite proud of it. The tones of grey and noir, it has a haunting quality, wouldn't you say?' I fingered my chin. My brilliant smile remained, though Gene's inertia was ruining my mood a touch.

He started to groan but he didn't move an inch.

'You really should get closer, it's an interactive piece. Touch it. The textures really are superb. Flaky in places, molten in others, a dusty feature exhibits itself on the surface but if you press down lightly with your index finger, I think you'll find it's soft inside. It might even give up some juices if you're really lucky. Now that's what I call a multi-sensory experience. I am really a superb artist.' I poked it for good measure, stooping over it, peering up at Eugene transfixed in horror, staring at Jim.

'So kind of Jim to donate his body to art. I am going to start a collection and I think you'll find that your girlfriend will fit in perfectly.'

I dashed at the door and bolted out dropping the locks behind me. Eugene had not the time to move his legs as he was rooted to the spot. I had one catch secured before he could protest. I locked a couple more of the padlocks so I felt it would hold and stalked off to find the lady. Gene hammered and shouted from inside as I went. How satisfying.

The lady was still waiting where she was told to, in the corridor by the great hall, looking as submissive as ever, an easy target. I got right up close to her, sniffing her neck. She looked petrified and disgusted as I invaded her personal space. So close was I, that I could feel her breath like dew on my shredded lips. She could smell the foulness of mine billowing out all over her décolletage and up her neck to find her nostrils.

'Mmmm . . . I say madame, you smell deliciously of musk.' I spitted a little, revelling in her revulsion. I enjoyed her fright. I loved it. I would invade her. I would conquer. I had harnessed my insanity now so I could do whatever I pleased and it didn't count. I was aware of my moral corrosion but I would make an exception for this one. She was too demure to be true and she needed to be taught a lesson from the book of Steves. I slithered around her neck to the other side and sniffed once more.

' . . . and top notes of Lily of the Valley, I do believe.'

I liked her slim, graceful neck so I licked it with my yellow tongue. A string of saliva formed as I moved away slowly, like an umbilical cord connecting us. It grew thinner and thinner and broke off, left hanging from my mouth with traces of blood suspended inside, making it pink instead of clear as it should have been. I formed a toothless and bloody wide-mouthed grin. Her lips quivered as if she were about to cry. I hoped she would. I took her hand softly in mine and studied it. She saw my brown nails, earth buried deep underneath. She saw that some were missing, the blood that was all over where it had seeped from the wounds, dried now. Hers was dainty and porcelain and her fingers were long and elegant. The skin as soft as any child's. I brushed it against my cheek hard and slow, the stubble grating against that beautiful hand, hurting it. I held it there and looked directly into her watering eyes. She shook her head from side to side and flinched but she couldn't harness the words as my blood-flooded eyes stared at her menacingly. I knew what a sight it must have been. I could see the fear in her eyes. I grunted. I should have liked to have danced with her but I had never been much of a mover and there was no time for foreplay. I jerked her arm so hard it must have felt as though it would rip from the socket. I dragged her into the great hall. The door banged closed behind. With all the might that I possessed I slammed her onto the ground. Her head banged down hard onto the floor with a pleasant crack. What more reward did a man need. Oh, much more. I smiled at her invitingly. How could she refuse me, really, how could she.

I advanced from my lofty position, leering over her as she lay half concussed on the cold floor. No sooner had she regained her senses than she began wriggling away on her elbows, shuffling across the tile like a worm. Her head must have been splitting in half. There was a small cut above her forehead where she had impacted on the floor. I doubted she had clarity of vision but she certainly was a fighter, even though her struggle was futile. I clambered over her, stood tall with my legs straddled on either side as she continued her pitiful bid for escape.

'Lady, you know what your problem is, don't you.' I followed her slowly, still straddling her all the way. 'You are a woman with no discerning, no taste and for that you must be punished. I think that in the fullness of time you will come to see that you deserve this. I did not invite you here so you could join Eugene's harem. I invited you so that you may worship at my altar and you, my dear, have sinned. You have defied the most integral mores of the Empire. Like Eve, you are corrupt in the mind and of the body and you have colluded with the Judas himself. Do mark my words though dear, once you have paid your debt by the flesh, Eugene shall pay ten times over for I shall let him see the spoils of my wrath before I lop off every appendage from his putrid, bloated body. Do you have any final words for me before I dole you your justice?'

I didn't give her time for an answer, for even if she had one to give I was not interested in it. I grabbed her hair by its puritan bun and wrenched her up from the floor. That hair-style deserved to be messed up, it was so severe that it made her look twenty years older than she was. Out it came in my hands, a small bunch of it. The rest tumbled down. I pushed her back onto the lectern behind us and smashed her full in the face with my balled fist. She squealed an almost undetectable squeal. Her nose began to bleed.

'Now look what you made me do!' I grunted. 'You and your subliminal siren manipulations, demonic woman. Come on lady, won't you give us a scream? Even in your final moments are you not able to manage a sound? I shall make you sorry you shunned my amour, for now you have forced me to commit one of my own cardinal sins, for which even I may never forgive myself. You have driven me to strike a lady and for that there can be no recompense.'

I balled up my fist once again, ready to take another mighty blow. It didn't make any difference how many times I hit her now. I had crossed the line so I may as well continue until the job was done. I couldn't have her struggling free as I deflowered her; I had designs of putting her out for the count. I was about to let rip and as I drew it back I gazed at my fist and then focused in on that little mortified face. I zoned in, like a sniper targeting his victim through the viewfinder of his rifle. She was within my sights. As I pulled back my arm for the assault, a movement in the corner of my eye broke the concentration. Although my vision was not all it should be, gummed up with congealed blood as my lashes were, I detected a breach of security. I caught sight of it. It was Mother, back from the other realm. What the hell was she doing? She gesticulated wildly, crossing her palms back and forth in a halt gesture and then pointed, pointed, stabbing the air with her finger in the international signal for 'behind you'. Oh! I ducked as quickly as I could. Down came a mighty sword from behind. It missed Kathryn by inches and clanged against the lectern sending Eugene juddering to keep control of it. The fool, had he been any closer, he would have bisected his own girlfriend. I rolled across the floor, compromised by the length of my sword, still sheathed. As I recuperated for no more than a split second, I twirled round in the graceful and nimble style of the ninja and took my place to stand face to face with Eugene, a face-off. He was clearly moved by the close call but he had to stand his ground. I understood it. He had to honour his woman and claw back some self-respect. If this would be his way of doing it then so be it. I would fight him to the death and then I would fight him some more.

'Ruuuunnn!' He shrieked at Kathryn whilst all the time keeping his eyes squarely on me. She did just that, out of the great hall she fled, the cowardess.

We bore fixed gazes at each other. Who would be the first to flinch, it would not be I. It was clear that this man was not about to give up until I had been despatched, if he was capable of such a feat. That blow was intended to end me, it meant business. The pussyfooting around was over.

'You fool, you almost killed her and you didn't even give me a chance to rape her first you rascal. You are underhand, you coward, you are two peas in a pod.'

We circled like fencers do, jabbing the air every few seconds for effect. I think you'll find if you are ever in a similar situation you will do the same. It is theatre, darling, and there is no better time for that than at the final curtain.

Gene reached down to his belt and loosened it a notch, his sword still raised to attention. It was inhibiting his movement which was already moderately inhibited by his sturdy consti- tution and the huge parcel of what I presumed to be cocaine down his pants. It signified his readiness to fight.

'I will not let you rip apart my life any more, Steves. If you won't let us go I will just have to force you to.'

'I should like to see it. How did you get out of my office, you fraud?'

'I climbed out the window, you asshole. You can't do any- thing right Steves. If you really wanted Kathryn all to yourself you really ought to have locked the freaking hall door.'

'Right you are squire, I was overcome with desire.' I laughed.

'Well I'm going to protect my family. I'm going to . . . '

'With child!?' He nodded. 'You! She is to spawn the seed of Satan's little helper! Pah! I doubt you could get it up.'

He jabbed at me. His lips were quivering again. This bravado must really be taking it out of him. It was a virgin attempt and if I didn't know him better I might be quite convinced. We continued to circle. I tippy-toed around like a pro.

'You low-down, fucked-up asshole. Could you get any more warped?'

'Certainly, sir,' I taunted. 'I already have. You don't think a master can become so attuned to his game without practice, do you?' I jabbed back at him, my arm stretched out to the side. 'Do you remember your beloved Nancy, Nurse Nancy and her sticky end? That was my work. I'm rather proud of that one.'

'Euurrrrrgggghhhhhhhh!!!' He lunged at me. I leapt backward to avoid the blade. He would have to do better than that.

'You son of a bitch!' He had that that look in his eye. The look that said 'I'll kill you', it came when I announced I might have my way with his paramour too.

'There, there, that's not all. I would have killed your mother too if she hadn't expired before I got the chance. Hideous woman, hideous, I can see where you got your looks.'

'Euuurrghhhh!!!!!' He charged me again. This time I swiped at him with my sword, the superior of the two, they clattered together and we postured once more, still circling as we went. I sneered.

'And the dirty immoral fat bastard back at the apartment. I did away with the whore too. I forget where I left her corrupt remains.' Gene looked as though he may vomit. I hoped he wouldn't splatter my shoes. 'You know, Jim was never a murderer. You didn't know that did you, Gene. He didn't do a god damn thing to those old folks. That was a lie of mine.'

'Why the hell was he in prison then? And what the fuck did he ever do to deserve what you did to him. What the fuck did you do to him? I can't even tell. He's so fucked I didn't even know who it was until you told me. You killed him ten times over and then desecrated his body. If I ever get out of here alive, I'm gonna see that you rot in that nut house. You're worse than a snuff movie. You're more than insane. You're demented.'

248

His voice was determined always as we fought, as his brain fought to internalise something that it couldn't even begin to conceive. Shock had set in.

'He was in prison on my behalf. He was better suited to such an establishment than I. I am too enlightened to be incarcerated. My genius must have the freedom of expression.'

'Incarcerated?! You should be castrated and then shot. States would bring back the death penalty for you.'

I smiled. He was right. They should change the laws of entire states for me. I was that important and of course they should name the new statute after me. Perhaps those murderers could go to 'Steves Row'. I would be writing to the governor in due course with my suggestions.

Deadlock. He was tiring already. We continued our posturing.

'You mean, you were trying to make out that I was a kiddy-fiddler right there in front of Kathryn, when all the time you're a serial killer. You fucking maniac. You were trying to break us apart.'

'Well observed, sparring partner.'

'And all that time you knew that I wasn't a kiddy-fiddler at all.'

'I never said that.'

'You knew it Steves, you bastard. You know how they hounded me after the police came to question me. You know I didn't do it. You know about the threats and whatever, just 'cause I like to keep myself to myself, that doesn't make me a paedophile.'

'It's the power of suggestion that counts, my fat friend.'

'And all the time too, you were making me feel bad about

249

my size but you knew I'd got that way because I couldn't take the shame. I was frightened to death someone was gonna come in the night and lynch me. Once you've been accused it doesn't just go away. People think there must be something weird about me anyway, just because they took me down to the station. You knew I only sat in at home and ate myself half to death to make myself feel better. To numb that awful pain, the stigma that followed me everywhere. There was no point in going anywhere at all. I had to hide. It was awful Steves. It was the worst time of my life and I confided in you and you stabbed me in the back.'

'I stab everyone in the back Gene, it's nothing personal.'

'Well now I'm going to do it to you and I'm going to do it properly this time.'

He flew at me. He hurled himself in my direction and our swords met each other. They clashed so violently I almost went spinning backward onto my ass but I managed to keep upright, just. He packed more pounds than I, so I had to be nimble. I held my arm strong and true and took another blow to the steel. I locked my arm straight for his attacks. He was much stronger than I thought but I had agility on my side. Once again he came, barely giving me time to right myself. We clashed from the right side and then the left over and over. I jumped around all over the place and he came after me at half the speed but with twice the power. Back and forth, back and forth, bash, smash, slicing the air. Then I spun round. He was two feet behind me. I had time for small flourishes but this was no longer the game I thought it might be. He was dangerous. I stabbed at the air. He followed me, pushing me backward but I managed always to dance out of the corners of the hall into which he was trying to force me. I felt I had the edge as long as I could keep out in the open. It was room for furtive manoeuvre that I needed more than any other means, I needed means of escape. I was in defence and he was in attack and that would never do. He was punishing my sword. Mine was thicker and wider than his but his was fine and tapered, sharp like a skewer. Conversation would slow him down.

'Wait!' I continued to pace backward, *en garde*.

'What for, your endurance giving in?'

'You must be joking, you flaccid member,' I jested. 'There is nothing I cannot endure except stupidity. It's a wonder I didn't give out years ago with you around. You dimwit.'

'Ha! Flaccid member, dimwit, you're full of compliments, Steves. Always putting other people down to make yourself feel better. Works, does it? Makes you feel big and clever? Does it help you to forget about your mother? No, 'cause she's still alive, isn't she?'

'I don't think so my friend. I think your pop psychology may have failed you there. I shot her brains out twenty-one years ago almost to the day. That was shortly after I blew a hole in my father's head.'

I swiped at him and missed. If this persisted any longer I would have to take out my handgun. Now he was pissing me off.

'You know what always puzzled me about you, Steves? You never once had a girlfriend the whole time I've known you. Not once. Yet you keep going on about how virile you are and how you're such a man and all this shit. And then you're trying to get it on with my lady. How could you do that? I may be fat but at least I have a soul and I can get some when I want to but

you, you never had a relationship in your life, did you Steves?'
Now he was smiling and I wanted him dead.

'That's right, isn't it? You never got it on, ever.'

'You better stop there, man, if you know what's good for you.'

'Always going on about how it's dirty and below you, because
you're too . . . what was it? Ah, because you're too virtuous to
dirty yourself with things like that. You're the freak, Steves.
You'd be a virgin too if it wasn't for your mother.'

Outside the clouds were giving up their all; thunder, lightning
and the rain came down so hard you could hardly see ten feet
before you. I had summoned the heavens to cash in on the
ambience of doom. This inhibited Spangler no end in his murderous pursuit. I was still fighting with Eugene. I was about to
forget that I had any scruples. He had mentioned the unmentionable. It is hard to recount as it burns a hole so deep in my
heart and my soul that it finally reminded me that I had ever
had either and then reminded me that they were both lost.
Kathryn was outside the great hall, sobbing and pacing and
not knowing whether her beau was dead or alive. She was
losing the will to be a decent and compassionate person as she
had promised herself all those years ago. The temporary madness that had afflicted itself so cruelly on her loving family, all
burned to a crisp. It would be so easy to give up those morals,
those pledges. Was it worth the loss to save her one and only
love or would it be the end of her to act upon her urges; the
moment she realised she had lost faith in her own ability to
control herself. Control had been her bedfellow for so long.
She might have to abandon it for a higher cause. A trade-off
that could send her slowly and silently mad if it were to come

to no avail, bringing back the memories of a past best left forgotten. She became quietly hysterical as she mulled it over. Any more time lost and she may find herself with a carcass instead of a future husband so she had better make her mind up soon. She cried tears that made her eyes puff up to a magnitude that rendered her unsightly by the conventions of modern beauty. She covered her face and cowered in the corridor. Maybe someone would come and save her from her own guilt. Perhaps if she embraced her Catholicism once more she would gain redemption. That would give her a licence to do whatever she liked so long as she repented.

Dirk remained in the truck unawares of the warfare inside. He sat in the cab with the radio turned on full blast, listening to his favourite team almost win the baseball, but not quite. He sulked. They never won anyway. He was still losing his game of chess. He managed to confuse himself so much that he now couldn't remember which side he was on, so he changed affiliations according to which side had just played the best move. Since he had made all the moves, none of them were indicative of any skill. Knowing him, both teams would probably lose. But he didn't care, for he was proud to be able to deliver reliable service. He was guarding the truck from nothing much at all, minding his own business, lost in his own little innocent world of dreams and this gave him immense reward. Somebody had asked him to do something that he was actually capable of at last, sitting around doing nothing. The rain was lashing the vehicle and there he was warm and cosy inside with the heating turned up to maximum.

Spangler was toiling under the weight of wet, dead cops way out back in the undergrowth. He practiced his killing in solitude; he made a little den in branches and bushes we had forged from the arid desert soil with irrigation systems and water channels leading from the pond. He dragged them to the water's edge and weighted them down with stones in their pockets. A delightful pile of dead policemen, it was all in a day's work for him. The kind of work he had not had the pleasure of pursuing for many years. The dead wouldn't have borne his insignia if he hadn't taken a knife to them before he dumped their bodies. They had been on his mind for days. All trapped in that little shed. It was like showing a dog a bone and then telling him he couldn't have it. It would only be a matter of time before his hunger got the best of him and he stole out in the dead of night to claim his forbidden rewards. He kept each of the ring fingers from their left hands in his pocket. Some had wedding bands, some did not. He felt no more moved by those which were adorned than those that weren't. We shared some qualities in common he and I; the ability to murder without remorse, the lack of empathy, the lack of identification with another person on any human plane. A complete sense of self that neither needed nor wanted another; a self that actively shunned a connection on any level. Only in prison do such people meet, for serial killers are inclined to do their bidding alone and separated. We are not likely to be effusive about our recollections of such events. That would signify an attempt to prove or to explain oneself which we do not see as necessary or valuable. Although our styles and motives differed greatly, the denouement was the same.

I raised my sword to Eugene, that bastard. For now he had entered prohibited territory, the parameters of which, like Area

51, should never ever be violated. Those secrets are secrets for a reason. I plunged that blade forward. He was not ready for the super-annuated Steves driven on by the ultimate fury. I sliced his arm as I lunged. I had been taken over. The pressure and volatility caused my nose to bleed even though I had not taken a blow. It grazed him and cut him slightly but not enough to force him to desist. We went for it. Jabbing and prodding. I would have him. As we went full force lashing out for each other's throats, a contest to the death, I could see the ethereal mist gathering. Out of it came Mother and the widow Stead-man, fighting in unison with swords flexed and ready, mirroring our own toil, a battle of Steves versus Steadman. I trusted Mother to win that one. The widow Steadman was as thin as a reed and as desiccated as the Arizona landscape. Both teams went for it like synchronised dancers, as I lashed out so too did Mother and with Eugene's riposte came an attempt from the widow. I leapt over them to the other side. Gene crashed straight through his own mother for he did not have the vision to see, unenlightened was he. I snarled at him. I went low and tried to take out his feet. I felt contact briefly and I heard his scream shrilly reverberate around the hall. My sword had met with his ankle bone, great deflector, but it had gone into the skin enough for him to feel the pain course up his leg. It would not be enough to immobilise him. He crashed his sword down trying to get a good hit at my retracting arm but I was too fast. He had taken two hits and I had taken none, just as it should be. He countered me as I spun round to avoid his blow. He swiped his sword back up in an unexpected move and as he did so he caught me just under the armpit. It sliced me as I moved it fluidly in the same direction. Had my arm been bearing down I would have been lucky to keep it. The pain was sharp as it shot up my nerves to my brain, sensory receptors stimulated. I didn't look to see the wound as sight would add perception to my pain. If I ignored it I felt strong enough to go on. I was still in the game.

'You sire, have raised my majestic hackles and for that you must pay dear.' I growled. My armpit burned as I moved. A ligament had been severed or at least severely compromised in the assault. The onslaught continued as I lunged for him. I still had full use of my sword-bearing arm. Our weapons clashed and slid up one another to the quillion, bashing together at the hilt. We stood eye to eye and broke off as we uncrossed our wands and the blades slid down each other once more. Mother and the widow stood locked in similar moments of stand-off in unison. We circled, we eyed. We weighed up in our minds who had sustained the most injury and by this token who could survive the next assault with the least collateral damage.

'Tell it to your mother, Steves,' snapped Gene.

I saw blood-red tones of pure anger and vitriol in the dark recesses of my mind come forth and seize me. They were showing me the corpse of Eugene Steadman on a silver platter with an apple in his porcine mouth. I captured its strength in the pit of my stomach and hurled it out through my arm. The power surged down into the sword I wielded. I gave Mother a sideways glance. She met it and winked at me. Then I rolled onto the floor taking Eugene by surprise as I did so, emerging from behind him. His bulk could not move as fast as I had spun round him. I had sidestepped my opponent in an Olympian move and he knew he had lost this battle. I jabbed my sword into his side at least four inches before I pulled it out and went in for another strike. I checked Mother's progress only to see her stood over the bleeding body of the widow, plunging her implement into her chest as a precursor to my victory. She turned and twisted it in the wound. The ghost of the widow, slain once again, rose up to the sky and departed this dimension. Mother followed her. Gene fell to the ground rolling around, murmuring. He clasped his side with both hands. The blood ran out and dispersed into his lemon jerkin. I had him now. He looked as vulnerable as a small child. I leered down at him. He was still mumbling incoherently and trying to stem the flow with his chubby digits.

'Ah, the precious elixir of life flowing freely I see.' I panted, recapturing my breath. 'Soon there will be none left my friend. You should probably see a doctor about that, looks nasty. Ha! Ha! Ha! You troll. I told you I'd win. I always do.'

'Fuck you, Steves,' he flinched as he struggled to insult me, 'Youch! Ahhhhh.' He winced. 'You bastard.'

'That's chief bastard to you. But thank you anyway. I wonder if I may put you out of your misery now.'

I poked him with the edge of my sword, enough to make an impression on his skin but not so hard as to break the surface.

'Come on, what are you waiting for? You're making it too easy for me. Get up and play with me some more. A victory as swift as this counts for so much less than a real fight to the death. I would like my triumph to be monumental. Will you spar?'

My armpit burned as I hurled my bravado at Gene. I was doing a fine job of covering up my anguish as I goaded him from above. The truth is my wound was killing me and I feared I may jettison blood everywhere if I didn't keep the left arm firmly by my side.

'Look what you've done,' said I, studying my garments. 'You have sliced up my robe. You are like an errant wife who has discovered an affair and put her lover's suits and ties through the shredder for retribution. I should have you for that alone if you hadn't committed every sin in the book already and the uniform is fucked. This will never do. Where is my stylist?' Gene groaned. 'Well if you won't play then I suppose I have no need of you any more. You really shouldn't have mentioned Mother, Gene. That was a very big mistake.'

I rested the tip of my sword on his chest and stood directly above him. My wand was perpendicular to his body, perfectly vertical. With only a slight application of pressure it would slice its way down into his trunk, come out the other side and strike the floorboards. I would leave him pinned down until the police arrived.

Gene sobbed uncontrollably. Thoughts of his one true love ran through his mind. There was nothing he could do. Now she would be at my mercy and I did not have any of which to speak. He had failed in his mission to become a man. As I began to increase the pressure on my weapon I closed my eyes and thought nice things. I was beginning to drift away, gradually increasing the pressure little by little. I would make his final moments linger on for as long as possible and when I opened my eyes, he would be no more. Moments like these to be cherished.

The next thing I knew I was ten feet across the room and I couldn't see a god damn thing. BOOM!!! I was almost deafened by the blast.

'Aaarrrggghhhh!!!' I screamed at full volume. What had

happened? My God. Say it isn't so. I felt around in the blackness. It was only black because something stung my eyes and prevented me from opening them. I must find my weapon. I must see. I touched me eyes tentatively and recoiled almost immediately as a spasm of pain sent itself through my body, round my head and down my arms. The epicentre was tiny but the pain was enormous. It superseded the pain in the hollow of my arm by approximately 9.8 times. I knew it immediately to be a shard of glass, a shard of glass to the eye. I must pull it out. I would have it in but a second. Oh my! 'Arrrggghhhh!!!' I felt piercing pain as I tried to get a grip on the little blighter. My hands shook. This was going to hurt. I couldn't open the unaffected eye because the natural reaction is to open both. If I did so I would blink or wince and the pain would surge forth again. My head banged as though it would explode like the windows of the great hall just had. I centred my focus on the offending shard and concentrated hard. I delicately grabbed for it with pincer fingers. I missed. I tried it again and managed to get a little purchase, as the pain shot up my hands jerked away. One more try Steves, you know you can do it. Try not to tremble, the thing might get lodged in further. My eyes were streaming with tears but they would not wash it away. Another explosion came and another shower of glass. I could hear something retreating and the clinking and crushing of the shards under it. It was not coming my way. Fuck, some more glass rained down. A fireball screamed across the ceiling above my head. I was down low. I needed to escape but I needed to extricate this thing first or I would never make it. The air around me was getting incredibly hot. One more concerted effort. Even though my eyes were closed I could sense the brightness around me. I could see the blackness, now tinted with an orange glow around the edges. Colour was all I could see, the orange glow getting redder and redder beneath my eyelids, filtering through my blood vessels. I crouched and put the fire out of my mind for a second, I had to. I condensed all of my thoughts together and concentrated intensely on the small shard of glass stuck out of my eye and the colours all round. I focused as though it were the only thing that existed in the world. I pinched my fingers together and grasped, tiny grasps a couple of times. I got hold of it and coaxed it out a little. I screamed in pain. I tried again. This time the small shaft was slightly lengthier and I had it. It slithered out. It was all of one centimetre long but felt as though it were a six-inch blade. My eyes burned hotter than that fire outside and the fluid seeped from inside as I opened my lashes and it rolled down my face. Another bloody tear. As I surveyed the room for a split second, I saw the door swinging as though it had just been exited and Gene was nowhere to be seen. The floor was covered with glass. I hid my face behind my arm to shield it from the melting heat. All of the windows were blown out and the fire outside, now taking hold of the building, was raging. A Eugene shaped clearing in the glass debris was visible before me and a path had been formed leading from it, across the room and out the door. I only had sight in my left eye. I lurched for the doors as another explosion blew a plume of flames into the hall. It slammed behind me, propelled by the thrust of the blast, the flames licking round it as I went.

My body slammed the corridor wall. Holding my eye, holding my arm, I lurched around hitting the walls with my shoulder, sliding along it. My sight had been greatly compromised as I had been blinded by both the light and by my punctured eye-ball. As I made my way along it I could hear the flicker of flames all around the house. The front of the building had not yet taken hold so I would be safe as long as I kept bearing in that direction. I could barely see anything before me for the fumes were closing in and disappearing out of the door. As I struggled to see and to breathe, I kept losing footing and sliding around. Something was coming between my foot and the floor beneath. They rolled when I rested my weight on them. Surely Kathryn hadn't booby trapped the corridor with marbles or some such obstacle to freedom. I crouched down to get a closer look and to escape the rising heat. My vision was so impaired I had to crouch on all fours. I focused on the object, it was a pawn, and another, and another, leading round the corner, all the way to my office, pieces of Dirk's chess set. Oh no. I rushed outside as quickly as I could, considering that I would need a glass eye and my arms stitching up in the event that I did seek medical attention. Everything hurt. My lungs were working heavy and hard to extract oxygen from the contaminated air. It became clearer the closer I got to the ground so I kept low. I flung myself outside, still on all fours. I took the deepest of inhalations. Fatigued, I managed to scamper up and jog toward the truck, except the truck wasn't there. Tyre tracks were grooved into the mud. Whoever stole my wheels was obviously in a hurry to get away. Dirk. God damn it. I spun round to see the ranch going up like a tinder box but it still hadn't taken hold of the front of the ranch where I stood. I figured I could make it quickly back to the office and still have time to escape the furnace. True heroes rush in and I did just that, crawling under the smoke once again, distant explosions going off everywhere. The emergency services were bound to find out about this sooner rather than later. Our elevated position on the hilltop would ensure those low lying busybodies would detect the funeral pyre that the ranch had come to resemble. I had no idea who was trapped inside. If I could save one acolyte, I may still have an Empire to salvage, lest I had to begin all over again. Concluding that the exercise had been something of a failure, it might not be a bad idea but I forged ahead regardless. I might be able to salvage some of my belongings from the blaze.

Crawling below the smoke I went, passing pawn after pawn until I reached the door of my office. It was open. Some blaggard had forced it. A violation of the highest order had been committed. I felt raped. But that did not matter at this moment as I was bound to lose some kudos ferreting around on my hands and knees. I hoped no one saw me. I pushed it open and crept inside. My hub had been abandoned long ago. Flames licked round the windows. One hand in front of the other I went on the carpet. Something was moist underneath. I got my head right down to it so my nose was almost touching the pile. My eyesight was failing. I had come nearer to the fire than I'd liked. There it was coming into focus, melted wax and blood. I looked ahead of me. My throne was overturned in what was sure to be an ultimate act of defiance. On the table, after the last pawn had been laid on the floor there stood two figurines, the king and the bishop lying on their sides. Someone's idea of ironic symbolism no doubt. When I found the swine, I would kill him with my kinetic energies alone. The place was full of smoke and Bronson was gone, half-melted if the pools of shimmering wax on the carpet were anything to go by. This was Gene's work, but not all, not quite. As the smoke billowed and my eyesight half evaded me still, I could just make out the pieces. By pieces I mean, pieces of a human being. Not whole. Shredded; a finger here, a lump of scalp there, a large muddy sneaker. Dear God, it was Dirk. It used to be Dirk. I felt sickened to the core. The undeserved innocent. I couldn't look at it. Jim was different, he was mine but this, this was someone else's opus. I could not identify with it. Just as any other human being would, I viewed this as perversion, not an art, a stomach-churning offence. I could only give credence to my own insanity, not to another's. I had no grudge against the boy. He had not crossed me; mine was retribution, reactionary murder for crimes committed against my person or an affront to my sensibilities or both. Spangler did not need a reason, no matter how twisted mine may be, they were reasons all the same. I had motive, he had none. He killed for pleasure and I for atonement, although I took some comfort from my endeavours, it's true.

The flames came round from the porch and licked through the window. I watched the spoils of my empire proceed to burn. Jim's body began to take hold. I knew I had to channel the speed of light to escape for he would go up in flames in no time since he was half-scorched already. I rolled for it, taking out the pawns like tiny pins to a giant human bowling ball. I knew the way out. I didn't need to see. I could feel the warm breeze against my skin and the burning, scolding air clipping at my heels from behind. I was wringing with sweat. My police uniform and robe had been soaked with more bodily fluids, from more pieces of meat, than a butcher's apron at an abattoir. I got into the open air and carried on running, shredded robe flapping about in the breeze. Alone was I and with nothing to my name. Who would pay for this, I wondered.

Sirens in the far, far distance began to sound, the FBI and a fleet of fire fighters hot on our trail. I looked down to see their headlights winding up the steep clifftop road on the horizon. The blaze would have destroyed any evidence by the time they reached the scene. I shot a look back to see the raging inferno behind me. There was barely anything left of the timber frame. I had escaped just in time and I had doused the walls of my office in kerosene naturally, so any remnants that Theodore Steves had ever been there were sure to be evaporated and destroyed, just as I had designed it. My Empire engulfed in flames. I refused to cry. I would not show weakness or fear. I loped across the plain. I was making good headway with my injuries hindering me less than they should but I was super-human after all. The pressure in my head built as I laboured the sprint. The eye was weeping and seeping. There would be no way to save it; I knew that now for it could no longer lend me vision, not even a hazy, distorted view. It was redundant. I kept my left arm close to my side as I went, throwing off the sword as ballast. I still had the shotgun strapped to my back and the handgun too; these were now my worldly effects along with the ruined snakeskins. I must have run three miles or so, the pitch black before me. I stumbled over stray rocks, dried up plants and knots of dead roots holding onto the last vestiges of life in the hot desert sand. Behind me an ear-shattering boom rang out across the county. That would be the armoury and its fine collection of munitions passing over to the arsenal in the sky. The explosives went off like rockets lighting up the nightscape one after another, a massive display in every

264

conceivable colour of the rainbow. I wouldn't have liked to have been in the vicinity when that supernova went off. The emus were sure to be fried, along with the deceased acolytes' remains. How handy for me and for Spangler, wherever he may be. They continued to explode as I disappeared over the ridge to the edge of a low eroded cliff. I rested for a moment. I was free. I scanned around in the sudden darkness but I could see nothing of note. I stooped over, a hideous wreck but no one could see me so it didn't matter. I rested a while and surveyed below.

Yes. No one could see me that was true . . . but I could sure as hell see them! As sure as night turns to day, there they were on a ledge directly below me, the escapees, Eugene and Kathryn and the concealed spawn of Satan's little helper taking a rest. They were completely unaware that I had discovered them. Thinking they were safe and patting themselves on the back for their cunning. I guess it was Spangler who stole the truck after all. I prayed to the god of all fine things for my providence and I thanked him for sparing my weapons. I would need them more than ever this day.

I watched them for a while. Eugene was laid out on the floor. In all the time I had been spying he hadn't moved an inch. The half-melted torso of Bronson was at his side and Kathryn was stooped over him, obscuring the mid portion of his body. I crept down trying not to dislodge any rocks or rubble as I went. I wanted to surprise them. I slid down tentatively and swung round the shotgun that was hanging around my shoulders and across my back, ready for action. I crept. I made it almost twenty feet from where they were situated before Kathryn heard the treading of gravel under my shoes. She turned her head and gave a look of horror. We stared at each other for a while.

'Lady, we meet again, so soon. What a pleasure.' I saluted her but she did not return my greeting. She had been crying, though I couldn't see her tears in the darkness I knew they were there.

'How do you intend to pay me back for burning down my Empire, miss? I think Eugene's life is worth the exact price of the ranch. Do you agree?' I advanced with my gun poised.

'He's dead.' She whispered and shook her head.

She moved away from Eugene's body as I made it right up to her. I peered over him.

'Oh dear, I am vexed! How could that have happened?' I laughed right in her face. 'I think you'll find that Eugene still owes me a king's ransom, back payment for the unfortunate demise of my greatest dream, the rise and fall of the Empire of Steves.' I wafted my hands about with dramatic licence. 'I shall write a book and dedicate it to your memory. Yes. Of course I hold you both personally responsible. So for starters my sweet, I think you'll find that belongs to me.'

I whipped out the package from Eugene's belt. It was sodden. The fool had bled to death, although he had not done the decent thing and allowed me to watch his tormented end, the ignorance. I peered closer. He was lying face up in a large pool of blood, holding his ear. His clothes were soaked right through. Kathryn had tried in vain to form a tight seal on his wounds by binding him tightly round the midriff with the glowing lemon jerkin but his vital organs had been ruptured. He had evidently died from both internal and external bleeding.

'Why, I'm surprised my sword made it through the blubber.' I jested but she did not look as if she cared for anything in the universe now. She seemed to have given up. I suspect that I could have done anything to her and she wouldn't even have offered me the satisfaction of a struggle. So I did nothing at all. She was braced for it though, stiff as a board. She clasped tightly onto her stomach.

'Oh dear once again, fearing for the child, are we. You better not get too stressed lady, you might miscarry. We wouldn't want that, would we?'

What better way to secure Eugene's departure from all of existence than to wipe his repulsive genetics from the face of our planet. I held my shotgun aloft and aimed it at her head.

'You know, this reminds me of a time, oh, many years ago, many, many years ago.' I gave a little smile. I was transported back in time to the small kitchen in Virginia. It seemed like another world and another life. She began to cry uncontrollably, still crouched down there on the ground. I saw Mother's face where hers should have been, mutated. I was sixteen again. I suppose I could have walked away. After all, I did have a good five pounds of cocaine in my hands. It would be enough to set myself up in small business, source a clientele and begin life over again as a dealer to create a base for the second wave. That would be the plan. I had chosen LA for the Empire's new gleaming headquarters. This would cater for my party lifestyle, once the Empire's affiliations with the power elite had made me a mint. She wouldn't tell anyone. At least I didn't think she would. Well she might. I presumed her frailty of mind would lead her to some mental institution or other where she would end her days haunted by the spectre of Steves. I would derive immense pleasure from that. But there are no happy endings in life, only in movies. As I pointed the barrel at her temple, Eugene's body become my father's and Kathryn became my mother. I knew my mother was dead. I knew she wasn't really there with me, stood behind me with a hand on my shoulder, watching herself die again. Well, sometimes I knew it in moments of clarity that swiftly became confused and flew away. At those moments I also knew what she had done to me and I knew that it was all her fault. No other woman would ever come close to her. No other woman would ever get close to me. I was her special one, always. I am God. I know that because she told me so and because she is always right.

I turned to walk away but Mother prevented me. She blocked my way and gave me that look with her big eyes, shaking her head slowly in chastisement. A chasm appeared in her head and her shoulder hung slumped as it had when I shot her. The blood trickled down her forehead. She smiled. She had me entranced, under her spell as she always had. I must do what I was told. I took up my gun and pointed it directly at Kathryn's swollen belly. I did not hesitate. I would not make the same mistake twice, for this time I would do the job properly. I did not waver and I did not feel any sorrow. I pushed the barrel as far into her abdomen as I could. Then I pulled the trigger and blew them away. For it was time to set off in my snakeskins, hand in hand with Mother across the desert to Hollywood and beyond, without ever looking back.